JESSICA BARRY

Jessica Barry is a pseudonym for an American author who previously worked in publishing in London. *Look for Me*, previously published as *Freefall*, her debut thriller, has sold in more than twenty-two territories around the world and has also secured a major Hollywood film deal. She lives in Maine with her husband and their two cats.

ALSO BY JESSICA BARRY

Look For Me

JESSICA BARRY

Don't Turn Around

VINTAGE

1 3 5 7 9 10 8 6 4 2

Vintage is part of the Penguin Random House group of companies
whose addresses can be found at global.penguinrandomhouse.com

Penguin
Random House
UK

Copyright © Hudson & Guide Post Limited 2020

Jessica Barry has asserted her right to be identified as the
author of this Work in accordance with the Copyright,
Designs and Patents Act 1988

First published in Vintage in 2021
First published in hardback by Harvill Secker in 2020

penguin.co.uk/vintage

A CIP catalogue record for this book is available from the
British Library

ISBN 9781784709488 (B format)

Printed and bound in Great Britain by Clays Ltd, Elcograf S.p.A.

The authorised representative in the EEA is Penguin Random House
Ireland, Morrison Chambers, 32 Nassau Street, Dublin D02 YH68.

Penguin Random House is committed to a sustainable future for our
business, our readers and our planet. This book is made from Forest
Stewardship Council® certified paper.

DON'T
TURN
AROUND

The smell hits her first: burnt rubber and gasoline. Then the pain comes. The roar of blood in her ears, the gurgled strangle of her breath.

She squints out of the splintered windshield. For a split second, she can't remember where she is. When she does, fear rushes over her, a black, suffocating wave.

And then she hears it: a long, shivering scrape of metal against metal.

She sees a face at the window.

It's him.

He's outside, and he's trying to get in.

Cait kept the engine running.

She'd had the Jeep since college, bought it used the summer before her freshman year with the proceeds of hundreds of hours working retail at Richland Mall, and sometimes it acted up. Normally, she didn't mind. She relished popping the hood and peering underneath, knowing more times than not that she would be able to fix the problem. Her father had her out in the garage from the time she was six. But at this particular moment, there was no way in hell she would risk the engine stalling.

Outside, there was a glitter of frost on the lawn. The house wasn't what she was used to, though by now she knew that she should expect anything. Usually, the places were cramped and run-down, cinder block apartment buildings or chipped-stucco bungalows, in neighborhoods where she wouldn't want to linger after dark.

There was one place about a month ago, on the outskirts of Abilene, that was tucked behind the railroad tracks on Route 20. She drove straight past it the first time, despite the number 22 painted clearly on the side of the mailbox. No way someone lived there, she figured—it wasn't much more than a shack, and it looked abandoned, the windows boarded up, a rusted-out pickup truck squatting outside, tires long gone. She followed the road another quarter mile, watching for the house, but there was nothing but empty farmland. She double-checked the address: it was right, though she'd known that already. They didn't make mistakes about things like that back at the office. So she turned around and parked outside the shack, and sure enough, a girl who didn't look a day over eighteen ran out from behind the house and climbed silently into the Jeep. Cait could still picture the girl's nervous smile, the long shining braid that fell down her back, the half-moons of dirt nestled beneath her fingernails.

But this place was different: a McMansion in a modern development, complete with a two-car garage and a light-up reindeer on the lawn. One of the tasteful ones made of wire and tiny white lights, not the inflatable kind her parents used to stick on top of their house back in Waco, two sagging reindeer pulling a bloated Santa across the roof. The house itself was built of red brick and topped with a series of peaked roofs, and there was a small paved path curving up to the imposing front door. Property was cheaper here than in Austin—most places were cheap compared to Austin—but this was definitely the house of someone who wasn't shy with a few bucks.

It threw her off a little, this house.

Cait scanned the street for any sign of movement. The windows on the houses were squeezed shut, and the only light came from the pretty streetlamps that lined the sidewalk. A child's red tricycle lay in a driveway, forgotten until tomorrow. She pictured a plump-cheeked toddler riding up and down the sidewalk, legs pumping, little fingers clutching the handlebars, wind rushing past as she sped up, shrieking with joy or terror, or maybe both.

The road had emptied out pretty quickly once she was out of Austin's sprawl, and soon it was just her and a few fellow travelers driving along the long, flat, endless road. The view didn't change much, just empty plains stretching out as far as she could see, briefly interrupted by the green of watered lawns and neatly plotted houses that signaled a town.

Eight hours later, and here she was, waiting. She shifted in her seat, scratched an itch, stifled a yawn. She'd need to get coffee once they were on the road. She didn't want to stop until they were clear of the city.

She checked the clock on the dashboard: 12:10. Pickup had been at midnight, but she'd gotten there a few minutes early, just in case. She'd been waiting for a while now. It happened sometimes. People got nervous, had second thoughts. If they changed their minds, they were meant to give her a signal: flick the lights three times quick, and she'd know they weren't coming. Two flicks meant there was trouble and she should call the police.

So far that night, there'd been nothing.

She wasn't worried, at least not yet. She scanned the road again. All quiet in Pleasantville. Every car tucked up in its garage, every person tucked up in bed.

Out of the corner of her eye, she caught something. One hand gripped the wheel, the other the gearshift. This could be it. Her heart pounded in her chest.

She watched a possum slinking under a thick hedge and shuddered. She'd grown up with possums, but that didn't mean she didn't hate them. They were cute enough as babies, but when they were full-grown, they were mean little suckers. Still, a possum wasn't going to give her any trouble.

Eyes back on the house. Still dark, still nothing. The clock read 12:15. She'd give it another five. They weren't meant to linger. Lingering attracted attention. If one of the neighbors happened to get up to use the bathroom and see a beat-up old Jeep parked out front, they'd call the cops quicker than a lightning bug in July.

And nobody wanted the cops involved in something like this. You never knew which way they'd swing.

One of the curtains in the house twitched, and a moment later, a light came on downstairs. This was it: now or never. She straightened up in her seat and wiped the mascara smudges from under her eyes.

Get ready. As soon as she gets in the car, you've got to go.

A few seconds later, a blond woman wearing a pressed white shirt and khakis emerged. She had a bag slung over her shoulder that looked expensive. Actually, her whole person looked expensive—slick and golden and whistle-clean. Cait watched the woman lock the door behind her, hesitate, check again that it was locked.

Sweat pricked at the small of Cait's back. *Comeoncomeoncomeon.*

The woman stole glances at the neighboring houses and hurried down the path.

Cait reached over and swung the passenger door open from the inside. The woman's face appeared.

"Hi, Rebecca?" Cait made sure to smile when she said the woman's name. It was important to put them at ease as quickly as possible. The woman nodded and climbed in. Her smell filled the Jeep, cotton and vanilla and sandalwood. "I'm Caitlyn," she said, though the woman would have known that already. "But you can call me Cait." The woman nodded again and pulled her bag tight to her lap. "The seat belt comes from the back," Cait said, and the woman frowned before reaching behind and snapping the belt into the clasp. She stared straight ahead, through the windshield, at the deserted suburban street.

Cait shifted into drive and pulled away from the curb. "Do you have a phone?"

The woman blinked.

"A cell phone," Cait prompted. Sometimes they got nervous and

6

froze. She had learned to coax them. "If you do, you need to turn it off."

The woman's eyes widened. "Why?"

"GPS."

The woman's frown deepened. "Is that really—"

"Yeah, it is. Sorry, I know it seems a little extreme, but—" She left the rest of the sentence hanging in the air. Both of them knew that these were extreme circumstances.

The woman fumbled around in her bag and pulled out her phone. Cait kept one eye on the road and watched until she'd switched it off.

"How long will the drive take?"

"About six hours. Maybe a little less. There's bottled water in the back if you want it. Help yourself."

Rebecca hugged her bag tighter to her chest. "I'm fine, thank you."

In the rearview mirror, Cait saw a light snap on in a neighboring house and a face appear at the window.

Take it easy. Just drive normally; don't read anything into it.

"Are you close with your neighbors?" She kept her voice casual.

Rebecca looked at her, surprised. "Not really."

Cait's eyes were locked on the rearview. The curtain fell back across the window, the light flicked off. She let out a sigh. "It looks like the kind of place where you'd all be friendly. Block parties, that kind of thing. Is there a neighborhood watch?"

Rebecca shook her head. "I don't think so."

"Good." She'd run into trouble with neighborhood watches in the past. Give a guy a fake badge and a pinch of authority and things could go sideways fast. The rest of the houses stayed dark. No cars on the road, either. They were almost out of the development. It would be easier once they got on the major roads. "Do you mind if I put the radio on? It helps keep me awake."

The woman shook her head. Cait reached over and clicked on the dial. The drone of a talk radio host filled the Jeep—the great scourge of Texas. She flicked through the stations until she landed on the local Magic station. The crooning voice of Billy Joel came through the speakers, singing about drinking alone. She left it on. She figured she couldn't go wrong with Billy Joel.

The house was on the southeast side of Lubbock, so they had to pass straight through downtown to get to Highway 60. She turned onto Broadway and drove past a banner hanging in the window of a local law firm: WELCOME TO BEAUTIFUL DOWNTOWN! NO WIN, NO FEE! There were stoplights every other block, and all of them seemed to turn red as soon as they got close, plotting together to keep them within the city limits.

"C'mon, c'mon," Cait muttered, hand tapping the wheel. She didn't like how quiet it was. That was the hardest part about these night drives: the quiet. It was easier to blend in if there were other signs of life.

A man dressed in a Santa hat walked past holding a filthy cloth in one hand and a sign in the other: HUNGRY, PLEASE HELP. He knocked on the window as they waited for the light to change. Cait tried to wave him away, but he mimed the action of cleaning and started wiping the cloth across the windshield, leaving streaks of grease on the glass. She glanced over at Rebecca, who was cowering in the passenger seat, knuckles white on the straps of her bag.

Cait rolled down the window and shoved a couple of dollar bills at him. "Thanks for the sterling work." He took them with a tip of an imaginary hat and shuffled off just as the light switched to green. "You okay?" she asked Rebecca.

Rebecca nodded, but her jaw was set tight and she was staring straight ahead, her eyes glassy and unseeing. She hadn't so much as blinked since leaving the house. "Almost out of Lubbock now," Cait said.

The wide double lanes were lined with the cash-and-carries and the megachurches and the little Mexican restaurants advertising Taco Tuesday, just like every other town in Texas. Occasionally, a neon-lit billboard would flood a sickly light down on them, conjuring up strange, flickering shadows. The Christmas lights were out—multicolored stars and pale blue snowflakes, an angel strung high above the avenue, her wings sparkling gold—and the signs in the shopwindows advertised half-price champagne and cheap diamond bracelets.

Cait hated Christmas. It was amateur hour for drinking, full of awkward office parties and old guys looking to cop a feel after one too many whiskeys. Her old manager had insisted on hanging a sprig of mistletoe at the edge of the bar, and every time she'd go to open the champagne fridge, there'd be some guy lurking, hoping to try his luck. There was a new manager now, a woman, so maybe it would be different, though given that the staff uniform involved mandatory crop tops and Stetsons, she wasn't holding her breath. At least the tips would be decent.

She stretched, winced. Her back was killing her already. She'd been driving for hours, pushing through rush hour traffic out of Austin and on to 183. She'd lived in the city for eight years and every year it seemed to get worse, the roads thick with pickup trucks and beaters and shiny new sports cars, clogging up the city's arteries, strangling its heart.

Friends talked about leaving the city. They said they couldn't take the traffic anymore, or the ever rising rents for ever shittier apartments, or the Tesla charging stations that had sprung up like dandelions and were perpetually full. It was all talk, though. No one ever left. Where would they go? Someplace like this?

They passed Church's Chicken and the Eleganté Hotel. The city was starting to lose its grip a little, pockets of land stretching wider between buildings and the buildings themselves growing longer and wider. Cait saw Rebecca's shoulders inch away from her ears and the grip on her handbag start to loosen.

Finally, they saw the sign for the Lubbock city limit. "We're out," Cait said. "The hardest part is over now." Rebecca cracked a smile.

They drove through Littlefield, past a John Deere dealership and a sign advertising vacancy at the Plains Motel. She'd done this stretch a couple times before—once with a sweet-faced college kid who spent the whole time cramming for her biology exam, and another with a woman from Odessa who wept for most of the journey.

That had been a tough one. But there had been worse.

Some of her clients—those who had jobs flexible enough to allow them a few days off, or partners who weren't breathing down their necks—stayed within state lines, and she ferried them to Austin or Dallas or Fort Worth. Most went to New Mexico, where the rules weren't so strict. It was a longer drive but quicker in the long run. Lubbock was in a dead zone: a five-hour drive no matter what direction she drove. It was the client's choice. Tonight she was heading west.

She glanced in the rearview. There was a tractor trailer behind them. She stepped on the gas, and its headlights receded. No tail that she could detect. She allowed herself to relax a little. It was always most dangerous nearest the home. The more miles they had under their belts, the safer they would be. Until they got to where they were going, of course, but that was a headache she wouldn't worry about until morning.

Cait had left in a hurry—late, as always—and hadn't managed to get dinner. Hunger was mixed in with exhaustion, gritting her eyes and making her bones heavy. A cup of coffee and maybe a slice of pie would be enough to keep her going. "Do you mind if we stop once we're over the border?"

Rebecca's head snapped toward her. "Why?"

"I need a cup of coffee. I've been on the road since six o'clock."

The corners of her pretty mouth turned down. "I guess. If you need to."

"Thanks. It'll be quick, I promise. I know you're nervous, but we're out of the danger zone now."

"How do you know?"

"Ninety percent of all incidents occur within the first ten minutes of the journey. Most of the trouble I've seen has happened right outside the front door. Now that we're out of Lubbock, it should be smooth sailing."

Rebecca nodded but didn't look convinced. She had the kind of profile that belonged on a Roman coin, all straight nose and firm jaw. Patrician. Cait smiled at her own description: it was good, she should write it down. Maybe she could use it.

In the meantime, she needed to work out that piece she'd been writing about labor conditions at the organic farm outside of Austin. The editor had been requesting the copy for weeks, but she hadn't been able to land it. Not that he had much of a right to complain considering how much he was paying her, which was nothing. Still, she couldn't risk pissing him off. It was rare that someone gave her a chance, especially these days.

A sign announced that they were leaving Littlefield. They were edging toward the desert now. Pretty soon there'd be nothing but scrub and sky. Her stomach rumbled. She couldn't get to Clovis fast enough. It would be her last chance to get a decent cup of coffee that night.

She glanced over at the woman sitting next to her. "You comfortable? You want me to put the heat on or anything?"

Rebecca shook her head. "I'm fine, thanks."

"Just let me know. It's supposed to get down to the twenties tonight. They're saying it might even snow." She reached out and patted the dashboard. "Don't worry, she's good in the snow."

Rebecca gave her a weak smile. "That's good to know," she said, before turning her face back toward the window.

So she wasn't a talker. That was fine. There was plenty of time for that.

Cait rolled off the bed and stumbled into the bathroom. The bulb had blown, so she had to feel her way to the toilet in the dark, careful not to hit her head on the sloped wall. She could hear his soft snores over the sound of her piss hitting the bowl. Good. She hadn't woken him up.

When she was finished, she stood up carefully and turned to look at herself in the mirror. Her eyes had adjusted to the light now, and she could see the dark hollows of her eyes and a glint of teeth in the reflection. She pressed her forehead to the glass. *What the fuck are you doing here?* she asked herself, but she didn't have an answer. The snores continued.

It was Alyssa's fault. She was the one who had insisted they go to Cedar Street for her birthday, even though the place was a hellhole filled with drunk college kids and tourists looking for an "authentic experience." She had whined about it for weeks until Caitlyn finally threw in the towel, which was exactly what Alyssa knew she would do, if only to shut her up. Alyssa had squealed and thrown her arms around Cait's neck when she agreed, and seeing her friend happy almost made up for the prospect of one of her precious nights off being spent dodging frat boys sloshing tequila over her sneakers.

What could she say? When it came to her friends, she was a sucker. That's what her mother said when she'd come home from school having traded her brand-new silver pencil case for Melissa Brandino's beat-up old red one after Melissa convinced her that silver matched her polished Mary Janes better than Cait's beat-up Keds. "Oh, Caity," her mother had said, shaking her head and sighing. "You're too nice sometimes."

In fairness, it had been a long time since someone had described her as too nice.

So they went to Cedar Street, and sure enough, within ten minutes someone had spilled tequila on her brand-new Nikes and she'd watched a girl projectile-vomit onto the door of the bathroom stall. "Remind me why we're here again?" she'd said to Alyssa, but Alyssa was too busy showing off her Birthday Girl badge to a bunch of tech bros to notice. Cait slinked off to the bar and ordered herself a double Maker's, neat, and tipped it down her throat in one burning gulp. If you can't beat 'em, join 'em. That was when she spotted Jake striding across the courtyard, every pair of female eyes in a twenty-foot radius trailing after him. Hers, too.

She knew about him already. A guy who came into the bar was a music journalist for the Digg, and he'd been singing Jake's praises over one too many Sierras the other night, saying he was the next big thing. She was curious, so when she finished her shift, she went home and looked him up on Spotify. Country music wasn't exactly her jam, despite—or maybe because of—growing up deep in the heart of Texas, but even she could admit he had something special. His voice was a low growl over the delicate guitar riffs, deep and compelling and sexy as all hell.

She'd checked on Alyssa, who now had her tongue shoved firmly down the throat of one of the tech bros, before ducking out of the bar and following Jake a few blocks to the Pearl on Fourth Street. She wasn't sure why she was doing it—she didn't make a habit out of following strange men—but something about seeing him like that had made it feel a little like fate, as corny as that sounded to her.

She stayed in the back as he took the stage and went through his sound check. Given the level of drunkenness she'd witnessed at Cedar Street, she figured it was well past midnight, but when she checked the time on her phone, it was just a little past ten o'clock. She signaled the bartender for a beer and settled her back against the bar as he strummed the opening chords.

The Pearl was relatively empty—it was a Monday night, after all—but the place started filling up quickly, drawn by the sound of his voice. She was drawn, too, and soon found herself in front of the stage, swaying her hips to the music and watching sweat roll down his face from the lights.

They locked eyes, and she saw a little smirk flash across his lips. Cocky. She liked that. She kept dancing, feeling his eyes roaming across her body, seeing the desire start to flare. She swerved her hips and ran her fingers through her hair. *You're mine*, she thought, and the power thrilled her.

He finished the set and climbed down off the stage and the inevitable happened: the sweaty make-out session in the back and the fumbling cab ride to his apartment, which was still very much the place of a struggling musician and not one about to make the big time.

The sex started out routine enough—she was on top for a while, and then he flipped her over onto her back. It was good, though there was something about the way he focused on a spot just slightly above her head rather than looking her in the eye that made her think she could be anyone, really, and he wouldn't care. She didn't care, either, particularly—this was sex, not a betrothal—but

15

she wouldn't have minded him paying a little more attention to getting her off.

And then, just when she thought he was about to finish, he put his hands around her neck and tightened them so she almost—but not quite—lost consciousness. She struggled at first, clawing at his back, gripping his hands and trying to pry them away from her neck, but the struggle only seemed to excite him more, and the lack of oxygen to her brain made her weaker and weaker until she finally went limp. He let go long enough to shove his cock in her mouth and call her a fucking whore as he came, and then he kissed her on the cheek—not the mouth, not after she'd swallowed—and rolled over and went to sleep.

She took her clothes into the living room and, body huddled from the air-conditioning, pulled on her jeans and hooked her bra and slipped her shirt over her head, keeping her head very still as she did, so as not to strain her sore neck. There would be bruises in the morning, bruises she'd dot carefully with concealer to avoid answering the inevitable questions—jokes, more likely—from the guys at the bar.

He hadn't asked if she was into that sort of thing. He'd clearly just assumed she would be or hadn't cared if she wasn't. So much for the sensitive-singer-songwriter bullshit. He was just another straight-up asshole in a long line of assholes who took what they wanted without bothering to ask. She was sick and tired of it. She remembered the music journalist back at the bar saying Jake was just about to land a big tour, that he'd be a national name in a couple of months. No wonder he thought he could get away with this kind of shit.

This time, she decided, it was going to cost him.

She ordered a Lyft from the curb outside his apartment. Nine minutes away: plenty of time. She pulled a notebook and a pen out of her bag and made a few notes. By the time the car arrived, she was halfway to writing the article that would change her life.

Rebecca had watched the silhouette of the city disappear in the side-view mirror until it was swallowed up by the night sky. Only then did she let herself take a full breath.

It was easier now that they were out of Lubbock. It was the first step, and the biggest.

When the Jeep had pulled up outside the house, she'd sat in the dark of their bedroom, hands folded neatly in her lap, and listened to the faint rumble of the Jeep's engine. This was what she had wanted—what she had carefully planned—but now that it was here, she was paralyzed. Five minutes passed, then ten. They had told her the driver would wait for twenty minutes—no longer. At the fifteen-minute mark, she grabbed her bag and ran to the door. If she hesitated for even a second, she knew she'd never make it. When she stepped out into the freezing night, there was no bolt of lightning waiting to strike. No corrective zap from an electric fence. Just a girl in a Jeep, waiting for her.

Rebecca couldn't believe how quiet the neighborhood was at that time of night. The low thrum of the engine and the distant cry of a skulk of foxes. She could hear her heart pounding in her chest as she checked the lock on the door, and the soft pad of her footsteps as she walked across the pavement. It was easy, in the end.

Still, the same worries snagged in her head. *What if he comes home early? What if someone found out my plans and told him? They promised total confidentiality over the phone, but I know how people operate. No one can be trusted, especially not if there might be money involved. And with this, there would be.*

Rebecca looked over at the girl. She was young: somewhere in her mid-twenties. Just a baby, really. She had expected someone older. It felt strange being driven by someone so much younger, a reversal of the natural order.

She turned her eyes back to the road. Nothing. Nothing. Silo. Nothing. Nothing. Storage unit. She felt tiny out here, like one of those paper dolls she had played with as a girl.

Nearly three years in Texas and the place still felt as strange and alien as it had the first time she'd set foot in it.

She still felt like a stranger in the place she was meant to call home.

Patrick's eyes blue and burning-earnest when he said it, a smudge of cream sauce in the corner of his beautiful mouth. "It's time, sweetheart," he said, leaning across the table and taking her hand.

Rebecca stopped mid-bite, fork hovering in the air. "I didn't realize there was a clock."

"I know it sounds crazy, but I promise you, you'll love it there. Wide-open spaces, fresh air, salt-of-the-earth people . . . Come on, Becs. You've seen how the place is changing, the same as me. It's like living in a museum. No one real lives here anymore."

It was true: San Francisco had changed. She had seen it every day at the high school where she taught English: families forced to move because of the skyrocketing rents, the homeless population exploding, the mental health of her students pushed aside in pursuit of ever higher test scores. Tech had flooded the city with its venture capitalist riches, whitewashing away its grimy charm. Even the restaurant they were eating in had a sign on the door announcing a relocation to Oakland. When they asked the waiter about it, he shrugged and said, "Progress."

Still, the Bay Area was the only place she'd ever called home. "Our lives are here."

"Our lives are wherever we are, as long as we're together." He shook his head. "I want to go home, Becs. Please. My grandma's on her own out there, and she's getting old. I need to step up and take responsibility."

"My dad's on his own, too."

"Your dad is in his early sixties and in better shape than I am. Gram is going to be eighty next year. You saw the state the house was in when we went back last Christmas. She can't look after the place anymore."

"We could hire someone to help her," she suggested. "Or she could move into one of those assisted living facilities. I've heard some of them are really nice these days. More like luxury hotels than nursing homes." She was grasping at straws.

"You know Gram will never leave that house. She's always said they'd have to carry her out in a pine box, and I have no doubt that she means it." He took her hand again, the warmth of his skin on hers so familiar. "I know I'm asking a lot, but I really do think you'll love it in Lubbock. The people are genuine, and there's so much space . . . so many more opportunities . . ." He took a breath. "Working for the DA—it's not enough. There's more I could be doing. If I were a congressman, or a senator—"

"Because congressmen are renowned for their efficacy," she pointed out, a little too sourly.

He held up his hands. "I know, I know. But I still think I could be more effective in an elected position than I can be here try-ing to cut deals with low-level drug dealers and prostitutes. It's just—there's no way I could get elected here. You know how en-trenched politics are in California. Back in Texas, I'd be a local boy, one with a proven record in a blue state. It'd make me a strong candidate. The demographics are shifting. I really think I have a shot."

She pictured him shaking hands and holding babies, a banner

with his name stretched across the stage behind him. Their friends always said he should go into politics. She just hadn't realized it was what he wanted, too.

She reached for the gold cross around her neck. She tried to see herself standing up on a stage next to him, smiling proudly as the crowd showered him with love. Because they *would* love him. She knew that as sure as she knew her own name. Everyone loved Patrick. He was one of life's golden boys. It was what had drawn her to him in the first place. Out of all the women in the world, he had chosen her. She knew that made her lucky.

She should have known that eventually, he would want the world, too.

She stared at him across the table. His eyes were eager, searching, but there was something else there. The quiet confidence of someone who always wins and knows his streak isn't about to end. He was used to getting what he wanted, and she had always been willing to give it to him.

"Two years," she said, folding her napkin and placing it on the table. "I'll give it two years, but if I hate it, we move back here for good."

"Deal." His smile nearly split his face in two. "Becky, honey, I promise you won't regret this. I really do believe I could have a gift for political work. If I can get in a position of power, I can make a real difference."

She convinced herself that it was a victory. Two years was nothing in the grand scheme of things, and maybe a change of scene would do them both good. Didn't she keep complaining about how the city was grinding her down? The school budgets had been slashed to ribbons, she hadn't had a raise in years, the classroom sizes were ballooning just as resources were dwindling. It wouldn't be hard to get her teaching accreditation in Texas. She could have a couple easy years teaching in a nice suburban school, maybe take a few grad classes on the side. They could get a bigger place there—a house, even, with a front yard and a garage and a car. No more brushing their teeth on top of each other. No more sweaty bus rides uptown lugging bags of groceries.

Big skies. Open plains. Patrick by her side.

Two years was nothing. A blip on the radar screen.

She didn't know then just how quickly a life could be obliterated, like a sandcastle at high tide.

Rebecca glanced at the clock. It was close to one a.m., which would be eleven on the West Coast. Maybe he was asleep already, or maybe he was in the hotel bar drinking a vodka tonic with one of those "Hello, My Name Is" labels still stuck to his shirt, as if the people there wouldn't know the name of the keynote speaker. She had spoken to him earlier that evening, after he'd given his talk but before he'd gone to dinner. He was fresh from the shower—he always showered before dinner—and she could hear him getting dressed over the speaker, the sound of silk slipping through his fingers as he looped his tie around his neck. She'd answered his usual questions—Was she taking it easy? Had she eaten lunch? Had she set the house alarm?—and promised to call him first thing in the morning. She told him that she loved him, and that she missed him, even if the truth was more complicated.

She reached into her bag, wrapped her fingers around the hard plastic of her cell phone, dropped it. It was late—if he was going to call, he would have done so already. He didn't like to wake her up. Still, cold fingers of fear brushed against her neck. If he called and she didn't answer, would he send someone to the house to check on her? And if they saw she wasn't at home, would they find a way to track her down?

She thought of the papers tucked into her bag. Maybe he already had. Maybe they were already on their way.

She gripped the handle on the door, knuckles white. Her lungs tightened. It was happening again: the walls closing in, the darkness creeping at the edge of her vision. The Jeep was suddenly too small, a tiny metal cage, there wasn't enough air for them both. She was inhaling Cait's breath, and Cait was inhaling hers, and that meant they were using up all the oxygen. They were going to suffocate in this stupid tin can that smelled like stale cigarette smoke and fake pine and Cait's shampoo and the perfume that Patrick had given her for her thirty-fifth birthday and God how could she survive this, how could she survive?

She felt the girl's eyes on the side of her face, watching. *Don't look at me. Don't look.* The walls pressed in tighter. She was a baby bird nestled tight inside its egg. Her lungs began to scream.

California.

This was a trick she'd taught herself after the first few panic attacks. If she needed to escape the confines of her mind, she would take herself to California. She pictured the palm trees arcing above the parks and the Victorian houses painted in shades of sherbet and the smell of salt water everywhere. If she closed her eyes and thought hard enough, she could conjure up the view of San Francisco from Crown Beach: skyscrapers shrouded in mist, the swell of Nob Hill, the wide arc of the Bay Bridge.

She felt her rib cage start to relax, her breathing ease. She felt strong enough to talk. "Do you mind if I roll down the window a little? I think I need some air."

Cait nodded. "Sorry, I know it's stuffy in here."

The air was bracingly cold, and Rebecca felt shocked back into her body with every breath.

Cait's eyes were still on her. "You okay? You look a little—"

A streak of movement in the headlights. Flash of teeth and dark fur. A sickening thud. A whimper. Cait slammed on the brakes, the screech of tires on tarmac splintering the night, too late. Silence.

"What was that?"

Cait shook her head. She looked pale and stricken. "I don't know. A coyote, maybe?"

She opened the door and walked slowly to the front of the Jeep, legs shaking visibly from the shock. Rebecca followed close behind. They saw it at the same time: a smear of blood across the front end and a tuft of coarse hair caught in the grille. A mass of spiky reddish fur. A single limp paw.

It was a fox. From this angle, lying motionless beneath the undercarriage, it looked like it was sleeping. Only the dark red blood staining the muzzle gave it away.

"Oh, God."

Cait looked back to see Rebecca standing behind her. Cait shook her head. "Get back in the car."

"Is it—?" She didn't need the answer. She already knew.

"Get back in the car. You shouldn't be out here."

The fox was small—probably a female, and a young one at that. Rebecca thought of the den that used to be underneath the old trampoline in her parents' backyard. Her dad always pretended that they drove him crazy—"Mangy, overgrown rats," he'd mutter when he found a fresh lump of scat—but she had caught him smiling at them from the back window on more than one occasion. One summer, she woke up to find the cubs jumping on the trampoline, their little legs flying up in the air as they did flips and somersaults, their mother crouched watchfully nearby. "They're not much different from dogs," her mother had said, placing a hand on her shoulder. "Just a little wilder."

Rebecca reached out a hand and touched its chest. Its fur was soft underneath her fingers and still warm.

Cait stared down at the dead fox and up at the deserted street. "We can't just leave it here in the middle of the road." She looked at Rebecca. "Are you okay? You aren't hurt?"

"I'm fine. Are you?"

"I'm okay. I'm just sorry this happened. I should have . . ." She trailed off. The headlights cast two interlocking circles of light in front of them, stretching their shadows long. The only sounds, the hum of the engine and the faint static coming from the radio.

Cait straightened up suddenly and dusted off her jeans. "Why don't you get back in the car," she said, trying to steer her toward the door. "I'll take care of this."

Rebecca shook her head. "You can't move it on your own."

"Sure I can."

"Please." She leaned down and placed a hand on the fox's skull. "Let me help."

They worked silently, Cait gripping the fox's hindquarters while she took the neck. Together, they gathered the body out from under the Jeep and carried it over to the side of the road. It was surprisingly heavy; its fur was almost achingly soft.

"It looks like it was quick. Painless."

Cait nodded. "I hope so."

They placed the fox at the edge of a small patch of grass in front of a trailer park. "Maybe someone will find it in the morning and give it a proper burial," Cait said, tilting her chin toward the row of houses.

"Maybe."

They both knew that was unlikely. Dead foxes were a dime a dozen on a road like this—its body would be left for the vultures to pick over or tossed in the trash for the next municipal pickup.

Rebecca stared down at the fox and fought the sudden urge

to howl. It looked so lonely there, all alone in the grass. So small. Like its mother had never licked its soft fur clean, or given it an affectionate nip while it played with the other cubs. She looked away. It was awful, this world. Sometimes unbearably so.

She heard the sound of the Jeep's door closing and turned to see Cait walking toward her with a bundle of fabric in her arms. An old Baylor sweatshirt. She bent down and tucked the sweatshirt around the fox's body. The look in her eyes was both embarrassed and defiant. "I didn't want it to get cold."

As they pulled out of town, Rebecca could still make out the outline of the fox's shape in the moonlight, growing smaller and smaller. Soon it was out of sight.

Rebecca's palms were slick with sweat, and she wiped them discreetly down the sides of her dress. She was glad she'd worn black, even if Patrick had worried it would look funereal.

"I'm going for Jackie O," she told him as she fastened a strand of pearls around her neck.

Patrick winked at her. "You're gorgeous, whoever you're supposed to be."

The campaign manager he'd had for a few weeks—Rich Cadogan, one of the best in the business, according to Patrick—strolled in and handed Patrick a few notecards. "Make sure you hit the beats," he said, slapping him hard on the back.

Patrick ticked them off on his fingers. "Lower taxes for hardworking families. Better health care. Community outreach. Stricter penalties for repeat offenders. 'Tough on crime, tough on the causes of crime.'"

"You got it!" Rich beamed. He turned his attention to Rebecca. "Lose the pearls," he said, shaking his head. "People will think you're elitist, wearing them. Same with the shoes. Remember, people have to like you as much as they like Patrick. And the people *love* Patrick. Am I right, my man?"

Patrick grinned. "Only thanks to you." He caught the look on Rebecca's face and tempered his smile. "I think Rebecca looks great, though. Classy. Like Jackie O."

"The Kennedy thing doesn't play down here. We need to appeal to the suburban moms, and with you guys not having kids of your own, we're already at a disadvantage. If she goes out there looking like that, they're going to assume she's a bitch." Rich threw her a look. "No offense."

Rebecca felt her cheeks grow hot. "This is the only dress I brought. I don't have anything else to wear."

"Let me see what I can do." Rich slid out of the room, leaving a gust of Tom Ford in his wake.

Patrick watched as she unfastened the pearls. "He doesn't mean anything by it," he said, putting a tentative hand on her arm. "He's just doing his job."

"I know." She felt hot tears swelling behind her eyes. "I just want to get it right."

He turned her around and pressed her against his chest. "You will, sweetheart. You will."

But not yet. That's what he was saying, wasn't it? She would get it right in the end, but she hadn't gotten it right yet. The worst of it was that she knew he was right. The week before, Rich had arranged for a journalist to stop by the house to interview them as a couple, and as soon as the woman stepped over the threshold, Rebecca could feel her weighing up every inch of the place and finding it wanting. The kitchen was too sterile. The living room, with its open bookshelves and lack of television, was stuffy and try-hard. The cookies Rebecca offered her—bought specially from the nice bakery on Eighty-Second Street—were greeted with a polite grimace, and Rebecca knew instantly that it would have been better to have baked a batch of Betty Crocker chocolate chip from a boxed mix.

When the profile finally came out, Rebecca winced at the woman's description of her. She was "poised" and "reserved," and her blond hair was twice described as "sleek." (Lazy copyediting, Rebecca had chided, before she could catch herself.) Much was made of the fact that she'd been born and raised on the West Coast and educated at Berkeley. "Rebecca McRae spent six years teaching English at a progressive high school in downtown San Francisco." She could hear the eye rolls from ten miles away.

Patrick, on the other hand, had been painted as a returning hero, a local boy who'd fought off the demon coastal elites and returned triumphant to the Lone Star State. The writer described his eyes in elaborate detail and made particular mention of his strong forearms, visible thanks to his rolled-up shirtsleeves.

Rebecca had locked herself in the bathroom that night and stared at her reflection. Was this really who she was now: a stuck-up housewife with bad taste in baked goods? She should have pushed harder to find a teaching job in Lubbock, but transferring her credentials had been more difficult than she'd anticipated, and by the time she was certified, a new school year had begun and nobody was hiring. And then Patrick had been tapped to run for Congress, and he told her she'd be too busy helping him campaign to work.

"Once I'm elected, you'll have a platform to talk about education," he said. "You can use your brilliance to help thousands of kids in Lubbock, not just the thirty who are lucky enough to get you in the classroom." He'd reached out and held her chin in his hand. "We're going to make one helluva team, you and me. Texas won't know what hit it."

Now Rich flew back into the room and tossed a baby-blue cardigan and a pair of ballet flats toward her. "I stole them from the intern," he said.

She slid the cardigan on—the intern wore Shalimar, which had always given her a headache—and squeezed her feet into the too-small shoes. Patrick smiled. "You look perfect," he said, kissing her on the cheek.

Rich gave her a thumbs-up from across the room. "It'll work for today. I'll get a wardrobe consultant on board for next time."

Rebecca looked at herself in the full-length mirror. She didn't recognize the woman staring back.

She heard Patrick's name being announced and the swell of applause and felt his hand around hers as he tugged her out onto the stage. She stood behind him, chin tilted down, face carefully arranged to project pride and seriousness and approachability and family values and all the countless other attributes Rich had coached her on. She didn't have to speak—in fact, they would prefer if she didn't—just stand there and look at the back of Patrick's head adoringly as she sweated quietly into the intern's cardigan. Her feet already ached.

Patrick approached the lectern with a practiced wave and launched into the speech she'd heard him rehearsing in the shower that morning. "Good afternoon. My name is Patrick McRae, and I'm here with my beautiful wife, Rebecca, to ask that you elect me your next congressman for the great state of Texas!"

Rebecca hadn't said a word since they'd left the fox by the side of the road, and the mood inside the Jeep was grim. Her silence felt pointed. Judgmental. Like she blamed Cait for what had happened, even though it had clearly been an accident. That said, if she hadn't been so caught up in her own thoughts, maybe she'd have seen the fox in time.

She had to admit, she'd been surprised when Rebecca had gotten out of the car after the accident, and even more surprised when she'd insisted on helping carry the body to the side of the road. She didn't seem like someone who would be comfortable getting her hands dirty. Seemed more like a sidelines kind of woman, used to other people doing things for her. Especially the nasty stuff.

But she'd helped, all right—had barely even flinched as she lifted the fox's shoulders. Cait could still feel the weight of it in her arms, the soft fur tickling the insides of her elbows.

Guilt twisted her stomach. She should have been paying closer attention to the road.

She shook away the thought. Keep it light, that was her motto. If you let it get on top of you, you'll drown.

"Well, that wasn't exactly an auspicious start to the trip." She was trying for flippant, but when she sneaked a glance at Rebecca, she worried she'd missed the mark. The woman's face was as still and solemn as one of those ceremonial death masks.

A beat went by. "I'll be marking down your Uber rating, that's for sure."

Cait was quick to catch it. "Hey, don't forget I offered you bottled water earlier. That's worth at least a couple of stars." The joke surprised her: she hadn't pegged Rebecca as the joking kind, either. It was good, though. It was an opening. She could work with it. "So, terrible driving service aside, how are you feeling? Do you need anything?"

Rebecca shook her head. "I'm okay for now, thanks." The smile disappeared.

Cait nodded, easy. "Okay, well, just let me know. That's what I'm here for."

"I will."

Silence. She rode it out. She could sense Rebecca wanting to say something, felt it welling up inside of her. She just had to be patient.

Finally, Rebecca took a breath. "Have you ever had something bad happen?"

Cait looked at her. "Driving, you mean?"

Rebecca nodded.

Cait reached over and fiddled with the radio dial. Nothing but static. She was stalling for time. "Nothing serious."

"So something *has* happened?"

Cait shrugged. "One woman's boyfriend chased her out of the house with a baseball bat. I don't know if he was meaning to use it, or if it was just for show, but we didn't stick around to see. She dove into the car and I drove off as fast as I could."

"Jesus. Anything else?"

Cait shook her head. There was no point in scaring the poor woman. So she didn't mention the brick somebody had thrown through her windshield, as technically, that hadn't happened during a drive. A technicality, maybe, but an important one.

"Did the woman go back to him?"

"The boyfriend?" Cait shrugged. "I don't know. I tried to tell her that we could provide her with other services, that our help wouldn't just end once the procedure was finished, but she didn't want to talk about it. She didn't want to talk at all, actually—as soon as she was in the car and away from that house, she closed her eyes and slept all the way to Albuquerque. I don't know if she was faking it or if she really was that exhausted." Cait thought about it for a minute. "Probably both."

"So you dropped her off back at the house when it was finished?"

Cait heard the implied criticism and felt a flash of irritation. "We're here to help as much as we can, but we're also here to do what the client tells us. She told me to drop her back at the house, so that's what I did." *I did my job*, she added silently. *Just like I'm doing now.*

"Was the boyfriend waiting for her?"

"I don't know. I didn't see him. I waited at the curb for a few minutes after she went inside, just in case, but . . ." She shrugged again. "Nothing."

She could still remember the feeling of powerlessness as she'd watched the woman walk up the drive, the gentle slope of her shoulders signaling nothing but resignation. Cait had wanted to jump out of the Jeep and grab her and shake her. Instead, she just watched her disappear into the darkened house, and after sitting outside for ten minutes, she'd driven back to Austin and spent the evening sinking beers and trying to forget.

It was a feeling she was all too familiar with.

It was supposed to be a tongue-in-cheek personal essay: nothing more. It was a little clickbaity, maybe, but that's how Internet journalism worked. You wrote a piece about something, your editor stuck a controversial headline on it, and you got eyeballs. Eyeballs meant advertiser money, and advertiser money meant the website could pay their writers. Not much, obviously. Five hundred dollars was the most she'd ever gotten for a story, and that was a spon-con thing for a hotel chain. The stuff she'd cared about got much less—sometimes nothing.

She got a hundred dollars for this one.

She typed up the story as soon as the Lyft dropped her back at her apartment, the alcohol wearing off after a strong cup of coffee, leaving her buzzing and jittery. She wrote the whole thing in an hour and sent it to her editor—well, the woman she hoped would be her editor—at a website that specialized in confessional essays and gossip.

"Thought you'd like this," she wrote, and after she hit send, she took a long, hot shower and went to bed.

She didn't have high hopes for it—Jake was well known in Austin, but he was only starting to break out nationally, and country music was generally considered pretty niche. But the timing worked in her favor, and editors were clamoring for Me Too content, especially when it involved a famous (or even semi-famous) man and salacious sexual details.

In the morning, there was an email waiting in her inbox: "Loved this," the editor wrote, "but I think we should publish anonymously. I spoke to our legal team and we can't cover your liability. We'll pay you two hundred for your trouble. Sound okay?" She said it would go live later that day.

Cait was a little bummed that she wouldn't get the byline, but she was still getting paid to be published, so she took herself for fancy coffee to celebrate. She sat in the café texting Alyssa and swapping stories with her about their night. Alyssa had ended up ditching the tech bro at Cedar Street and then gotten in a limo with a bunch of Israelis who were about to ship back to their home country and start their stints in the national army. "Those guys can really party," Alyssa typed, along with a long string of emojis. "What happened to you?" she added. "You disappeared! *poof of smoke emoji*"

Cait filled Alyssa in on the details of her evening and told her to look out for the article later that day. At two p.m., the piece went live under the headline "WORST. DATE. EVER." The thumbnail was a photograph of Jake's brooding face with a pair of devil horns Photoshopped on the top of his head.

Cait clicked on the link with a fizz of nerves. The website wasn't in the big leagues, but it was gaining some cultural traction, and she was hoping that the article could put her on the ground floor of the new Jezebel or Man Repeller. She skim-read it, making note of what the editor had changed and what she hadn't. She thought it held up—it was funny and caustic and, yeah, maybe a little brutal, but the guy was a total asshole. He deserved to get it with both barrels.

She read it again, sent it to Alyssa, put on her uniform, and went to work at the bar.

When she checked her phone, after the bar was shut and the bottles had been married up and the back mirrors wiped as clean as she could get them, she realized that the piece had blown up.

It was what every writer wanted, right? As many eyes on the work as possible. But not in this way, not like this. The comment section was filled with his fans calling her worse than he had. A lot of them were women. There were men on there, too, telling her that she was a whore, that she deserved to be raped in order to be taught a lesson, that women like her were dirt, that women like her deserved to die. The word "skullfuck" was used in more ways than Cait had previously thought possible.

She felt sick to her stomach. Who were these people, and why did they hate her so much? Okay, so maybe she'd played it up a little in the article, but everything she'd written was fundamentally true. He *had* choked her when they were having sex. She *had* been scared, though maybe not quite as scared as she'd made herself out to be. Though that was only because she knew how these things usually played out. Jake hadn't wanted to kill her or even hurt her. He'd just wanted to show her he could, because he got off on the power. He wasn't exactly a rarity in that respect.

Still, a wave of shame washed over her, hot and thick. She must have done something wrong for people to hate her like this. It must somehow be her fault.

She was asking for it.

She read that line over and over. She had pursued Jake, it was true. She'd known what she was doing when she was dancing in front of him, had known the kind of promises she was making with her body. She had gone home with him willingly, had sex with him without asking any questions. Did she really have a right to complain just because his version of pleasure was different from her own? Hadn't she always known something like this would happen to her one day? Wasn't she lucky that it wasn't worse?

There was an email from the editor waiting in her inbox. The subject line was "Holy Shit." "Your story has had more clicks in the past eight hours than anything we've published before!"

And a text from Alyssa. "No one knows you wrote that piece, right? You need to keep it that way, because people are going CRAZY."

Cait pulled a glass off the stack, poured herself a few fingers of bourbon, sank it in a few swift swallows. Poured herself another. She'd have to write it off as wastage so JB wouldn't get pissy when he did the stock take. She felt the liquor slide down into her stomach, warming her fingers and toes, loosening the knot at the base of her throat.

Alyssa was right: she was lucky no one knew she was the one who'd written that article. Because right now, it was looking like a huge mistake.

Rebecca's mind kept tugging her back to the dead fox lying by the side of the road back in Sudan. She could see the steam rising from the pool of blood and the dull black beads of its eyes. She had first seen those eyes as a kid, when Bugs, her pet bunny, was mauled by the neighbor's dog. She saw that dog every day, twice a day, walking to and from the bus stop. His name was Fletch and he would track her the length of his yard, growling, penned in by a chain-link fence. One morning, she heard a commotion coming from the backyard and made it just in time to watch the dog shake Bugs until his brittle neck snapped. Fletch had dropped the bunny and run off when she'd charged at him screaming, but it had been too late. She watched the light go out of Bugs's eyes, quick and final as a birthday candle. One minute Bugs was her pet rabbit who loved bell peppers and chin scratches and whose whiskers tickled her when he twitched his nose, the next it was just a collection of bones and flesh and fur. That's why, later, when her mother tried to convince her that Bugs had taken the rainbow bridge to heaven, she knew it was a lie. She'd seen an animal die and now she couldn't unsee it—she knew that life could go from something to nothing, just like that, and that there was no use pretending there was something waiting beyond.

She put a hand to her stomach.

They passed a processing plant on the horizon with a line of silos rising in the dark sky like a row of blunt teeth. On the other side of the road, a restaurant welcomed potential customers: THURSDAYS = STEAK NIGHT.

A small green sign announced they were leaving Farwell, Texas, and entering Texico, New Mexico.

"We're through," Cait said, nodding toward the sign and giving her a small and gentle smile. "You can relax now."

Something tightened in Rebecca's chest.

Cait was wrong about danger lying closest to home. For her, crossing the state line meant the threat was suddenly, terrifyingly real.

SAN DIEGO, CALIFORNIA

Patrick sat down heavily on the hotel bed and rubbed his tired eyes. The conference had promised a four-star, but from the feel of the cheap linen, it was probably more like three. It didn't matter much to him. The places where they held these events were always the same: marble foyers—this one with a tinsel-laden artificial Christmas tree, to mark the season—and long echoing corridors and tiny soaps wrapped in paper. Tomorrow morning, there'd be breakfast with limp bacon and congealed eggs, and he'd eat it while people came up to his table and shook his hand. Some of them would linger, hoping to be invited to sit. He didn't mind. This was what it was all about, wasn't it? Connecting with people. Touching lives.

He checked the clock. Half past ten. It would be after midnight in Lubbock. She'd be asleep by now, or at least in bed. He knew she didn't sleep much these days.

He reached for the phone. He wanted to hear her voice, even if it was just for a minute. The way things had been with them recently . . . it tore him up inside, it really did. If he could just make her see things the way he saw them, if he could just make her believe, they wouldn't have to be like this with each other.

He wouldn't have to be like this. They could be happy, like they were before. Like they'd been back in San Francisco, all those years ago.

He clicked the call button and listened to the phone ring. She usually picked up on the second ring. Maybe she'd fallen asleep. Still, the phone should wake her up. He waited for the answering machine to pick up, but instead he heard the monotonous drone of an automated service. "We're sorry, your call cannot be answered at the minute. Please leave a message after the tone."

He held the phone in his hand for a second before disconnecting the call. Why hadn't the answering machine picked up? Maybe the power had gone out and the machine had reverted back to factory settings. But that automated voice . . . he'd heard it before.

It was her cell phone. She'd tried to set up voicemail when she'd first gotten it, but she'd given up. "There are too many buttons on this thing," she'd said, brandishing the Samsung in the air. "I give up. I'll just have to be a robot."

He checked the number he called. Definitely the house phone.

He scrolled down to her cell number and hit dial. It rang a few times and then the same robot told him to leave a message after the tone. He hung up and tossed the phone across the bed.

Why would she have forwarded the house phone to her cell? She'd promised him that she would stay at home while he was away. She needed rest. There was no reason for her not to be picking up the phone right now.

Unless.

He put his head in his hands. *God, no. Please. No.*

He reached over and grabbed his phone off the comforter, scrolled through his recent calls until he found Rich's number. He'd still be awake. From what Patrick could tell, his campaign manager never slept.

Rich picked up on the first ring. "Hey, champ! How's California? Did you knock 'em dead?"

"The conference went fine. Look, I'm sorry to call you this late—"

"No apology necessary. You know I'm available to you twenty-four/seven."

"I tried calling Rebecca at the house and she's not answering. I think . . . I think we might have a situation on our hands."

"Leave it with me. The wheels of justice are already in motion."

"It might be nothing. She might be at home, asleep. She might have accidentally turned the ringer off or left the phone off the hook . . ." Even as he said the words, he knew they weren't true. "I'm probably just wasting your time."

"You did the right thing by calling. Now go get some shut-eye, okay? You've got an early flight tomorrow, and we need you looking fresh for the judge."

"Could you let me know when you find her?"

The line went dead. Patrick cradled the phone in his hand for a minute before placing it on the nightstand and walking across the room to the minibar. He took out a couple of miniatures, poured them into a glass, and bolted the whole thing. And then got down on his knees and began to pray.

Cait knew a lot of people who didn't like driving—they hated the road rage and the boredom and the stiff necks and the pins-and-needles legs—but she enjoyed it, especially once she was clear of the city and out on the open road. There were times when she would be steering straight on one of these wide Texan roads for hours, staring at the dotted white line leading all the way to the horizon, and a Zen-like calm would come over her. It was the closest she'd come to meditating. She had used one of those apps once—a woman's voice in her ear, telling her to picture crashing waves or fields of wildflowers—but as hard as she tried, she kept thinking about all the shit she could be doing instead, and eventually, she switched it off and made a to-do list and went to bed.

You could take the girl out of Waco, but you couldn't make her believe in new-age-wellness horseshit, she guessed.

Out on the road, her mind would empty until it was just the sound of the engine and the feel of the Jeep hurtling forward through space. Sometimes she imagined herself in the car as a single still point in the universe while the rest of the world rushed past. She liked those moments the best, though after a while it started doing weird things to her head, like one of those Magic

Eye paintings they ran in the newspaper when she was a kid, and she'd have to squeeze her eyes shut for a second to reset.

Mainly, though, she liked the fact that driving was the only time she was ever truly, genuinely alone. At the bar, she was a sitting duck for whatever lonely soul happened to wander in looking for a drink and a little small talk, and when she wasn't serving customers, she was laughing politely at the manager's bad jokes or hassling the barbacks for fresh ice. Even in her cramped one-bedroom apartment, she never lost the sense of being surrounded by people. The walls were thin, and every time her neighbors made a smoothie or had sex or went to the bathroom, she could hear it, loud and clear. The sounds of other people's lives were with her all the time, pushing their way into her head.

In the Jeep, there was silence. It was like floating in her own little bubble, untouchable, even when she was sharing the road with hundreds of other cars. Even now, with Rebecca sitting silently next to her staring out the window, she could almost pretend she was on her own. Almost.

Cait pulled off at the exit for the first town she'd seen since crossing the border into New Mexico, then steered the Jeep through the deserted streets to the glowing blue-and-red smile of an IHOP sign. "Here okay?" she asked, already pulling into a space in a lot that was empty except for a pickup truck and a beat-up El Camino.

When they walked in, the waitress didn't bother to get up from the stool where she was filling out a crossword puzzle, just pointed at a pile of menus on the greeter stand and told them to sit wherever they wanted. Cait scanned the room, taking in the cook blowing cigarette smoke out through the emergency exit in back and a four-top of shift workers still wearing their high-vis vests. Cait picked a booth by the window and made sure to sit with her back to the wall, so she could keep a lookout.

The waitress eventually came over and took their order—coffee and a slice of cherry pie for Cait, ice water with lemon for Rebecca—and the two of them sat in silence while they waited, the swirl of Muzak filling their heads. The waitress shoved their drinks on the table with a grunt. Not expecting a big tip, then. Cait couldn't blame her. She knew from her own waitressing days that when you got a table of women, they weren't usually big tickets—appetizers split four ways and salads-as-mains and single glasses of house white. They tended to split the bill, too, and calculate the tip down to the penny. It wasn't like serving a table full of men, all dick-swinging and red meat and bottles of Barolo. Not that they'd be serving Barolo in a place like this, but the principle remained. Men wanted to show off for each other, and—if you were lucky—that meant a fat tip for the cute waitress. If you weren't so lucky, it meant fending off stray hands when you bent over to clear the table.

Cait always tipped big. She'd give the waitress 25 percent, easy, even though the woman hadn't said a civil word to them yet. She'd do it to prove a point more than anything else. Maybe next time a couple of women walked in here in the middle of the night, the waitress would be a little nicer to them. "Smile, sweetheart. It can't be that bad." How many times had she heard that when she was serving tables? Let the smile falter for one second and they were onto her. They thought she owed them that smile. That she should be grateful.

Bartending wasn't as bad. She controlled the alcohol, which meant that she was the most powerful person in the place. If somebody told her to smile, she could tell him to fuck off, and all they could do was laugh it off, because they wanted their liquor. Plus, there was a bar separating her from the customer. She still got the occasional hand reaching over when she bent down to fetch a beer from the fridge, but it was rare.

Cait poured a long stream of sugar into her coffee and stirred it with a spoon. She didn't normally take it so sweet, but the adrenaline from the fox was long gone and the exhaustion had set in right behind her eyes and she was left feeling like she was swimming in murky pond water.

"I'm sorry you've got to drive at this time of night," Rebecca said, scraping with her fingernail at a spot of syrup that had congealed on the table. "You know, I can drive for a while if you're getting tired."

"I'll be fine once I get some coffee into my system." There was no way in hell she was letting someone else drive her baby. "I'm basically nocturnal, anyway. This is no big deal."

"Do you mind it?"

"Being nocturnal?"

Rebecca nodded.

"It's fine. I'm a bartender, so it's an occupational hazard."

"You are? Where?"

"Back in Austin." Cait took a long pull of coffee.

"There are some nice bars in Austin, I've heard."

"Yeah, well, mine is the kind of bar where the bartenders wear Stetsons and Daisy Dukes. Not exactly the height of sophistication."

Rebecca looked horrified. "Seriously? That's so . . . so . . ."

"Gross? Degrading? Yeah, pretty much."

"Why are you working there?"

"The money's decent, and my landlord's pretty attached to getting paid his rent."

"Oh. Of course. Sorry, I didn't mean—"

"It's fine." Cait tried not to roll her eyes. Of course this woman would ask her something like that. She'd probably never had to work a day in her life. She'd probably never even set foot in a place like the Dark Horse, or an IHOP, for that matter. She probably assumed the world just ordered itself around her, one long red carpet rolling out in front of her, ready to be stepped on.

When she was growing up, Cait's family had been the poor ones in the neighborhood. They'd lived in one of the nicer areas in Waco—her father had inherited the house from his own father—and she'd been surrounded by the children of accountants and doctors and oil executives. She could still picture the look on the popular girls' faces when it was her mom's turn to host her Girl Scout troop. Mindy had wrinkled her cute little nose when she saw the linoleum kitchen floor and the ancient toaster oven languishing on the countertop. Cait had overheard her telling the other girls that it was a "trash house," and the girls had all laughed. She'd never heard that term before, but she knew instantly what it meant and that it was probably true. After they'd gone home, her mom had given her a couple of scoops of ice cream and told her not to listen to "those little bitches," but of course she had, and from then on she felt like she saw everything in her life through Mindy's eyes. The couch where she'd curl up with her mother and watch old movies suddenly looked tattered, the bedroom her three brothers shared suddenly seemed cramped and sad—no one else in her class had to share a room, never mind a *bunk bed*—and her mom's Friday tuna noodle casserole, which had been her favorite, suddenly tasted weird and cheap. Trash food, she would think as she sank her fork into it.

Nine was the year when she discovered that all of the things she'd loved about her life were actually not good enough.

She drained her coffee, sediment leaving a bitter trail down her throat, and signaled the waitress for a refill. She mashed her fork into the slice of pie. Now that it was in front of her, she didn't want it. The cherries were near-fluorescent red and covered in thick, syrupy goop. She pushed her plate away. The coffee would have to be enough to get her through.

48

She scanned the room. The four-top was still there in the back, the table littered with torn-up sugar packets and half-drunk cups of coffee. She saw one of them pass a flask under the table. She upped the tip she'd leave for the waitress, who had a long shift ahead of her, trying to get those guys out the door.

The cook had come back in from his cigarette break and was now standing at the pass, cell phone in hand. The waitress was at the refill station, taking her sweet time picking up the coffeepot. Cait's eyes snagged on a man sitting at the counter. She hadn't noticed him before. Middle-aged. Jeans and T-shirt. Nothing special about him. Still, she felt a seed of unease start to germinate in her stomach. She had to be alert all the time—wasn't that the motto at Sisters of Service? "Ever watchful, ever vigilant." When she'd become a driver for them, she'd sat through eight hours of training on an overcast Sunday, where they went over and over the necessary safety precautions. The drivers would be using their own cars—the organization couldn't afford a fleet—but would be given plates registered to a dummy address in Dallas. They weren't allowed to tell anyone where they were going or whom they were driving. No cell phones. No photos. No last names. And always, always assume the worst. At the time, she'd thought it was a little excessive, but she'd learned to appreciate the stakes. Especially since the man at the counter had turned to stare at Rebecca.

It wasn't the kind of pervy once-over she'd had so often herself and would expect a woman as pretty as Rebecca to get all the time. There was something behind his eyes that went beyond trying to imagine a woman naked. He looked like he wanted to strip her down to the bone.

Cait intercepted his gaze and didn't smile. That was what she did when guys did things like this: she challenged them. If growing up in a houseful of meathead brothers had taught her anything, it was not to back down from a fight. If they smell weakness on you, you're a goner.

She kept her eyes locked on him. He had the good sense to look away, but after a couple of beats, his eyes were back on Rebecca. There was something desperate behind them, hungry. It scared the hell out of her.

Calm down, she told herself. *Focus. Use your eyes to assess the situation. What do you see?*

Okay. No obvious holster. He might be carrying, of course, on the ankle or in the waistband. Could just be a creep not used to seeing a pretty woman. Could be some kind of weirdo with specific ideas about when women should be outside, making a point about them being out here on their own past midnight. Could be that Rebecca reminded him of someone.

Or maybe he knew where they were going and had made it his business to stop them.

Cait looked at Rebecca, still lost in her own thoughts. She hadn't clocked the guy yet. Good. It meant she would have less time to freak out when Cait made her move. In the dark glass of the window, she could see that the man had turned his body away from them, but also that the mirrored chrome above the pass-through to the kitchen allowed him to watch them. She caught his eye in the reflection and felt the hairs on the back of her neck stand up.

Time to go.

Rebecca looked at Cait, and Cait gave her the look. It was the sort of look a woman learns to feel rather than see. Cait flicked her eyes toward the man at the counter and then gave a barely perceptible shake of her head. Rebecca's face transformed into a mask of raw fear.

"What do you say?" Cait asked, as calmly as she could manage. "Back on the road?"

Rebecca nodded, her eyes still fixed on Cait's. She was scared—
that was obvious—but she was keeping her cool. Cait was impressed. She reached a hand across the table and lightly tapped
her wrist.

"Don't look," Cait said quietly.

Rebecca nodded. "I'll get the check," she said. Her voice was
shaking a little but steady.

"No time." Cait dropped a twenty-dollar bill on the table. No
time to wait for change—the waitress really would be getting a
good tip. "Ready?"

Rebecca went first, Cait close behind while she kept one eye
locked on the man. He didn't seem to see Cait at all: his gaze was
all for Rebecca. He tracked her all the way across the diner, but he
didn't make a move. He just watched. That was worse, in a way. If
he tried something here, there would be witnesses. Those guys in
the back might decide to play the role of hero. The chef would at
least have a knife at hand, and she'd be surprised if there wasn't
a gun tucked under the counter. Place like this, out in the middle
of nowhere, people usually didn't take chances.

Cait glanced out the window at the empty stretch of parking
lot. Once they were outside, they'd be on their own.

The door jangled as Rebecca opened it. The waitress looked
up from her crossword and, once she clocked the money lying on
their table, gave them a half-hearted wave. Cait couldn't remember the door jangling earlier. How had she not heard him come
in? She'd let her guard down, gotten too comfortable. She'd been
sloppy, and now they were going to pay for it.

A step across the threshold and they were outside, the air sharp
and cold on their faces, sprinting across the parking lot together.
The El Camino was long gone, but the pickup was still there.
Other than that, it was empty. The Jeep was on the far side of
the lot. Cait berated herself for not parking closer to the building.

The tarmac stretched in front of them, endless and black. Cait gripped her keys between her fingers and listened for his footsteps, sure she was about to feel his hands on her throat. She could hear Rebecca's ragged breath, and the echo of their shoes slapping against the pavement, but the door behind them didn't chime. He was still inside.

Unless he'd used the back exit.

Just a few more steps.

She hit the unlock button on the key ring and the headlights flashed on.

The two women dove inside and slammed the doors behind them.

Rebecca hit the locks.

Cait threw the Jeep into reverse.

She cast one last glance through the window as they peeled out onto the road. The counter was empty. The man was gone.

JAKE

"The thing that gets me," Jake said, dangling his beer bottle by its neck, "is I feel like she tricked me. You know?"

Craig ducked his head, which was his way of showing he was listening. It reminded Jake of being in confession as a kid, lying about how many times he'd punched his brother, leaving out the impure thoughts.

"I'm not even mad that she wrote about me, though my manager said I should start getting chicks to sign an NDA, and honestly, it's not a bad idea. It's the principle of the whole thing. It's like nothing's sacred anymore or something." He raised his beer to his lips and took a long pull.

Craig shook his head. That meant sympathy.

"I could tell she was crazy, but I thought it was the good kind of crazy, you know?" Jake shot a significant look at the crown of Craig's head. "You saw her that night, man. Dancing in front of the stage, making a show of herself. She came to fuck. So we fucked! And then what does she do?" He slapped his hand down on the table. "BAM! She twists things around so it looks like *I'm* the bad guy."

Craig lifted his head. "It's fucked up, man."

"It *is* fucked up!" Jake shook his head, baffled. "I swear, I will never understand women."

Craig made a noise that meant *I agree*. Craig had problems of his own—his ex-girlfriend from a couple months back had called earlier to say she'd been to the doctor and it turned out she had chlamydia, so he should probably go see a doctor himself so he could get some antibiotics. "It's very treatable," she'd said, as if that were some kind of consolation. He wasn't about to tell Jake, though. What, and get his balls busted for the next six months? Nah.

"The more I think about it, the more I feel like *I'm* the one who got violated or whatever, you know? Think about it: I let her into my house, I have sex with her, *which she was begging for,* and then I'm the one who gets the shit kicked out of him. She gets to tell her side of the story and suddenly everybody thinks I'm some kind of sick pervert. How is that fair?"

Craig grunted. He didn't have insurance at the minute. Fuck. How much was this doctor's appointment going to cost him? Maybe he could try the free clinic, though somebody might spot him there and he'd have to explain . . .

Craig took a swig of his beer. He'd Googled chlamydia after getting off the phone with her, and now he couldn't get the pictures out of his head. Holy fuck, man. That shit was no joke.

Jake leaned back in his chair. "What's crazy is, all the attention from the article has made the new single blow up," he continued. "My manager called this afternoon to tell me he got a couple calls from promoters, wanting to set up a national tour. So maybe I owe her a thank-you."

Did it mean that she'd been sleeping with other guys when they were still together? Was that how she'd picked it up? Craig made a mental note to Google the gestation time when he got home, and then changed his mind. He didn't want to know.

"Have you read the comments section? They're crucifying her. Not that they know who she is. 'Anonymous,' my ass." Jake shook his head again and finished off his beer. He signaled the waitress for another round. "I told my manager I was going to out her, but he told me it might make me less sympathetic. People might want to interview her, and she might make up some bullshit that would make me look worse." He shrugged. "I still wish somebody would out her, though. It'd be funny as hell."

Craig's brother-in-law was a pharmacist. Maybe he could just call him up, ask him to swipe a pack of antibiotics for him. It wasn't like he was asking for Oxy or anything.

Jake grinned at the waitress as she set their beers down on the table, and she smiled back. "Might have to get her number," he murmured to himself as he watched her walk away.

Nah, his brother-in-law would never agree to that. He was too much of a wuss.

"Okay, so maybe I was a little rough, but most chicks love that shit. Women like being dominated, period. They act like they want to be all independent, but deep down, they want a man to tell them what to do and how to do it. It's just human nature. Ain't nothing wrong with it." Long swig of beer, suppressed belch. "But what's crazy is that what she did to me is legal. Can you believe that? I mean, I believe in free speech as much as the next guy, but this shit is like . . . slander or something."

Craig picked up his beer bottle and started picking at the label. Shit. He'd have to risk the free clinic.

"I'm just saying, somebody needs to teach her a lesson. Put her back in her place." Jake twisted toward him. "You know what I'm saying?"

Craig was silent.

Jake nudged him with his foot. "Hey, man, are you listening?"

CANNON AIR FORCE BASE, NEW MEXICO—
217 MILES FROM ALBUQUERQUE

They'd been silent for the first couple miles back on the road, eyes trained on the mirrors, watching out for headlights, waiting for the man from the diner to appear on the road intent on killing them, but the lights of Clovis had faded and the road behind them had remained stubbornly empty. Rebecca felt herself breathe again.

Cait looked over at her. "Did you recognize him?"

"No." It was the truth: Rebecca hadn't recognized that man in the diner, but she'd known as soon as she'd seen him that he was there for her. The look in his eyes, caught in a fraction of a glance, was enough to tell her that.

Patrick must have called the house phone and realized she was gone. But how would he have found her so quickly? She looked at the dashboard clock. They hadn't been on the road longer than a couple of hours. It wasn't enough time for him to have sent someone to the house, let alone track her down like this.

Unless he already knew where they were headed.

Cait shook her head. "I didn't recognize him, either. Well, he's gone now, anyway. Are you okay?"

"A little shaken up. You?"

"I'm fine," Cait said, a little too quickly. She was still rattled and trying hard to hide it. "Honestly? He was probably just some creep." She sneaked a glance Rebecca's way, testing out whether she was buying it.

"Probably," Rebecca said vaguely. She didn't want to let Cait in on her suspicions, not until she knew for sure what was out there. She couldn't risk Cait deciding it was too dangerous. They'd read a disclaimer to her over the phone when she'd set up the appointment. "Sisters of Service holds the right to terminate a drive at any point if the client's safety or the driver's safety is in immediate danger. If a direct threat is made to the client or driver, Sisters of Service will contact the authorities immediately." Rebecca had agreed to the terms because this was her only choice. She couldn't afford to lose it.

"There are a lot of creeps in this world, but most of them are harmless. We get them at the bar all the time," Cait said. "Guys who think that just because you're serving them a drink, it means they own a piece of you. I had this one guy who spent the whole night tipping a buck on five-drink rounds. The bar closes, I'm walking to my car, and the guy staggers up to me and offers me a hundred bucks for a blow job."

Rebecca was horrified. "What did you say?"

"I told him I wouldn't touch his dick for a million bucks, and to get the hell away from me before I called the cops."

"Weren't you scared?"

"Of what? The guy could barely stand up straight."

"I would have been worried about making him angry. He could have hurt you."

Cait shrugged. "Like I said, he could barely walk, let alone take a swing at me. Besides, I grew up with three brothers. I can take care of myself."

Rebecca didn't challenge her. She knew Cait was saying it so she felt safe in her care, but something about the bravado rubbed Rebecca the wrong way.

She tried to remember herself at Cait's age. She'd been teaching by then, putting in fifty-plus hours a week in a dingy classroom and still working weekends at the bar for extra cash. Had she met Patrick by then? Probably. She'd been—what—twenty-five? So maybe a little younger than Cait. Twenty-five and waiting for her life to start.

It was his smile she saw first. It was blinding white, like something out of a toothpaste ad, a row of perfect teeth grinning at her from across the room. She looked away—that's what she'd been taught to do if she saw a man she was interested in, make eye contact and look away—and when she looked back, he was still smiling. With something close to awe, she watched him walk across the room.

Square shoulders, crisp button-down, that smile that led to a pair of deep dimples. He had eyes that could be credibly described as sparkling. He extended his hand and she reached for it without looking, and as soon as their palms touched, a thrill ran through her that she'd never felt before. "I'm Patrick," he said, and she said her name in a voice she barely recognized.

She was used to men approaching her. She was blond and thin and pretty—she acknowledged this about herself, she didn't engage in the false modesty that most pretty women insisted upon—and, despite her mother's worries, her air of detachment worked like catnip on men. She could sense it inside them when they looked at her, this desire to know what she was thinking. There were times when she caught a man she'd been talking to sizing her up like she was a specimen awaiting dissection and he was wondering which tool to use to pry open her skull. Sometimes she would give them her number, and sometimes she would even answer when they called. Mostly, though, she kept herself separate. Love, in her mind, was something powerful and all-encompassing, an earthquake or a hurricane. She was waiting for it to strike her.

With Patrick, it did, full force. By the end of the evening, he'd kissed her. She couldn't remember when she'd been kissed like that, his hands cupping her face, his eyelashes brushing against her skin as he pulled away, and she knew immediately that she was a goner.

Later, she'd ask herself if she'd had a choice in the matter. The more she knew him, the more she realized that Patrick had a singular vision for his life, and when he saw her from across the room at that party, she slid into it like fingers into a glove.

TWO YEARS EARLIER

The cut and scrape of silverware on good china. The tinkling of champagne glasses clinking together in a toast. The murmur of polite conversation, gentle as a babbling brook.

The thrum of a headache pressing against her sinuses. The nipped-in waist of her dress digging into her rib cage. The bile rising in her throat.

"Excuse me," Rebecca whispered as she pushed back from the table. Patrick barely noticed: he was elbow-deep in conversation with a major donor, some oil impresario whose name she'd already forgotten. The man's wife—Sara, she thought, or maybe it was Tara—gave her a tight smile and went back to staring at her plate of langoustines. She seemed to have taken an immediate dislike to Rebecca, or maybe she was just exhausted by the thought of another evening of making small talk while the men flexed their muscles and did their deals. Rebecca could sympathize.

She asked a passing waiter for directions to the bathroom, and he pointed to a door across the ballroom. She plucked her way through the tables, pleasant smile slapped on her face, and hoped she'd make it before she passed out.

The bathroom was one of those strangely formal affairs, complete with velveteen armchairs and vanity mirrors lined with light-bulbs, like something out of a Marilyn Monroe film. The designer had misjudged his audience. None of the women frequenting this bathroom wanted to inspect their faces under harsh incandescents.

There were only three stalls, so the line felt interminable. The women smiled at one another and then tucked in their chin and stared at the floor or their phones. No one wanted to make conversation while waiting for the bathroom. It was too personal, too humiliating. Besides, there was enough conversation waiting for them back in the ballroom. This was meant to be an escape.

Rebecca leaned against the wall while she waited, checking first to make sure it wouldn't smudge her dress. Another pastel number, high-necked and below-the-knee, and sprigged with spring flowers even though it was February. Rich had sent it over earlier, along with a note reminding her to wear hose. She'd rolled her eyes but had gone to her underwear drawer and double-checked that she had a pair without a run.

Four months. He'd been a congressman for four months. A minute and a lifetime. Long enough for her to have gotten the hang of being a politician's wife, especially if you factored in the months of campaigning. Some things were easier. She knew how to navigate her way through an interview now, and where to stand onstage so that she was visible but didn't overshadow Patrick. She had learned how to navigate these fund-raising dinners, even if they left her hollowed out with exhaustion.

Tonight was different, though. Tonight she'd felt exhausted before setting foot in the car. Her head was pounding. The bathroom smelled of intermingled perfumes and bleach and potpourri, and she could feel the bile rising in her throat again, her stomach cramping, something inside her bucking and twisting.

A gray-haired woman in a twinset emerged from a stall, and

Rebecca pushed past the line of women and slammed the door behind her. She didn't have time to twist the lock before she was on her knees, retching up the buttered dinner roll and the sparkling water and the half a langoustine she'd managed to choke down. Tears stung her eyes.

There was a knock on the door. "Are you all right? Can I get you something?"

"I'm fine," she bleated, just before her stomach revolted again. She was spitting up bile now, nothing more. She pressed her forehead against the cool porcelain.

Another knock. "Would you like me to get your husband?"

"No, thank you." She wondered briefly how they would know which husband belonged to her, but of course, all of them knew about her and Patrick. They had watched him onstage barely a half an hour ago. "My beautiful wife," he had said, pointing toward her, and they had joined in the polite applause while she practiced her demure smile.

Humiliation swept through her like a wildfire. She needed to get up off the floor and get cleaned up and go back out there before the news spread. As quietly as she could, she spat one last time in the bowl and then flushed. She pulled herself up and wiped the sweat off her brow and straightened the neckline of her dress and sailed out of the stall as gracefully as she could. "I'm sorry about that," she murmured apologetically. "There's a stomach bug going around. I must have picked it up."

The women cooed sympathetically as she dabbed water to her wrists and temples, but she could feel their eyes on her in the mirror, watching, weighing her up. She could feel the questions pressing inside them. Had they seen the waiter refill her wineglass more than once? Had she seemed unsteady on her feet or glassy-eyed? Worse: had the langoustines been bad? They had eaten them, too—did the same fate await them?

Rebecca checked her reflection in the mirror and tucked a stray hair back into place. She looked pale but not too bad. One of the women walked up to her and handed her a mint. "Your breath, dear," she said, and Rebecca flushed with embarrassment but accepted it gratefully.

When she got back to the table, Patrick was watching her, eyes anxious. "You okay?" he whispered as she slid in beside him.

"Fine," she said brightly. "Just a little upset stomach."

But a thought had occurred to her on her walk back from the bathroom, and she was already doing the mental math.

Her mother had told her once that the term "morning sickness" was a misnomer. "When I was pregnant with you, it was more like all-the-damn-time sickness. I couldn't keep down anything but saltine crackers for the first three months."

Six weeks on Sunday. Usually, she was like clockwork.

She stared into the distance as the waiter whisked away her plate.

ST. VRAIN, NEW MEXICO—
207 MILES TO ALBUQUERQUE

Cait sensed it before it happened, something tingling at the back of her neck. The sound hit her next. It was nothing at first, the buzz of an insect above the hum of the engine, but it grew louder, quickly, and just like that a pair of headlights was blinding in her rearview mirror. The truck was charging up the road toward them, fast. Too fast. The buzz became a roar.

The truck passed on her left, a blur of sound and steel, before swerving back into her lane and hitting the brakes. Cait had to slam on her own brakes to keep from rear-ending it. "What the fuck?"

The truck was moving slowly now, the speedometer barely edging thirty. "What is he doing?" Rebecca asked.

"I have no idea." It was a two-lane highway, and there was no one else out there. Plenty of room to pass. Cait moved into the left lane. He swerved in front of her. She moved back into the right. The truck followed. She leaned on the horn, hard. "What the hell is he doing?" The truck slowed down again. Twenty now. Fifteen. "Jesus Christ."

"Maybe he wants you to pull over," Rebecca suggested, but Cait shook her head.

"We shouldn't stop. We don't know . . ." She didn't have to finish the sentence. They'd read articles, watched films, read books, listened to podcasts, existed in the world as women. They both knew how the story could go if they pulled over.

Cait's eyes scanned the road. There wasn't a barrier in place, so if she could get up onto the hard shoulder, she might be able to get enough room to pass . . .

She hit the gas and jerked the wheel to the right. Rebecca let out a little yelp as the Jeep surged forward. Cait didn't have time to apologize. She was even with the truck now, though he was drifting toward her into the shoulder. She wrenched the wheel again and the Jeep stuttered into the dirt, the wheels slipping underneath until they found traction. She swept in front of the truck and hit the gas.

"What an asshole," Cait muttered as the truck's headlights dropped back.

But the truck accelerated, and soon it was tucked tight behind them. "Shit. I can't see a damn thing," she said, squinting to see through the windshield. The truck's headlights mixed in with the Jeep's, casting an eerie yellowish glow on the tarmac. The truck's high beams flashed on and off, and its horn began to blare.

Cait stepped on the gas, but the engine was slow to respond, and the truck surged ahead, keeping pace with her for a few long minutes before it passed them clean on the left-hand side and swung back in front of them.

Once again, the truck's speed slowed to forty, thirty, twenty. "What are you doing?" she shouted. They were crawling now. She moved into the passing lane. He moved, too. She moved back into the right lane. He did, too. She laid on the horn, hard. Nothing.

They were down to ten miles an hour now, and he was straddling the median, blocking her from passing on either side. She squinted out of the windshield, trying to get a glimpse of the driver in his mirror, but there was nothing but black glass reflecting her own headlights back at her.

"What do you think he wants?"

"I don't know." Cait saw Rebecca close her eyes.

She scanned the road. The last time she'd seen another car was a half hour ago. Clovis was twenty miles back, and the next town was still a good ways up the road. Plenty of time for him to do whatever it was he wanted to do. There wasn't a single other living thing except the jackrabbits burrowed in their dens and rattlesnakes coiled tight underneath the shrubs, and neither was of any use to them if they found themselves stranded out here because the psychopath in front of them had driven them off the road or worse.

She'd have to try to get past him. She tossed a glance at Rebecca. "You're wearing your seat belt?"

Rebecca nodded.

"Hold on. C'mon, baby," she murmured, and cranked the wheel to the right. The tires spat gravel as she swerved off the shoulder and back onto the road. The truck swerved, too, but not quickly enough. It clipped the back edge of the Jeep as it slipped past, a little nudge that Cait knew wouldn't leave more than a scrape in the already-dinged-up fender.

The truck's horn blared.

She sank the pedal to the floor. The Jeep could still move when she needed it to. Soon they were up to seventy. The truck was dropping back in the rearview. "I think we got him," she murmured. She stayed at a steady high speed with her eyes trained on the mirror until the headlights were nothing more than pinpricks fading into the night. "We lost him."

"What . . . who was that?"

Cait exhaled. She hadn't realized she'd been holding her breath. Her heartbeat was a flutter caught high in her throat, and her palms were slick with sweat. She'd thought they were goners back there. "I don't know."

"Do you think it was the man from the diner?"

"I don't know," she said again. She'd been wondering about it herself, but she couldn't see why he would have waited that long to make his move. Unless . . . unless he wanted to make sure they were out in the middle of nowhere, where no one could hear them. But how would he have tracked them this far without her seeing him? "I don't think it was the man from the diner," she said finally, as convincingly as she could.

Rebecca didn't look convinced. "I couldn't see the driver at all. Could you?"

"No, nothing." She glanced in the rearview again. Nothing but empty road behind them now. Whatever it was, it was over. No need to dwell on it. No need to scare the poor woman even more than she already was. "Honestly?" she said, making her voice light. She needed to keep things on course; she couldn't let them get off track. "It was probably just a bored teenager looking to cause trouble. We did stuff like that all the time when I was a kid—drag racing, playing chicken. It's what happens when you live in the middle of nowhere: you make your own entertainment."

"They could have killed us. We could have been run off the road. We could have—"

"I know, but we're okay now. Nothing happened." Cait took a deep breath, willed her pulse to ease up a little. "Teenagers, that's what I'm betting. Little shits. We'll be fine now. They'll find somebody else to pick on."

The two of them looked out at the long stretch of dark road. Neither of them pointed out that, out here at this time of night, there wasn't anyone else.

NINE MONTHS EARLIER

Cait was checking the bottles in the speedrail, making sure she had enough cheap tequila to make it through happy hour. It was something the barback was supposed to do, same as he was supposed to slice the lemons and limes and restock the ice well, but Jimmy had called in sick that day, so she was stuck doing it herself. It didn't matter much—it was a Tuesday after spring break, and all the college kids were hiding out nursing their hangovers, which meant she was going to spend her shift watching the TVs mounted behind the bar and trying to stay awake until close. She'd be lucky to walk out with twenty dollars in tips, but it was part of the deal. You had to take the crappy shifts along with the good ones. Saturday, the UT students would come flooding in, eager to show off their tans and swap stories about doing shots off a stranger's stomach in Cancún, and she'd walk out with three hundred dollars, easy. So she could suck up a slow Tuesday.

It was March Madness, which meant nothing but college basketball on the TVs, something Cait couldn't care less about, but at least it made the time pass. She watched De'Andre Hunter sink a three-pointer as she wiped down the bar top for the hundredth time and thought about checking her phone.

It had been a week since the article came out, and while the full force of the firestorm had passed, a few embers were still blowing around. Miraculously, no one had pegged her to it; she was still officially "Anonymous." It was a relief. They were welcome to write the occasional shitty line about her on 4chan, so long as no one came knocking on her door.

She checked the back bar, saw they were low on tequila, jotted it down on the stock notepad. JB was up in his office somewhere, probably smoking weed and watching porn, the manager's two great passions in life. He'd be able to see her on the security cameras, but she knew he never watched them. He wasn't the most effective manager she'd ever had, but he was the easiest. Stay out of his hair and he'd stay out of yours: that was pretty much the motto of the place.

Anyway, she'd been there for, what, two years now? She could be running the place if she wanted—the owner had said as much the last time he was in—but she knew that moving up to management would mean accepting this as her actual job, rather than a way to make easy cash while she waited for her real life as a writer to begin.

And she was close to it now, so close. Hers was the most-clicked-on article ever published by the website. Her editor had said that she'd made their name, though she had yet to see any of the cash. It had been a flat-fee rate, no share of the ad revenue, so while the website was raking it in, she was stuck with her two hundred bucks. She'd thought maybe she'd be able to convert it into more commissions, but so far, the editor hadn't liked any of her pitches. "Too worthy," she'd responded to Cait's pitch about sex trafficking across the border. "Do you have anything sexier?" Cait had feelers out with a dozen other editors, had even dropped a couple of not-so-subtle hints that she was the woman behind the Jake Forsythe piece, but so far she hadn't had any luck.

Still, she had to be close. Something she'd written had gone viral—surely that couldn't just be down to dumb luck. No, she didn't want JB's job. She was going to be a writer, a real one. One who got bylines and paychecks.

She felt a blast of warm air cut through the air-conditioning and looked up to see a couple of guys walk through the door. She tossed the rag under the bar and started pulling a couple drafts of Bud.

"Hey, Caity." Ken took up his usual stool at the bar, Nick sliding in next to him. "How're you doing this fine evening?"

"Bored out of my skull," she said, placing the cold beers in front of them. "How about you?"

"Ah, you know," Ken said, taking a long pull from his drink. "Same shit, different day."

"I hear you. You want a chaser to go with that? Two for one on whiskey shots. Thirsty Tuesday."

"Why the hell not."

Cait poured out two shots of Jim Beam, and the two men sank them and placed the empty glasses upside down on the bar. She tossed them in the dishwasher and wiped the bar top clean again.

"Where's the big man?" Ken asked. He meant JB.

"Up in his office, I think."

"Working hard or hardly working."

"You're telling me."

It went on like this for a while, Ken tossing patter across the bar and her tossing it back while Nick sat nursing his beer and staring silently at the screen above her head. Nick wasn't much of a talker, and she'd known him long enough not to try to force it. That was her job, more than pouring drinks. She was there to either talk or not talk, and to read her customers well enough to know which one they wanted at any given moment.

Ken always wanted to talk. He'd been coming in most weeks

for the past year, sitting in the same spot and drinking Bud drafts with whiskey chasers until his eyes went a little hazy, at which point he'd climb down from his stool, slap a ten-spot on the counter as a tip, and make his way back to wherever it was he came from. He talked a lot of hot air, Ken, but she liked him. He kept her occupied, especially on the slow shifts.

"Hey, you heard about this whole thing with Jake Forsythe?"

She arranged her features in what she hoped was bland disinterest. "No. What's that?"

He shook his head. "You know he's a musician, right? I saw him down on Fourth Street a few months back, pretty good, too, though the guy needs a haircut and he was wearing his jeans a little too tight." He flicked a glance at Nick. "Not that I was looking at his ass or anything. Anyway, this chick goes home with him—completely willingly, by the way, she even says so herself—and they have sex—again, completely willingly—and the next thing he knows, she writes some article claiming she's been violated or something." He threw his hands up in the air. "Call me crazy, but I just don't think that's right. I mean, the poor guy's just trying to get laid, and this girl uses him to get attention for herself."

Cait tried to swallow her pounding heart. "Maybe she didn't like what happened when they were having sex. Maybe it wasn't a good experience for her."

Ken pulled a face. "If I complained every time I didn't have a 'good experience'"—he put air quotes around the words—"I wouldn't have time to go to work or brush my teeth in the morning. Jesus Christ, Caity, how often does anyone have a good experience in this world?"

"That's a pretty cynical view."

"Hey, it is what it is, and I'm not complaining. These two people wanted to have sex with each other, so they had sex. That should have been the end of it. Instead, just because this girl didn't see stars during it, or wasn't showered with roses afterward, she goes off and writes some article tearing him a new asshole and puts it out there so the whole world can read it." He shook his head. "If a man did that to a woman, there'd be hell to pay."

"Yeah, well, if a woman tried to choke a man during sex, it probably wouldn't have been as traumatic. He had fifty pounds on this woman. He could have killed her."

He looked at her sharply. "I thought you said you hadn't heard about it."

She turned her attention back to wiping down the bar, but she could still feel him staring at her. "I remembered something about it when you were talking."

"How do you know he had fifty pounds on her? They don't know who the girl is who wrote the article. She did it anonymously, which is even worse in my opinion. Cowardly."

"I was speaking generally," she blustered. She felt a trickle of sweat run down the small of her back. "Usually, men weigh more than women, and they're stronger. I've seen a picture of Jake, and he's not exactly a small guy."

"Yeah, fair enough." Ken's eyes trailed up to the screen above her head. "Still think it was bullshit, though. Political correctness gone crazy."

"I'm going to go on break. You want another before I go?"

He waved her away. "Nah, it's fine. You go ahead. Sorry for getting heated. It's just things like that just really boil my piss."

"Don't worry about it," she said, forcing a smile. "I'll be back in twenty."

She ducked into the break room, a cigarette already in her mouth. She lit it and took a long drag. Her pulse was still racing, and the nicotine made her feel woozy and a little nauseated.

That was close. Too close.

You're okay, Rebecca told herself, steadying her shaking hands under her armpits. *You're alive. There's no reason to panic.*

Of course, that was a lie.

She didn't believe Cait's story about teenagers driving that truck. She knew deep down, at the center of her core, that the truck had come after them deliberately. And as much as she wanted to think it might not be the case, she knew it was her they were after.

She reached down into her bag and switched her phone on. No missed calls. No text messages. Just the lock screen of Patrick's face pressed against hers, both smiling for the camera. Reception: no service.

They were out of range. If he tried to call now, it would go directly to voicemail. It wouldn't even ring—he would think that she'd turned off her phone. She could tell him the battery had died, but if he called the home phone and she didn't pick up there, either . . . No. She had to hope he was asleep in his hotel room. Dead to the world. She breathed out a long, shuddering sigh and shoved the phone back in her bag. She'd keep it on, just in case.

"You waiting for a call?" Cait asked. There was no warmth in her voice.

Rebecca kept her head down. "I just wanted to see if I had any reception," she said. "I don't."

"How long has your phone been switched on?"

"I just turned it on."

"You sure about that?" Cait's voice was icy.

"Yes," she said, as forcefully as she could manage. "I'm sure."

"There's a reason I asked you to turn your phone off. Do you understand that reason?"

"I'm not stupid," Rebecca said. She was hot with shame.

"I'm not saying you're stupid," Cait said evenly. "I'm just wondering if you fully appreciate the dangers of the situation."

"Of course I do," she snapped.

Cait lifted a shoulder in a shrug. "Well, I'm not too sure of that, all things considered."

Rebecca wanted to slap her. It was Rebecca's life that was on the line here, not hers. Cait was just a glorified taxi driver with a chip on her shoulder and an ancient Jeep that smelled like the inside of a gym locker. Rebecca should be doing this on her own, not reliant on some stranger's charity. She hated the fact that she was in this position, hated the fact that she was weak, hated the fact—most of all—that she knew deep down that Cait was right. She was in danger, and she had to be careful. More careful than she'd ever been in her life.

She took a deep breath and arranged her features in her best approximation of contrition. "I'm sorry I turned my phone on," she said quietly. "I just wanted to make sure no one had tried to contact me. If someone had, they might wonder why I didn't answer and get suspicious."

"It's the middle of the night," Cait pointed out. "Why would someone be suspicious about you not answering your phone?"

She was like a dog with a bone. Rebecca's palms began to tingle, something they always did when she was nervous. "I don't know," she said carefully. "I guess I just wanted to make sure."

Cait made a noise that was more like a grunt, and Rebecca saw that she believed her. "Well, just keep it switched off from now on, okay?"

Rebecca nodded and pulled the phone out of her bag.

"Wait."

Rebecca looked up at Cait, her finger hovering over the power button. "What?"

Cait ran a hand across her mouth. "While you've got it out, can you look up the nearest gas station?"

She shook her head. "I still don't have service."

Cait cursed under her breath.

"Are we running really low?" Rebecca asked, a flutter of nerves batting around in her stomach.

"No, not too bad." There was a tightness in her voice that Rebecca didn't like. Her eyes moved to the gas needle. It was deep in the red. Cait caught the look on Rebecca's face and smiled. "Don't worry," she said, "I've driven on empty for miles and miles before. The gauge isn't right."

"How long do you think until the next town?"

"I'm not sure. It can't be too far, though, and I think the next town along is pretty big. We shouldn't have a problem finding somewhere to fill up."

Rebecca could tell Cait was bluffing. She didn't like the idea of stopping—not after the man in the diner, not after the truck—but she liked the idea of running out of gas in the middle of the desert even less.

Her eyes wandered over to the needle on the gas gauge. "Do you have a map in the glove compartment? I could see if there's anything marked out on it."

Cait shook her head. "I've done this route before," she said. "It's just a straight shot on 60. I didn't think I'd need a map." She had the good grace to look faintly embarrassed. *Of course she wouldn't have a map*, Rebecca reminded herself. *She's a kid*. Though, saying that, when was the last time she herself had used a map?

She had a flash of the trips she'd taken with her parents as a kid, her dad driving while her mom wrestled to read one of the huge maps they'd been sent by AAA. Her mother hadn't liked to fly. No matter how many times Rebecca's father had explained the mechanics to her, she still didn't trust the idea of something that big and that heavy somehow ascending into the sky. When her father was still in the navy and scattered all over the globe, her mother had forced herself to fly—she'd pop a Valium, go to sleep, and wake up in a different time zone, groggy and disoriented and faintly surprised by her survival—but once he retired and they settled in Alameda, she declared her flying days were over. "Emergencies only," she used to say, though she would never be drawn out on what constituted an emergency. She didn't board another plane for the rest of her life.

That meant that Rebecca's childhood vacations were limited to places within driving distance of their house. Not that there wasn't a ton to see around there—they'd gone to Big Sur and Joshua Tree and the Grand Canyon by the time she was ten. These trips were rarely planned. She would just wake up one Saturday morning and the station wagon would be packed and she would be told to brush her teeth and wash her face and be down in the car in ten minutes. She would grab a stack of books and her Discman and the pillow from her bed, and within the hour they'd be driving over the San Rafael Bridge or down through San Jose, the morning light streaming through the windows while U2 played tinnily through her headphones.

Once, when her mother had declared a desire to see snow, they had driven up through Northern California and Oregon and most of Washington to the border with British Columbia. Rebecca could still remember the slap of cold air on her cheeks when she opened the car door, and the soft crunch of the snow underneath her unsuitably thin sneakers.

She felt the familiar ache in the center of her breastbone. God, she missed them.

Cait was watching her again. The earlier severeness had been washed away, replaced by a careful, solicitous kindness. "Are you feeling okay?" she asked gently, and Rebecca realized that she was apologizing.

The truth was, she was too hot and nauseated, and there was a headache blooming at the center of her forehead, right between her eyes. "I'm okay," she lied.

"Well, just let me know if you need anything."

Rebecca nodded. "Thanks." She let the silence lie between them for a few seconds. "It's my husband," she said finally. "That's why I keep checking my phone. He's away on business, and sometimes he calls me late at night if he can't sleep, and if I don't answer . . ." She waited to see how Cait would react. A lot of people knew her husband—and knew her by extension—and she'd been wondering if Cait was one of them.

But Cait's face stayed neutral. "I get it. How about this? You turn off your location information, and I'll stop hassling you about leaving your phone on." She shrugged. "I can't promise he'll be able to get through if he calls, considering there's no reception, but it'll give you a better shot."

Rebecca felt a rush of relief. "Would that be okay?" She was already reaching for her phone.

"Yeah, should be."

Rebecca flicked off the little green switch and slid the phone into her bag again. "Thanks."

Cait nodded. "No problem."

Rebecca waited for the follow-up questions, but none came. If Cait was surprised about the fact that she was married, she hid it well. She felt a swell of gratitude as she turned her face back toward the window and watched the bleached-out desert sail by.

She felt safer already.

Rebecca was eight weeks pregnant when she got the call.

She didn't answer it at first—she didn't recognize the number and assumed it was a robocall trying to sell her insurance—but it flashed up again a minute later, and this time she picked up.

The woman introduced herself as Kelly. "We live next door to your father," she explained, and the bottom dropped out of Rebecca's stomach.

"What happened? Is he okay?"

There was a pause on the line. It was only for a second, but it was long enough for Rebecca to know her life was about to change. "There's been an accident," Kelly said gently, and Rebecca started to cry.

A car had hit a dog outside her father's house. He must have been watching from the window, because as soon as it happened, he was out the door and running down the porch steps to help. In his hurry, he missed a step and fell headfirst onto the concrete sidewalk below. The driver of the car called an ambulance. Kelly followed it to the hospital, which was where she was calling from. "The doctors won't tell me much," she said. "They say they can only discuss his condition with family." Another pause. "I'd get out here quick if you can."

Rebecca flew out that night. Patrick was in Aspermont and couldn't make it back in time, so she went on her own. By the time she got to the hospital, her father had been on life support for nearly twelve hours. He had a DNR on his file, but the EMTs had intubated before they'd had the chance to check, and now it would require a family member to make the decision.

Rebecca was the only family he had left.

She gave herself an hour with him, but no longer. She knew if she let it stretch beyond that, she wouldn't be able to bring herself to let him go. It was what he wanted, though—to be let go. He'd told her as much several times over the years, first when her mother got sick and they'd sat sentry at her bedside and watched the cancer eat her down to the bones, and again a few years later when he had a minor heart attack. "Don't ever let me rot in a hospital bed," he'd said to her. "When it's my time, it's my time."

She held his hand and talked to him. She told him about Texas, about the big house he'd never gotten the chance to see and the tamale place down the road he would have loved. She talked to him about Patrick's work as a congressman and imagined him rolling his eyes.

He'd never warmed to Patrick. On her wedding day, right before he walked her down the aisle, he'd held her back and told her there was still time to call it off. "I love him," she'd told him, laughing. She was his little girl. She understood that letting go was hard. "This is what I want." He'd leaned over and brushed a kiss against her cheek and said, "Okay, sweetheart. Whatever you want. Just know I'll always be there for you, okay?" Patrick later told her that her father had shaken his hand so hard at the top of the aisle, he thought he could hear bones snap.

Now she told him her favorite stories from when she was a

kid. Him and her mother swinging her through the surf at Crown Beach. The time they went to Disneyland and she'd made him ride Big Thunder Mountain with her and he'd thrown up in the garbage can as soon as the ride finished. The cake they'd made for her mother's birthday, lopsided and Pepto-pink and tasting somehow of sawdust.

She tried not to look at his face, slack and pale, or notice how small his body looked in the bed. He'd been a big man, her father, broad-shouldered and six feet even. A military man to his core. But, she realized, age had started to chip away at him. She allowed herself to feel grateful that he wouldn't have to suffer through the indignities of being elderly. He would have hated it.

Right before she signaled for the doctor, she curled herself around his body and hugged him close. "I'm pregnant," she whispered in his ear. "You're going to be a granddad." She was sure that she saw his eyelids flutter, but when she looked again, his face was as still and placid as a lake.

She watched them pull the tube from his throat and listened to the heart monitor flatline, and then she'd taken a cab back to her father's house and curled up in the bed he had shared with her mother and tried not to think about the fact that she was an orphan now at the age of thirty-three. The house smelled like him, and she found herself burrowing her face in an old sweater of his, trying to breathe him into her.

At some point, she fell asleep.

When she woke up in the early hours of the following morning, she was cramping, and when she stumbled into the bathroom, her underwear was spotted with blood.

OUTSKIRTS OF TOLAR, NEW MEXICO—
180 MILES TO ALBUQUERQUE

The engine gave out twenty minutes later, letting out a sad cough before coasting them to the side of the road.

Cait ran a hand across her face. "Shit."

"Do you have a gas can in the car?" Even as the words left her mouth, Rebecca knew the answer. If there was a gas can, Cait wouldn't be swearing.

Cait winced. "I usually do, but . . ."

Rebecca felt a prickle of irritation. She knew she was meant to feel grateful to this girl—and yes, that's what Cait was, a girl, not a woman, not a grown-up—but this was irresponsible. How could she have been so careless? Now they were stuck in the middle of nowhere, with no hope of flagging someone down to help, and even if they did see someone, how could they be sure it wouldn't be some maniac? The man in the diner, whoever had been driving that truck . . . they were coming for her, right now, and there was no place to hide.

The air inside the Jeep suddenly felt stagnant and soup-thick. The seat belt was tight on her shoulder, and the skin underneath chafed. The world outside started to recede, frame by frame, and her field of vision filled with black stars. Her hand scrambled at the door. She had to get out. She couldn't breathe.

"Wait, Rebecca—" She heard Cait's voice behind her shoulder, but it sounded faint and far away. The black stars were getting bigger. She had to get out of this goddamn Jeep. She had to get away.

The handle popped open underneath her grip and the door swung open. The night air was like a glass of ice water thrown into her face: cold enough to shock her out of her own mind. She took a few deep lungfuls of clean, crisp air, so sharp they almost hurt.

"What are you doing? Are you okay?" Cait had climbed out of the car, too, and was watching her with a combination of bafflement and concern.

She took a deep breath. The stars were receding, and her mind had cleared. "Sorry, I get a little claustrophobic sometimes. I just needed to get some air."

"You *are* really pale. Do you want some water?"

"I'm fine now, honestly."

"Okay. Just let me know if I can get you anything."

How can you get me anything if you can't even get us where we're going? "What are we going to do?"

"Call a tow truck, I guess. See if they'll send someone out with a gas tank, or tow us to the nearest station," Cait said, biting savagely at a cuticle. "I'm so sorry about this. I don't understand what happened. I filled up the tank before I picked you up, so we should have been fine."

"Do you think there was a leak?"

"Maybe. I don't remember hitting any big bumps or anything, though, so I don't know how that could have happened." Cait ducked back into the Jeep and started rummaging around in the glove compartment. Rebecca heard a muffled curse. "No signal," Cait said, holding up her phone. "What about you?"

Rebecca checked her phone. "Me, neither."

Cait kept her face neutral, but Rebecca could see the panic in her eyes. "Oh well," she said, her voice unnaturally high. "We'll just have to rely on the kindness of strangers. I'm sure someone will come by soon enough."

Rebecca felt a flicker of fear. This was the person who was responsible for getting her to Albuquerque alive, but right now she looked like a scared little kid struggling to keep it together. She shook her head. "It's too dangerous."

"We don't have a choice. Anyway, flagging someone down can't be any more dangerous than sitting on the side of the road in the middle of the night, waiting to freeze to death."

"What if the truck comes back?"

Cait scooped up a few pebbles and tossed them into the brush. "I told you, that was just teenage stuff."

"What if it wasn't?"

"What do you want me to say?" Cait snapped. "That we're fucked? That some ax murderer is going to come down the road any minute and chop us up into little pieces? Is that what you want to hear?" She tossed another pebble, harder this time. "Because I don't see how that shit is helpful."

The two women stared at each other, anger pulsing between them like a heartbeat.

Cait held up a hand. "Look, I'm sorry, but—"

Rebecca spun on her heel. "I'm going to see if I can find a signal." She needed space from the girl, the car, the road. She held the phone up as she walked, waiting for a bar to appear, but it remained stubbornly blank.

She picked her way across the dusty ground, the headlights dimly illuminating scraps of brittlebush and Apache plumes. The landscape was vast and frozen and cast in shades of black and white, like the surface of the moon. The light from the Jeep receded and soon it was just the slivered moon and the vast carpet of pinprick stars lighting her way. She had a sudden near-violent urge to break into a run and keep running out across the vast stretch of frozen dead land, straight on until she fell off the edge onto the other side.

One bright summer morning when she was five years old, she'd gone out into her parents' small backyard with the plastic bucket and spade her mother had bought for the beach, and she'd started digging. By lunchtime, there was a knee-deep hole in the ground. By afternoon snack, it was up to her waist. She went slowly, crouching beside the pile of scooped dirt and sifting through it for treasure.

Her father had come home from work early that day and found her sitting next to the hole she'd dug. "You dig any farther," he'd said, ruffling her hair as he headed back into the house, "you're going to fall out the other side."

She dug even harder.

That night, she dreamed of falling into the hole like Alice in Wonderland, and waking up in an upside-down world filled with Cheshire Cats and Mad Hatters. In the morning, she ran outside to find the hole filled in and the dirt tamped down tightly across it. She burst into tears.

Her father heard her and came outside to comfort her. "I didn't want you to hurt yourself," he'd said, placing an arm around her thin shoulders.

She'd turned her tear-streaked face to his. "But now I'll never see what's on the other side."

That's what she wanted to do now: reach the edge of the world and launch herself off the precipice. She could feel the plummet in her stomach, the giddy flip before impact.

She hated the fact that she was out here in the middle of no-where, forced to rely on a stranger's help. Cait didn't know what the hell she was doing—that was becoming more obvious by the minute—but the worst thing was that Rebecca had no choice. In that moment, she felt like a star shining down from the night sky: cold and remote and utterly alone.

"Rebecca?" She could hear the fear in Cait's voice as it rang out across the desert. She shouldn't have stormed off like that. Rebecca took one last look at the screen on her phone—still no bars—and headed back.

The Jeep's hood was up, Cait buried deep in its guts.

"What are you doing?"

Cait straightened up at the sound of her voice. Rebecca could see the relief in the girl's eyes. "Just seeing if I can figure out what happened with the tank. I've had a look underneath and it doesn't look like we have a leak or anything, at least not that I could see." She wiped her grease-smeared hands down the front of her jeans. "I'm sorry for not having a spare gas can in the car. I should have been better prepared."

Rebecca felt herself soften a little, but not enough to accept the apology. Not yet. "How do you know that stuff?" she asked, gesturing toward the hood.

Cait shrugged. "My dad taught me. It's not that hard, really, especially on an old car like this. Now they're all run by comput-ers, which makes it way harder to diagnose a problem. You need a technician with a scanner and all sorts of stuff."

"I don't even know how to change the oil in a car," Rebecca admitted. "I guess I'm not very practically minded."

"Yeah, well."

"So you don't think it's a leak? That's good, right?"

"Hopefully, though it doesn't explain why we ran out of gas."

Cait ducked her head back under the hood, and Rebecca could hear the scrape of metal on metal. "Hang on."

"Did you find something?"

Cait emerged holding what looked like a small electrical plug. "This isn't right."

"What is it?"

"It's the fuel relay. It was loose."

"Maybe when we hit the fox . . . ?"

Cait shook her head. "Stuff like this doesn't just come loose."

"What does that mean?"

"I think somebody's been messing with it." Cait kept her eyes on the plug nestled in her palm. "I think somebody might have drained the tank on purpose."

She fixed the plug back in place and slammed the hood shut.

KEN

Ken parked up outside the Dark Horse and killed the engine. He checked his watch: 5:23. A little early—Nick wouldn't turn up until six o'clock sharp, with the same clockwork precision that he did everything with—but Ken didn't mind. It wasn't like being in Nick's company was all that different from being alone, anyway.

Don't get him wrong, he loved the guy like a brother. Hell, he practically *was* his brother, he'd known him so long. They'd gone to school together, two little kids with skinned knees trading baseball cards on the playground. Nick had been quiet then, too—had taken some crap from the other kids for it—but Ken hadn't minded. Things at home were always so loud—his father shouting, his mother screaming and crying—and things in his head weren't much different. From as far back as Ken could remember, his mind had buzzed with a swarm of thoughts, and he usually couldn't stop those thoughts from coming straight out of his mouth the second they popped into his head. His mother used to tell him he had verbal diarrhea. Nice thing for a mother to say to her kid, right? She said a lot of things in her time, most of which he tried not to remember. It can get to you, that stuff. Wear you down.

Anyway, Nick was quiet, and Ken was loud, and they worked

well together like that. Their friendship was like one of those yin-yang stickers he'd see on the back of some hippie's van.

He walked across the parking lot and pushed open the door. The place was nearly empty, even though it was happy hour. He remembered a time when everybody stopped work at five on the dot, but it seemed like people were working later and later these days, stretching the workday well into the evening, out of pride or necessity, he didn't know. Ken, he didn't understand that. Don't get him wrong, he worked hard, but he didn't work a minute past what he was getting paid. Why should he? They weren't running a charity, and he sure as hell wasn't a volunteer.

Ten more years. That's what he told himself every morning when he pulled on his stupid brown shorts and buttoned up the itchy brown shirt and set off in his stupid brown truck. Ten more years and he'd be finished. It wasn't that he hated his job, though his knees were starting to give him trouble. He liked it for the most part, driving his route, seeing the same faces, making conversation with people, seeing the insides of people's houses and offices, catching little glimpses of their lives. He could tell a lot about people by what they had delivered. Some people were real addicts, buying stuff off the Internet and letting it pile up in the hallway. Some were just lazy. Ken, he'd rather go to the store to buy something, hold it in his hand and feel the weight of it, than click a button and sit on his ass waiting for someone like him to bring it to his doorstep.

He slid onto his stool at the bar, signaled the bartender to bring him a drink. It was some guy with bleached-blond hair, worn too long. His son wore his hair the same way, or at least he did the last time Ken saw him, which was . . . when? Last Christmas? Beth said it was his fault that Brian didn't come visit more often, but what was he supposed to do? Pretend that the life Brian was leading was just hunky-dory?

Thank God he had his little daughter. Though she wasn't so little anymore. Erin would be in college next year, which scared the daylights out of him. All grown up. No more Daddy's little girl. Just the other day, she came home and he swore he could smell rum on her, not that she'd admit it. Beth told him to leave her alone when he'd asked her about it, but how could he leave the girl alone, knowing how her brother turned out?

He took a long pull from his draft, made a face. The long-haired guy didn't pour them as nice as Cait. Didn't offer him a shooter, either, like she would have. He looked around for her, hoping to see her come out of the stockroom. She usually worked on Thursdays.

Sweet girl, Cait, or at least he'd thought so until he'd seen her standing in that parking lot. Since then, he'd learned a lot about his favorite bartender. Cast things in a whole new light, as they say.

He pulled out his phone and started scrolling through his notifications. It was strange to think he'd lived half his life without the Internet, had only owned one of these smartphones for—what? Five, six years? Now it was like another limb or something. He knew it wasn't good for him to spend so much time on it. Beth told him so all the time, though she didn't have a right to talk considering how much time she spent on Facebook. *That* he didn't get. Didn't looking at someone else's vacation photos used to be shorthand for "boring as hell"? He could still remember his parents setting up the projector so they could show off their photos of the Grand Canyon. He was sure nobody had fun looking at those, though maybe that was because his mother once threw the carousel wheel at his father's head during the middle of a viewing.

It had its uses, though, Facebook. It was good for organizing and recruitment. And of course he had his Saturday gang.

But 4chan. Finding that was a revelation. All the thoughts that swelled in his head throughout the day, that he had no one to share with when he was driving the truck: now he could just pull over, put it out there on a forum, and by the time he looked at his phone again, he'd have half a dozen replies. These people—not all of them, but most—were smart, too. They understood his point of view. Some of them had even given him an education, which wasn't something he'd been expecting.

All these years of talking, he'd never been sure if anyone was listening. Beth probably heard one out of every ten words that came out of his mouth. His kids sure as hell didn't listen to him, even his Erin. Most of the time, he wasn't sure Nick was listening to him, and even if he was, he didn't have much to contribute. Ken wasn't raggin' on the guy, it was the truth. He loved him like a brother, but he wasn't much of a conversationalist.

Online, though, people listened to him. Not only that, they *wanted* to listen to him. Even asked his opinions sometimes. He was respected there, like some kind of tribal elder. Finally, he felt like his words had meaning. They had weight.

He looked around the room at the young college kids pounding craft ale that tasted like mulch and cost the earth. They probably thought he was just some sad old guy sitting at the bar on his own like a loser. They didn't have a clue what he was capable of. Not a single goddamn clue.

OUTSKIRTS OF TOLAR, NEW MEXICO—
180 MILES TO ALBUQUERQUE

It was a low growl, faint at first, echoing through the desert.

The two women froze and turned their faces toward the sound.

A pair of headlights swept into view.

"Do you think it's—"

Cait shook her head. "I don't know." The headlights were coming up fast, but she couldn't see yet what was behind them. Whatever it was, it was big.

"It's a truck." Rebecca's voice was tight. "I think—it must be—"

The headlights grew brighter. The engine was a roar. Cait shook her head. "It's bigger than a pickup." She caught a glint of chrome coming off a pair of exhaust stacks. Her heart leaped. Cait scrambled back inside the Jeep and emerged clutching something lit up in her hand. An emergency flare.

Rebecca reached out to stop her. "No! Cait, don't!"

"It's an eighteen-wheeler. He's bound to stop."

"But we don't know who's driving it!"

Cait stared her down. "We don't have a choice." She arced the flare above her head and paced out into the road.

"You just said someone might have tampered with the gas tank! How do you know it's not whoever's driving that truck?"

Cait shook her head. "If somebody did drain the tank—and I'm not sure they did—it would have happened back at the IHOP. You're hearing that engine for yourself now. There's no way whoever was driving that thing could have sneaked into the parking lot, tampered with the gas tank, and gotten away without us hearing it."

"Maybe he switched vehicles."

Cait twisted her mouth. "Maybe. But I don't think so. It's hard to stash an eighteen-wheeler." She clocked the look of doubt on Rebecca's face. "It's fine, I promise." It wasn't, not really, but it was the closest to fine they were going to get. The truck was close now, only a couple hundred feet away. She could feel the vibrations underfoot. She waved the flare higher in the air.

The truck hissed to a stop. The door swung open and they watched a man step down from the cab.

Cait felt a twist of fear when his boots hit the ground. What if Rebecca was right and the guy was a total lunatic? She shook the thought from her head. Lunatic or not, he was the best shot they had. Besides, there were two of them and one of him. They'd be fine.

It was hard to tell his age from where she was—he could have been anywhere from a bad thirty to a good fifty. He was wearing a checked shirt and jeans and a Rangers cap with the brim peaked and pulled down low over a pair of light brown eyes. His skin bore the pockmarks of teenage acne, but she could see now that he was handsome in spite of it.

His eyes swept past her and landed on Rebecca. Something pinched at the base of Cait's spine. She knew that look, and she took it as a warning. The smell of his cologne invaded the air around her, something musky and synthetic that reminded her of junior high dances.

Cait pushed herself toward him. "Thanks for stopping. We're in kind of a jam."

His eyes were slow to find hers. "I guess that's right. What's happened—it break down?"

"We ran out of gas."

"Out here, at this time of night?" He let out a low whistle. "That's some poor planning, that is."

"Yeah, well. I don't suppose you have a spare gas can in your truck?"

"She runs on diesel," he said, nodding toward the truck. His eyes trailed across Cait back to Rebecca. "There's a gas station about fifteen miles up the road in Fort Sumner. I could give you ladies a ride."

Rebecca stepped forward. "We don't want to impose." There was a smile Cait hadn't seen on her face before, sugar-sweet and dimpled. "I'm sure you must be on a tight schedule. Maybe you have a cell phone we could use to call a tow truck?"

He shook his head. "No reception out here, and even if you could get it to call one, a tow truck likely wouldn't make it out here for a good few hours. I run this route pretty frequent. It's all just mom-and-pop mechanic shops, and they're all tucked up in bed like good little boys and girls." He shot her a wolfish smile. "Not like us night owls. I'm Scott, by the way."

The two women looked at each other, questioning. The truck driver saw their hesitation and laughed. "I don't bite, I promise. I'll get you back here safe and sound, scout's honor." He lifted two fingers to his forehead. "Anyway, don't expect you'll get many more opportunities for rescue tonight. Yours is the first car I've seen in fifty miles."

Cait glanced at Rebecca. "What do you think?" she whispered.

Rebecca shook her head. "I don't think we have a choice."

"You could stay here if you wanted. Lock the doors and wait for us to get back."

"If we're going, we're going together."

Cait slipped her hand in Rebecca's. Her palm was clammy, but her grip was strong. "Let's go."

The eighteen-wheeler was throwing off steam like a thoroughbred. Scott opened the passenger door of the cab and helped them up. Rebecca went in first, smiling that same sweet smile at him when she took his hand, and Cait slid in next to her.

"Everybody comfortable?" he said, sparking up the engine. He threw the gearshift back and pressed down on the gas without waiting for an answer, and the truck lurched forward on the long, dark road.

SIX MONTHS EARLIER

Cait stood awkwardly in front of the reception desk, ignoring the urge to pluck at the waistband of her tights. What had she been thinking when she pulled them on that morning? Temperatures were already in the eighties before the sun had risen in the sky, and yet she had chosen to wear the itchy shift dress her mother had bought for her when she graduated from college. "For job interviews," she'd told her, pushing the plastic Family Dollar bag into her arms. "There's a pair of hose in there, too." Cait hadn't had the heart to tell her that she didn't have a single interview lined up, and the Dark Horse didn't require nylons underneath the regulation Daisy Dukes.

It had seemed right, though, to put on the outfit that morning. She wanted to look professional. Competent. Trustworthy. Anyway, preparing for this appointment had done something strange to her, made her feel like she was Dolly Parton in *9 to 5* as she brewed her coffee bleary-eyed in the bright morning sunlight. She watched people file out of their front doors clutching laptop bags and bagged lunches and thermoses filled with coffee. *So this is what it's like to be a real person*, she marveled. *No, thank you.*

Adam, her next-door neighbor who sometimes watered her neglected lemon tree, spotted her in the window and raised a hand, whether in greeting or surprise she wasn't sure. She'd never been seen at seven-thirty a.m. on a Monday before.

She'd driven through rush hour traffic sipping from her own thermos full of coffee and pulled up to the address with ten minutes to spare. For the first time in her life, she was early for something. It meant that much to her.

The woman handed Cait a thick sheaf of papers, an ID badge, and a rainbow-striped tabard. "They were orange before," she said, nodding at the tabard, "but we had a few pretenders wearing them, so we switched to these. They're harder to copy, and it's easier for patients to identify you out on the lot."

"Works for me. Orange isn't really my color," Cait said.

The woman, whose name was Deborah and who had a head of close-cropped steel-gray hair and was wearing a pair of enormous owlish glasses, didn't crack a smile. "This is the manual," she said, tapping a finger on the bundle of papers. "Read it, and then read it again. You'll have a one-on-one training session, too. Your trainer will be"—she glanced down at the clipboard—"Lisa. She's one of our longest-serving volunteers, so you'll be in good hands. If you just take a seat, she'll be with you soon."

Cait nodded and lowered herself onto one of the hard plastic chairs that lined the room. The office was tucked away in a 1970s block in Westgate that also housed a dental practice and a Laundromat. It was a shabby, tired-looking place, its walls painted a dull beige, its carpet threadbare. The only decoration was "Sisters of Service" painted in bold purple letters above the receptionist's desk.

Cait pulled out her phone and started scrolling through Instagram while she waited. A few plates of artfully arranged food, an ad for "the best pajamas in the world," which Cait had to stop herself from clicking, Busy Philipps doing painful-looking exercises as she grimaced at the camera. An extremely cute dog.

"No cell phones." Cait looked up to see a woman with a mane of red hair towering above her, frowning.

"Sorry." She slipped the phone back in her bag.

"It's fine, you're new. You'll get used to it. I'm Lisa, by the way."

Cait shook her outstretched hand. "Cait Monaghan."

"Nice to meet you, Cait." She led them to a cramped office. The walls were papered with Frida Kahlo and Georgia O'Keeffe prints, and the single, small window overlooked the parking lot below. "So," Lisa said, moving a stack of papers off a chair so Cait could sit down. "How'd you hear about us?"

"I saw the article in Digg and thought it would be good to get involved." This was true, mostly. The attention surrounding her article had died down as the good people of the Internet had found someone else to hate, and she had been pretty much forgotten. She should have been relieved. Instead, she found a swirl of anger growing inside her like bacteria, ready to burst through the skin.

After her conversation with Ken at the bar, she'd gone home and read every single comment that had been written underneath that article, followed every single thread. She read until her eyes were blurry and her insides slick with nausea and then she clicked on another link and read some more. She read until she could read these things—things she always feared might be true about herself, things she would whisper to herself late at night, when her mind was soft and weak—unflinchingly and without pain. She read until the shame was replaced with a dull sort of numbness, and then she read on until that numbness turned to rage.

She'd been carrying that rage around with her for weeks now.

She needed somewhere to focus it, a grindstone on which to sharpen it.

Reading the article about the work the Sisters of Service were doing across Texas, she felt something stir inside her. Here was a bunch of women facing down a bunch of (mainly) men who wanted to tell them that what they did with their bodies was shameful and wicked and wrong. Here were women standing up for other women, strong and proud and brave. She wanted to be like them, to be involved in something noble and selfless.

Really, though, she wanted one of those protesters to spew some of their bile her way so she'd have an excuse to explode.

"Oh, cool. We've been getting some nice attention from that piece." Lisa's mouth twisted, like she was tasting something sour. "Some not so nice, too."

Cait attempted a rueful laugh, but it came out more like a splutter. She had read the comments underneath the piece, every hate-filled word. It was what had nudged her into sending the email asking if she could volunteer.

"Anyway, did Deborah run you through the basics? No last names, no personal details, no social media. Our job is to protect the patients, period. Their safety is our only priority, and we can't do anything that might jeopardize that."

"Absolutely."

"All right. Let's get going. We're starting you out on a weekday because they're quieter. Saturdays are a zoo. For today you'll just shadow me. See how I talk to the patients, get a feel for the route. If we're both feeling good after today, you'll go out on your own for the next shift. You work nights, right?"

Cait nodded. "I bartend down at the Dark Horse."

"Oh, man, I haven't been to that place since college. They still make you wear those Daisy Dukes?"

"Does a bear shit in the woods?"

Lisa laughed. "Yeah, it seemed like the kind of place that would remain untouched by progress, if you know what I mean. How long've you been there?"

Cait shrugged. "A few years. It's not so bad once you get over the uniform. The tips are usually good."

"Hey, money's money, right?"

"Amen."

Lisa led her to a beat-up, old Honda Civic. "Our chariot awaits," she said ruefully. "Sorry about the mess." Cait excavated some space on the passenger seat among the take-out wrappers and stacks of leaflets, and Lisa drove them downtown and parked in front of a Rite Aid. "You don't want them to see your car," she explained. "If they get your plates, you're cooked."

It was early still—not quite nine a.m.—but Cait could already see a few protesters starting to gather. "Time to suit up," Lisa said, slipping the rainbow tabard over her head. "You ready for this?"

Cait pulled on her tabard. The smell of cheap nylon filled her nostrils, and she felt a flutter of nerves. "I think so."

Lisa put her arm around her and steered her across the street. "You totally are."

The inside of the truck smelled like fast-food wrappers and synthetic lemon air freshener and Scott's cologne, which seemed to get stronger by the minute. His thigh pressed against Rebecca's and she held her breath, willing herself to shrink as small as possible.

Play nice, she reminded herself. *Don't do anything to upset him.*

She stared out the window. It was strange being up this high, like they were flying above the road rather than driving on it. She shifted in her seat and tried to angle her body away from his, but his thigh pressed in tighter.

"So, how do you two know each other?"

She saw Cait about to open her mouth, but Rebecca didn't trust her to say the right thing. They had to be careful, and Cait didn't strike her as the careful type, so Rebecca made sure she got in first. "Cousins. We're on our way to our grandfather's birthday party tomorrow in Tucson. That's why we're out here now—Cait's shift ended late, so we had to drive through the night to get there on time. It's a surprise, so we can't be late."

Cait made a noise in her throat that could be read as an affirmation. Rebecca could feel the girl's eyes on her, questioning, but she kept her own eyes locked on the road.

"Awful long drive," Scott said, rubbing a thick hand across his stubble. He cocked his head toward Cait. "What kind of shift work do you do?"

"She's a nurse," Rebecca said. Cait arranged her features in bland agreement. She knew enough to play along: good. "We both are."

Scott nodded. "God's work." He looked at Rebecca and winked. "Too bad you two aren't wearing your uniforms."

Cait laughed, too loud. Rebecca winced. "I'm not sure we'd be all that sexy in our scrubs," she said lightly. "Not when we've been on shift all night."

"Aw, pretty girls like you? I'm sure you'd be sexy in anything." Rebecca let this hang in the air. She knew what was coming next. "You two have boyfriends?"

"Yes," Cait said, too quickly. "We both do." Rebecca winced again. *Wrong answer, Cait, and said in the wrong tone of voice.*

"Is that right?" His eyes swiveled away from the road and turned sharp. "And they let you drive through the middle of the night on your own like this? No way I'd let my girlfriend do that, 'specially if she was as pretty as you two. It's a dangerous world out there, you know."

Rebecca placed a hand on Cait's leg. A warning. "That's why we're lucky you turned up," she said, smiling so her dimples showed. "Our knight in shining armor."

She could feel Cait's eyes on her again, disbelieving now. She knew what the girl would be thinking. She didn't care. She knew what she was doing.

"That's right," he said, teeth glinting in the half-light. "Come along with my big white horse to sweep you off your feet."

Rebecca giggled. "Have you got a girlfriend?" She hoped he would say yes. Maybe they could offer him a little relationship advice, play the big-sister card. Remind him of what he had waiting for him back at home.

Scott shook his head, and her heart sank a little. "I was married for a while, but the strain of being out on the road was too much. Divorce came through last year."

Rebecca cooed sympathetically. "That's tough. I'm sorry."

"Don't be," Scott said, waving her off. "I didn't much like being tied down, always having to check in and answer to somebody."

"I get that," Rebecca said, nodding along like he was some kind of guru. "Better to be single and happy than married and miserable." Validate his choices. Make him feel like he's a good guy. Honorable.

"Amen," Scott crooned. He looked at her, eyes full of admiration. "You know, it's not often I meet somebody I'm simpatico with. I feel like you and me, we're simpatico." He leaned back in his seat and grinned into the dark. "I sure am glad I stopped for you two. Next town should be in a couple miles." He nodded toward the road. "We'll get your tank filled up and get you back on the road in no time. I wouldn't want you missing your granddaddy's big day."

Rebecca felt an elbow digging into her ribs, but she didn't dare look at Cait, not when they were this close.

"Now," Scott said, shaking his head, "why is it that I can't find nice girls like you two back in Louisiana?"

"Give it time," Rebecca said. "A nice guy like you? I'm sure the right girl will come along any day now."

Scott looked over, his eyes shining, and Rebecca felt so much cold fear rushing through her. She'd played it wrong after all. "Maybe she already has," he said, and she felt his thigh press harder against her own.

Patrick came home, eyes wide and bright. "It's happening," he said, grabbing Rebecca by the waist and spinning her around. "It's actually happening!"

"What's happening?"

"The junior senator for the great state of Texas is going to resign at the end of the summer. Something about health problems, but Rich says there's been a financial scandal brewing for a while."

"What does that mean?"

He put her back down on the ground and hugged her close to his chest. "It means, baby girl, that you are looking at the newest candidate for the United States Senate. Rich filed the paperwork today. He says it'll be an uphill battle—I haven't been in my congressional seat for very long, and some people might take against that—but he thinks I have as good a shot as anyone." His eyes took on a far-off, dreamy cast. "Senator McRae. Has a nice ring to it, doesn't it? And you'll be my beautiful, brilliant wife!"

"That's wonderful!" Rebecca tried to hide her dismay behind a bright smile.

Two years as the wife of a congressman had been enough to convince her that she wasn't cut out for it, and the spotlight would be all the brighter when he ran for Senate. There had been a part of her that had hoped he'd get sick of it—sick of the travel, the bureaucracy, the hours hitting the phone banks, begging for money—but he seemed to love even the worst parts of politics. He was good at it, too: in the short time he'd been in Congress, he'd developed a reputation as an effective dealmaker, one of the rare people who could reach across the aisle and appeal to members of both parties. Rich said he was a natural.

Rebecca, on the other hand . . . well, she had yet to find her feet. She'd tried to set up the educational charity Patrick had promised, but she found it tough to drum up interest. Parents were focused on getting their kids into the best schools so they could get the best grades so they could go to the best colleges, period. When Rebecca started talking to them about empathetic learning or creative modeling, their eyes would glaze over. In her desperation, she'd even reached out to the local newspaper to see if they'd be interested in interviewing her about it, but the journalist they sent was more interested in talking about her role as Patrick's wife than as an educator.

Eventually, she gave up. She tried getting another teaching job, but with Patrick's job being so high-profile, schools didn't want to hire her for fear of attracting scrutiny. "The press'll be all over us like white on rice," one principal had said as he pushed her résumé back toward her. "I can see you're highly qualified, but we just can't take the risk."

So she'd become a full-time politician's wife, the plus-one he brought along to fund-raisers and rallies and charity events. She'd tried to do well, to make friends with the other wives, to make people like her, but somehow, she just never fit.

And now things were about to go into hyperdrive.

"Look," Patrick said, as if he could read her thoughts, "I know these past couple years have been tough on you—on both of us."

She put a hand on her stomach instinctively. She didn't want to think about that, not right now. "I know the last thing you want to do is get dragged around the campaign trail, so you just take this at your own pace, okay? I'm the one who's running for office here, not you. I don't want you to do anything you're not comfortable with."

She felt a rush of gratitude. He was a good man, her husband. He understood. "I'm so proud of you," she said, reaching up and running a hand through his hair. "You're going to be the best senator this state has ever seen, and I promise I'll do as much as I can to help make it happen."

"I know you will," he said, bending down to kiss her. "I know."

WELCOME TO FORT SUMNER: A SLEEPY LITTLE VILLAGE WITH A SHADY
LITTLE PAST.

Rebecca could have wept with happiness. It was a town, a real one, one she'd heard of before, however vaguely. There was bound to be a gas station here.

But the first few minutes in Fort Sumner weren't promising: the only buildings fringing the road were barns or warehouses, all of them dark. She caught a glimpse of a neon sign up ahead, but it was a Super 8 with VACANCY lit up underneath, the motel all dark except for a strip of emergency lights in reception. No sign of a gas station.

They passed the Billy the Kid Museum, its brick exterior in-explicably covered with wagon wheels. The yellow sign depicted a cartoon Billy in jeans and a bandanna, a rifle resting by his side, his ten-gallon jauntily perched on his head. He looked more like an amiable cowboy than a murderous outlaw. A sign underneath boasted that the museum had once appeared on prime-time TV.

Who came to these places? Rebecca wondered, but as soon as the thought ran through her head, she remembered going to places just like it when she was a kid and loving every one of them. Rebecca, aged seven, would have jumped at the chance to go to the Billy the Kid Museum, would have happily posed for a photo next to the wagon wheels, would have begged for her very own bandanna from the gift store.

Grief washed over her in a single powerful wave. How many times had she dreamed about her and Patrick bundling a pink-cheeked, still-drowsy toddler into the car one early weekend morning and pointing the car in a direction just to see where it would take them. Small hands sticky with roadside ice creams, cheap souvenirs that would be lost as soon as they were bought, the long, quiet ride back home, the radio on low, a gentle snore coming from the backseat. She reached her hand to the little gold cross around her neck and held on until the edges dug into her palm.

More buildings, no lights. She could feel Cait's body straining next to her, both of them waiting for something to appear.

She spotted an RV park half full of trailers, and a light on in one of them.

"We could ask them for gas?" Cait suggested, pointing toward it. "RVs usually keep extra gas on hand."

Scott shook his head. "The gas station's just ahead," he said. "Besides, I don't think they'd look too kindly on us knocking on their door at this hour of the night."

Cait settled back into her seat. Rebecca felt an itch building at the back of her throat. They'd been in the truck for too long now. Over twenty-five miles. The town stretched on. Fred's Restaurant. Fort Sumner High School. First United Methodist Church. A few auto parts stores that raised her hopes briefly before dashing them. Lights out everywhere. Not even the streetlamps were lit.

There wasn't a gas station in this town, and even if there were, Scott wasn't going to stop for it. She thought she'd sweet-talked him enough to keep them safe, but she'd been wrong. He was going to keep driving until he found whatever place he had marked out in his head, and then he was going to kill them. Her hands started to shake, and then her arms and legs, and soon her whole body was quaking like she was undergoing her own personal earthquake.

Cait placed a hand on Rebecca's knee to try to steady her, but it was no good. The truck felt suddenly, stiflingly hot. Sweat trickled down her spine and pooled in the seam of her cotton underwear. The stars pressed down on them through the windshield, suffocating. Her breath turned shallow.

Cait gripped her knee so hard she let out a yelp of pain. "Look." Rebecca followed Cait's outstretched finger to the glowing white-and-yellow sign that loomed ahead: ALLSUP'S.

Scott turned to them with a smile. "I guess it was further up the road than I thought. Sorry about that." He swung the eighteen-wheeler into the parking lot of the gas station and killed the engine. "I'll go in and talk to the guy about a gas can."

In the end, all three of them went inside. Scott held the door open for them, and Rebecca had to work to keep her legs from shaking as she walked in. The attendant was waiting for them, one eye watching the TV mounted above the register, the other trained on them. "Evening, ladies," he said, arching an eyebrow and tipping an imaginary hat toward them. Rebecca knew instantly that he had taken them for a pair of prostitutes.

"We ran out of gas a few miles back," Cait said, leaning an elbow on the countertop. "We need a can of regular to get us going again." She was trying to look confident, Rebecca saw, trying to take control of the situation, as if they weren't at the mercy of these two men and whatever the night could throw at them.

"Sure." The attendant's eyes drifted back to the TV screen. "But it'll cost."

Rebecca pulled out her wallet, impatient. "How much?" The

attendant looked at it, and she felt him immediately reassess his opinion of them—most prostitutes don't carry Italian leather wallets—and double his price. She didn't care if he fleeced them. She just wanted out of there.

"Sixty bucks," he said. "That includes the can, which you ladies can keep in case you find yourselves in a future fix."

Scott stepped forward. "That's twice what it's worth."

Rebecca shook her head. There was no point in fighting it. They were stuck, and he knew it. She pushed a few bills into his hand and watched him count them.

"All right, then." The attendant lumbered into the back and reappeared a few minutes later with a red plastic can. He handed it to Scott with a grunt.

"I'll do it," Cait said, reaching for the can, but Scott shook his head and pulled it out of reach.

"A gentleman doesn't let ladies do a man's work," he said. "I'll get this filled up and get us back on the road."

She saw Cait was about to argue and put a hand on her arm. "Let it go," Rebecca mouthed, and Cait had the good grace to look embarrassed.

So Rebecca and Cait stood outside and watched him pump the gas.

Cait pulled out a pack of Marlboro Lights, tapped one out, and offered the pack to Rebecca. She shook her head. She hadn't smoked since her twenties, though watching Cait light up, she felt a familiar tug of yearning in her chest. A curl of smoke emerged from the girl's mouth, and Rebecca's fingers twitched. He hated the smell of cigarette smoke. He'd be able to smell it on her, and he'd have questions she couldn't answer. She moved downwind.

"I'll pay you back for the gas," Cait said, grinding the cigarette underneath her heel.

"It's fine. Don't worry about it."

"You were good back there. In the truck. He likes you."

"It seemed like a good idea to make friends with him. I figured he'd be less likely to murder us."

Cait raised an eyebrow. "I don't know if it works that way."

"Maybe not. But better than making him an enemy."

When he was finished, Scott stashed the can behind the seats and sparked the key in the ignition. The attendant was watching them through the window.

"Now what, ladies?" Scott asked as he steered the truck back onto the road. He looked at Rebecca and smirked. "You know what they say—no favor should go unreciprocated. I hope you have something special up your sleeve for me."

Rebecca's whole body tensed, every muscle and tendon straining in anticipation, the adrenaline running hot through her veins. She eyed the passenger door. They were up high in the cab, and the truck was gaining speed. If they tried to jump, they'd be hurt, and they'd still be miles away from the pickup. He had the gas, too, stashed in the back. They could run back to the gas station—she could still see the lights in the rearview—but would the attendant be inclined to help? Maybe they'd been working together, the two of them. The truck driver patrolling the roads, the attendant lying in wait.

No, if that were the case, they would have made their move back at the station. Getting back there would be their only chance. They'd have to throw themselves on the attendant's mercy and hope he had some of God's grace hiding behind those mean eyes.

She saw Cait's hand reach down toward the door handle. *Go,* she willed her, *just go, we can do it, we can get away from him, there's still time,* but then Cait brought her hand up to where they could see it in the light. Rebecca saw a glint of silver.

Cait unwrapped the bar of Hershey's, clicked off a strip, and offered it to Scott, who took it with a grin.

"Will this make us even?" Cait said, a secret smile playing on her lips. She caught Rebecca's eye, and Rebecca felt a surge of affection for her.

Scott pushed the piece of chocolate into his mouth. "You give me another piece," he said, his voice thick with sugar, "and we will be."

"You guys ready to rock and roll?"

Patrick gave Rich a thumbs-up while Rebecca worked up a queasy smile. She'd been dreading this for days now: their first official "media training" session ahead of Patrick's Senate-run announcement. Rich had insisted that the training was for both of them—"We're in the big leagues now, team, it's a whole new ball game"—but Rebecca knew it was really for her. Everybody already loved Patrick. It was Rebecca who was the problem.

"Okay," Rich said, spinning around in his chair and clicking his mouse a few times. The screen behind him flashed into life: ENGAGEMENT.

He turned toward her. "Okay, you're up first. What does this word mean to you?"

"Um. It means . . ." Rebecca's palms began to sweat. This was ridiculous, she told herself. Absurd. She was a grown woman. She didn't need to be trained. "It means connection," she said, as confidently as she could muster.

"Good," Rich purred. "And how do we connect with people?" His eyes stayed fixed on her.

"By finding common ground, I guess."

"Exactly!" He smiled at her as if she were a puppy who'd just peed on command. "In order for people to connect to you, they need to know that you share common ground. We've done a few focus groups ahead of the announcement, just to get a sense of how people are feeling about the two of you."

About me, Rebecca thought. *You already know how they feel about Patrick. I'm the one that's the problem.*

"I'm going to read out some of the feedback," Rich said in the soothing tone of a doctor about to give his patient a particularly grim diagnosis. He clicked his mouse a few more times and a new slide appeared.

"'Cold,'" Rich read aloud. "'Bitchy.' 'Stuck up.' 'Californian.'" He lifted his eyes to hers and smiled. "I'm not sure we can do anything about that one. There's no changing the fact you're from California." He couldn't quite hide his regret. "'Snobby,'" he continued. "'Ice princess.'"

"But . . . it's not true," Rebecca said. Her voice came out as a bleat. "I don't think I'm better than anyone else." *In fact*, she added silently to herself, *these days I think I'm pretty worthless*.

"Hey, I know that what that slide says is a load of horseshit. Patrick knows it, too." Rich leaned forward, elbows on knees, and leveled her with his gaze. "The thing is, it seems like a lot of people think it's true, and that's a problem for us. We've all seen how the bitchy-wife narrative plays out in the polls. I know we're in another wave of feminism"—he smirked—"What is it now, the fourth? Fifth? But people still don't like a ballbuster. You can be smart, sure, but there needs to be some softness there, too." He flicked back to the first slide, reached up, and tapped the screen with his finger. "Remember what you said about engagement? You need to make a connection. Find common ground." He leaned forward again. "They need to see that you're just like them, with the same problems, the same flaws, the same heartaches . . ." His eyes flicked to Patrick, just for a second, but enough to tell her what was coming.

"No," she said, already shaking her head. She turned toward Patrick, who had the good grace to at least look embarrassed. "Please tell me you didn't tell him."

"Now, look," Rich said, holding up his hands. "Patrick didn't mean any harm. He was just opening up to me as a friend. He's been having a tough time dealing with your . . . difficulties, just the same as you."

She snapped back to him. "Don't tell me what kind of time I've been having. You have no idea what the past eighteen months have been like for me. You have no idea."

Patrick squeezed her hand. "Sweetheart, please—"

She wrenched her fingers free of his. "Don't."

"Hey, hey—let's not get heated," Rich said. "We're all on the same side here. Rebecca, you're right, I don't have any idea what you've been through, though I'm sure it's been hell."

Rebecca softened, just a little.

"See, the thing I'm trying to get at is . . ." Rich stopped. She could see him arranging the words in his head, like tiles in a mosaic. Making sure they all fit together to form an attractive picture. "We have a unique opportunity here. You have an experience to share—an awful experience, a universal experience. Just think how many women have had experiences similar to yours who are out there right now, hurting, feeling alone."

Patrick reached out and reclaimed her hand, and she let him take it.

"What I'm saying is, you could help those other women by sharing your experience."

"You want me to use my miscarriages to make me more likable." Her voice was flat, affectless. She knew she should feel outraged, but instead she just felt numb.

Patrick turned toward her, squeezing her hand in his. "I would never ask you to do something you're not comfortable with, so if this isn't something you want, just say the word and we'll drop it. It's just . . ." He reached up and ran a hand through his hair, something he always did when he was nervous. "I think Rich might be right, that sharing your story might be a good thing. Not because it will make you more likable, or even because it might help other women who are struggling. Becs, you've been carrying this weight around with you all on your own, and it's crushing you. I've been trying to help carry it, but it doesn't seem to be enough, and . . ." He shook his head. "I just think if you shared your story with the world, you'd be sharing that weight, too."

Silence. All Rebecca could hear was the faint whir of the computer and the hum of the fluorescents and the rush of blood in her ears. Five miscarriages in eighteen months. Her doctor said it was normal, nothing to worry about. "It takes longer for some women's bodies to get the hang of it," he'd said, as if carrying a child in your body were the same as learning to tie a cherry stem with your tongue, or recite the alphabet backward. A cute little knack. All the test results had come back normal. "There's nothing stopping you from having a baby," the doctor had added. "Just give it time."

Five miscarriages. Five dreams held for a moment, only to be lost.

Patrick was right: she had been carrying the weight of it on her own, and it was crushing her. She could feel it in the heaviness of her limbs, the way her bed called to her in the middle of the day, the way she flinched in bright sunlight as if burned.

Maybe her story could help someone feel a little less alone.

Maybe sharing it would make her feel a little less numb.

"Okay," she said finally. "I'll try."

OUTSKIRTS OF FORT SUMNER, NEW MEXICO—
165 MILES TO ALBUQUERQUE

Cait didn't know what had made her steal that candy bar.

First of all, she was pissed at herself for screwing up. She should have had a spare gas can in the back, but as soon as Rebecca asked, she could see it clear as day sitting in Alyssa's garage. Cait had loaned it to her for a camping trip and forgotten to ask for it back. Stupid of her. Careless. And then the gas station attendant had been such a creep, looking at them like they were trash, and screwing them by hiking up the price of gas. Scott insisted on filling up the gas can. She knew that he was just being nice, but it pissed her off nonetheless, and made her feel even more stupid and useless than she already did. It was her car, her drive: she should have been in control of it, but instead it had been Rebecca who paid for the gas and Rebecca who thought to sweet-talk Scott like that, because she didn't trust Cait to handle the situation. It had been a little much, Rebecca fawning over Scott like he was some kind of white knight and then saying she'd done it to "save" them, as if Cait needed to be saved.

Anyway, Cait had been pissed, so she'd told those two she had to pee and she'd swiped a candy bar and a pack of gum on the way out. She hadn't stolen anything since high school, when she and her friends had run rings around the poor security guard at Walmart. They stole makeup, mainly. Tubes of sticky lip gloss, shimmery bronzer, bottles of nail polish. Nothing that was worth much, but more than she could afford.

It wasn't her parents' fault that they were poor. They both worked, and worked hard, her father out on the telephone lines and her mother as a receptionist at the local dentist. They had tried to get ahead—they'd tried so hard—but every time they made a little headway, something happened to set them right back to zero: the boiler broke, or the roof started leaking, or her father's car needed a new transmission.

Her brothers never seemed to notice that they had nothing. They were good at sports—all three of them on the varsity football team—and that meant nobody cared that they bought their clothes from Walmart. She was the youngest, though, her parents' little "surprise," and by the time she got to high school, the Monaghan boys' sporting glory had faded from memory. A few of the teachers would sometimes reminisce with her about the time Kyle rushed a hundred yards in a single game, or the time Ben sacked the Liberty Hill QB in the final seconds of the fourth quarter, but none of the kids cared about that. All they cared about was the fact that she carried an army-green backpack rather than a leather Coach bag, and wore jeans bought from the discount store rather than at the mall, and liked reading books more than cheering on the football team.

She didn't care much about what the other kids thought about her, not really. She knew she was on a trajectory that would send her far beyond Waco. She loved her parents, but she didn't want their life, and she didn't want the lives of her brothers, either, four years at Baylor followed by jobs at the oil company. She knew she could have more, if she wanted it badly enough. That was how it worked, right? If you worked hard and got in to a good school, you could make a better life for yourself.

So she worked hard and got offered a full ride from UT, and when September rolled around, she drove herself halfway across the state in the used Jeep she'd worked all summer to buy, the trunk filled with a shower caddy and a study buddy and all the other crap that Target had told her she needed for her first year of college.

She left four years later with a degree in English lit and not a single goddamn clue about what she was going to do next.

She could have gone to law school and become a corporate shill defending oil companies for big money, but even that wasn't the safe option it had been a few years before. She knew kids who had law degrees from good schools and still couldn't get a decent job. The 2008 crash had been more like an earthquake, wiping out all the grand avenues to wealth and security and leaving behind a barren wasteland of scavenging and self-created, multi-hyphenated job titles. Basically, unless you could code, you were fucked. Cait couldn't code.

What she wanted to do was write, so that was what she did. She wrote for nothing during the day and slung drinks to assholes for cash at night, and after a few years, she finally felt she was getting somewhere. Editors knew her name, answered her emails. She even got a couple of commissions. She still wasn't making much money from it, but she thought that maybe, in a few more years, if she landed a couple of big pieces, she might be able to call herself a writer without feeling like she was playing pretend.

So far, it hadn't exactly worked out as she'd planned.

She was going to get there, though. Swear to God, she was going to get there, and she didn't care what she had to do to make that happen. Cait thought about the tape recorder stuck under the dash that had been running since she pulled up to the curb outside Rebecca's house, before that creep had scared the tar out of them. She had screwed up, sure—she'd let herself get distracted, and the nerves had made her sloppy—but she'd get her head back in the game. She'd get what she came for, whatever the cost.

Deep down, she knew exactly why she'd stolen that bar of chocolate. Because the world wasn't going to give her anything. She would have to take it herself, whatever way she could.

The sign for Fort Sumner hove into view, snapping her out of herself. Time was running out. She needed Rebecca to start talking. She thought back to her journalism professor back in college. "Build a bond," he used to say. "If they like you enough, they'll give you anything you want."

She tossed Rebecca a rueful smile. "It felt like it took longer to get here when Scott was driving," she said. She could still smell his cologne on her hair, in her throat. She could admit now that she'd been scared.

Rebecca nodded. "A lot longer."

Driving through the second time was like watching a movie you've already seen, Billy the Kid still glaring down from the museum sign, the banner flapping outside the high school. When they passed the gas station, Cait saw a figure hunched against the wall of the shop and the red glow of a cigarette cupped between hands.

Cait heard Rebecca mutter the word "prick" under her breath and turned to see that she was giving the attendant the finger, so Cait laughed and stuck hers out, too, not that he'd be able to see them in the dark. In the rearview mirror, she saw him toss his cigarette and head back inside, oblivious. "That guy was such an asshole."

The two women started to laugh, gently at first and then harder, until they were near-hysterical, and the atmosphere between them suddenly lifted.

Cait looked at the woman next to her wiping tears from her eyes and wondered, for the first time, if maybe they would have been friends had the circumstances been different. If maybe she liked this woman after all.

She brushed away the thought. It didn't matter if she liked Rebecca or not. She wasn't here to make friends.

She was here to take what she was owed.

FIVE MONTHS EARLIER

Cait pulled into the Rite Aid parking lot and killed the engine. It was 8:32 on a Saturday morning, and the streets of downtown Austin were deserted except for a few exhausted parents wheeling their babies to coffee shops and ponytailed women carrying organic tote bags and yoga mats.

Cait wiped the sleep out of the corners of her eyes. The Dark Horse had closed at two a.m., but by the time she'd broken down the bar and tipped out the barbacks, it was closer to three. She'd had four hours of sleep, tops, but most of it had been junk, her precious few hours in bed spent checking the time on her phone and worrying about missing her alarm. Lisa promised that she was ready for a Saturday, but Cait was less convinced. She'd had nightmares about the guy who'd thrown a pot of red paint over her a few Wednesdays before, screaming that she had blood on her hands. The cops had taken him away—the protesters weren't allowed to touch anyone, though you wouldn't know that by how close they got, so close she could tell what they'd eaten for dinner the night before, so close their spit peppered her face as they shouted—but it had rattled her, and he was just one of a handful that day. On Saturdays, Lisa had told her, they could have upward of a hundred protestors. How was she supposed to manage them all?

But she also knew that this was what she wanted. Doing this work over the past month had been more rewarding than anything she'd ever done. For the first time in her life, she felt like she was doing something that made a difference, as cheesy as that sounded. It was true, though: she saw it in the relief on the women's faces as she helped them from their cars and steered them into the clinic, the way they held her hand right up until the last moment, their nods when she blasted Pink or Madonna through her iPhone to drown out the protesters' screams.

So when Lisa told her that she'd been tapped for a Saturday shift, she'd jumped at the chance, despite her nerves and the fact that she'd be coming off a Friday double. Sisters of Service thought she was ready for it, and she wanted so badly to believe them.

She tugged the tabard over her head and walked the few blocks to the clinic. The protesters were already starting to gather out front, handing around thermoses of coffee and Tupperware full of muffins like they were in line for *Antiques Roadshow* rather than waiting to shout abuse at a bunch of frightened women.

Cait pushed past them, ignoring their jeers, and checked the barrier positions. The patients would have to drive past the protesters to park in the lot and would then walk the twenty feet to the entrance. A few volunteers would stand by the barriers to make sure the protesters stayed on the other side while the others—including Cait—would escort the women from their cars to the door.

Twenty feet wasn't much, but Cait had learned that a lot of damage could be done across a short distance. Some of the protesters tried to scare the women by telling them that they were damaging their health, saying they were destined to get cancer or to be infertile. Some used kindness as a weapon, offering boxes of doughnuts from Big Kahuna, knowing full well that if a woman took one bite, she wouldn't be able to go through with the procedure. You had to have an empty stomach, or it was too dangerous. Some just straight-up screamed in the women's faces and told them they were going to hell, which was the least effective at changing minds but the most upsetting, from what Cait had witnessed.

It was a hot day, not even nine a.m. and already in the nineties. Cait had hoped it might keep some of the protestors away, but they kept coming, and soon the barriers were lined on either side, and there was a spill-out onto the sidewalk, which meant the protesters would be the first thing the women saw before they even pulled in to the lot.

The first car of the day pulled up, a Honda Civic with Alabama plates. The crowd snapped to attention, signs raised like spears, and began to chant.

Cait went to work.

The women came to the clinic. They were brave and afraid, cowed and defiant, tearful and stony-faced. They were teenagers who came with their mothers and women in their thirties who came with their husbands and women Cait's age who came with friends. Some came alone. Cait stayed close to each of them, shielding them as best she could, distracting them with a joke or a smile or leading them to the door in silence. She felt able to divine what each woman needed from her, and she gave it to each of them as best she could, hour after hour on the baking tarmac, while the protesters howled.

At the end of the day, she could still remember the face of each woman she'd led through the doors, still feel the heat of their palms pressed against hers. She couldn't remember the face of a single protester. To her eyes, they had become a shapeless mass, a blur.

Maybe that was why she didn't notice when one of them followed her the three blocks to the parking lot where she'd parked the Jeep. Maybe it was the heat, or the exhaustion that had set in to the marrow of her bones. She wouldn't know.

All she knew was the sickening crack of the rock when it landed on her windshield, the glass splintering into a spiderweb, her heart pounding wildly in her chest as she peeled out of the parking lot, not daring to look back.

Rebecca sagged in her seat. All the adrenaline had leached out of her now, leaving her weak and exhausted. They had to be half-way there by now, or close. She pulled her phone out of her bag. There was a single reception bar. She waited to see if any missed calls would appear on the screen, but the little phone icon stayed blank, and after a while, she allowed herself to believe that maybe he hadn't called to check in on her. Maybe she'd get away with this after all.

Cait looked over at her. "You got anything?"

Rebecca nodded. "I've got a little reception now."

"Did he call? Your husband, I mean."

Rebecca shook her head. "It doesn't look like it."

"That's good. Right?"

"Yes," she said quietly. "It's good."

"So he doesn't know where you are." It wasn't a question.

Rebecca shook her head, hot shame flooding through her veins. Cait wouldn't understand the situation—couldn't possibly ever understand, because Rebecca barely understood herself. How did she get here? She wasn't meant to be this person. This wasn't meant to be her life.

"How long have you been married?"

"Ten years."

"Ten years is a long time."

Rebecca tried to conjure up the sharp, bright happiness she'd felt on her wedding day. Neither of them had two nickels to rub together, so they'd asked friends to stake out a spot in Washington Park early one Saturday and brought along a bunch of folding chairs and blankets for the guests to sit on. She'd worn a white slip dress she'd found at a vintage place in the Mission, baby's breath laced through her hair. Patrick had worn a suit he'd borrowed from a friend and a smile so big it looked like it might crack his face in two. She'd felt that they were the two luckiest people in the world.

"What does he do for a living?" Cait asked now.

Rebecca scanned her face, looking for some trace of slyness, but Cait just seemed curious. Maybe she really didn't know. Rebecca wasn't about to tell her now. "Oh, he works for the government," she said vaguely. "I don't really understand it. What about you?" she asked, desperate to change the subject. "Are you married?"

Cait barked out a laugh. "Me? God, no."

"You're too young, I guess." Though she couldn't have been much older than Rebecca had been at the time. But Rebecca had the sense that women Cait's age didn't aspire to marriage, not in the way her generation had. Theirs had been the last to invest in their parents' model for life: marriage, mortgage, kids. People Cait's age didn't seem to care about those things the way they had, or perhaps it was more accurate to say they had accepted that the promise those things offered was often empty and unachievable. Rebecca had read the articles about how hers was the first generation destined to be worse off than her parents'. She guessed they hadn't gotten the memo in time. Cait's generation had. "Do you have a boyfriend? Or a girlfriend?" Rebecca added hastily.

"Nothing to write home about."

"Well, you're still young. There's plenty of time."

"I guess. How long did you know your husband before you got married?"

"Just a couple of months. Not long."

"Jeez. I don't know if I like a pair of shoes until I've worn them for a couple of months. Never mind marry them." Cait winced. "Not that I'm comparing your husband to a pair of shoes."

"Don't worry, I know what you meant. You're right, it was fast. Our friends all thought we were crazy."

"Ten years," Cait marveled. "How old were you? Twelve?"

"Twenty-five."

"That's how old I am!" The way Cait said it made it clear that this was unfathomable to her. "God, it's just . . . I feel like I'm barely an adult, you know? Like, I'm still impressed when I pay a bill on time or remember to get the Jeep serviced."

"I guess we were pretty young, though I don't remember feeling that way at the time. The opposite, really: we were completely sure of ourselves and each other."

"How did you know he was the one? Like, this guy I just started seeing—I like him, but there's no lightning bolt, you know? I always thought that, when I met the right guy, it would be like getting struck by lightning." Cait tossed her an embarrassed look. "But in a good way, obviously."

"I guess it was a little like being hit by lightning," Rebecca said. "I guess people would call it love at first sight." She could remember those early weeks, when it felt like the entire universe had aligned itself toward the two of them. Neither of them slept longer than a few hours a night, too consumed by the newness of each other's bodies and minds and hearts. There was a feeling of something precious slipping through their fingers. When he proposed to her over a bottle of Ernest & Julio Gallo, holding

128

a dime-store plastic ring in his outstretched hand, it felt like a warm blanket spreading out, waiting to catch her.

Rebecca looked at the girl, one hand resting lazily on the steering wheel, the other fiddling with the mess of curls on top of her head. She tried to picture herself living Cait's life: single, scraping by on tips, making these long drives with strangers, ignoring the inherent dangers that lay around every corner for a woman like her. The truth was, even when Rebecca had been living a similar life, she hadn't really believed it was hers. She was waiting for her real life to begin, and when she met Patrick, she believed that it had. The thing she'd wanted more than anything was a love like her mother and father had. Even though it was embarrassing to admit, even though it went against all she and her college friends had purportedly railed against, all she'd ever wanted was to be a woman who was loved.

"What's he like?"

"My husband?"

Cait nodded.

"Oh, you know. He's great. Smart. Good-looking. Considerate." Were these things true? she wondered. He was certainly smart, and no one could deny that he was good-looking. Could she still think of him as considerate? In his way, she told herself. In his own way, he was. "My father never liked him, though."

"Really? How come?"

Rebecca smiled to herself. "Have you ever shot a gun?"

Cait's eyebrows shot toward her hairline. "No. Why?"

Now it was Rebecca's turn to be surprised. "You haven't? You said you grew up in Texas. I thought it was like a rite of passage. My husband's from Texas, and his grandmother had him out in the backyard with a rifle as soon as he was taller than it."

"My brothers shoot, but I never wanted to learn. They used to call me the conscientious objector." Cait thought about this for a second. "Probably still do. What does this have to do with your father not liking your husband?"

"My dad taught me how to shoot when I was sixteen."

Cait shook her head in disbelief. "You're telling me a girl from California learned how to shoot and I didn't?"

"My dad was a navy man. He thought it was his duty to show me how to protect myself. He bought me a gun when I turned twenty-one. A Smith and Wesson M and P nine-millimeter."

"You're kidding. What did you say?"

"I told him he could keep it. There was no way I was going to own a gun." Rebecca could still picture the light blue box wrapped with a white bow. When she first saw it, she thought it was from Tiffany. And then she felt the heft of it, heard the rattle of metal when she picked it up, and realized she was wrong. She should have known better. Her father was a practical man. He wanted to protect the people he loved, not indulge them.

"Was he disappointed?"

Rebecca thought about her dad's expression when she pushed the box back in his hands, a strange mix of annoyance and amusement and pride. "I don't know if he was disappointed, but he definitely wasn't surprised. Anyway, that was my dad all over. He wanted me to be independent, self-sufficient. He wanted me to be able to fend for myself." She shook her head. "My husband is one of those larger-than-life people, and I think my dad worried that I'd lose myself inside him."

Cait's eyes were tight on her face, watching. "Did you?"

Rebecca turned her head toward the window. "The jury's still out."

MIKE

It started with a photograph.

He was driving through Austin on his way to see his sister in Abilene when he passed a bunch of people holding signs and shouting something he couldn't catch over the sound of his radio. At first he didn't pay them any attention—he didn't consider himself political, and he didn't have time for people who did—but then he saw a picture on one of those signs of a little baby no bigger than a walnut curled up at the bottom of a wastebasket and the word MURDER written over it, and he thought of the babies he'd always thought he'd have until Bonnie died and his heart broke in a thousand pieces, and that was enough to make him stop. He pulled over to the side of the road and went up to one of the sign holders and asked him what it was all about and the man looked at him, eyes solemn as a funeral, and said, "We're trying to stop the murder of millions of innocent children."

Which was a pretty convincing argument to be starting out with. The guy handed him a couple pamphlets with pictures of fat, smiling babies on the front and told him his name was Ken and that the building over there was a clinic where women came to kill their unborn babies and did he know that a baby's heartbeat starts at six weeks and it's been said that they can feel pain from as early as eight and yet these women didn't care, and the doctors inside didn't have a conscience because how could they go through with something like that if they did? Ripping a baby out of its mother's womb, cutting it up with scissors, and throwing it in the trash like it was nothing. Like life was worth nothing.

That made Mike think of Bonnie and how she used to kiss him goodbye every time she left the house. Hell, every time she left the room, and how the man who'd killed her must have thought life was worth nothing if he was willing to get behind the wheel when he was three times over the legal limit—that's what the officer said during the trial, three times over the legal limit—and smash his car straight into Bonnie's going seventy-five on the wrong side of the road.

What Mike had been thinking must have shown on his face because Ken put a hand on his arm and squeezed, and when he looked into his eyes again he saw understanding there, which was rare. Most people didn't understand what he was feeling. It wasn't for lack of trying: Bonnie's friends had kept him fed for a few months after she died, and his own friends had turned up on his doorstep with a six-pack most nights for a long while, but he could tell they didn't want to understand his pain because understanding it would make it real, and making it real would mean there was the possibility it could happen to them, too, and they didn't want to think about that. He understood. He didn't want to think about it happening, either, but it had, so he didn't have a choice.

Anyway, Ken was a nice guy, grew up in Morgan City, Louisiana, which was where his uncle lived for a while back in the '90s before the floods got too much for him and he moved north. They talked for a while about the Morganza Spillway and whether or not it was a waste of taxpayers' money and how the Saints could have gone all the way last season but the team was still young and then a Jeep pulled up to the entrance and the crowd surged forward like a wave and started shouting all at once and waving their signs and the girl driving the car—she couldn't have been more than twenty—flipped them the bird and kept driving. Nearly hit some poor woman who was just trying to express her disgust for what was going on in that building, which was her right as an American the last time he checked.

They watched as the girl got out of the driver's side and went around to open the passenger door and a lady with a coat slung over her head so no one could see her face came out and the girl and two women, wearing high-vis vests, ushered her through the doors of the clinic, none of them listening to a word the people around them were saying, or looking at the pictures of these innocent babies, or paying them any heed at all, just heads down and straight inside like they couldn't wait to murder another baby. Like they didn't care in the least.

Well, after that, he'd seen enough. He took the pamphlets and Ken's number and shook hands with the people standing out there in the baking heat and he promised them all that he would read up on things and maybe join them next time. They were all such nice people. Very welcoming, which he thought everyone could agree was rare these days.

His sister wasn't too pleased when he took the pamphlets out after dinner and started flipping through them. Said something about those people being zealots and having no right to tell her what she could or could not do with her body and how she wouldn't stand having that propaganda in her house and that Bonnie would have agreed with her, too, which was when he got really mad, because why did she have to bring Bonnie into all this? How could she presume to know more about his wife than he did?

There were a lot of things he could have said to her then, but instead he got up from the sofa and shook his brother-in-law's hand and told him to kiss his nieces for him at breakfast and he walked out the front door, his sister shouting at him at first and then telling him to stop being such a damn fool, it was dark out and too late for him to drive all the way to Columbus, but he didn't so much as turn his head toward her, he was so mad. He'd never been so mad in his life, and he thought about it the whole ride home, and about the pictures on those signs of those poor helpless little babies, and that girl driving the Jeep and the way she had just dismissed all of them like they were nothing at all.

The next morning, he called Ken and made plans to come back up to Austin the following weekend.

He got used to the new routine pretty quick. On Saturday mornings, he'd get up early, stop by the gas station to fill up the tank and pour a couple of regular coffees in his thermos for the drive, and then he'd hit the road. Most of the time he went to Austin, where Ken and the rest of the group would be gathering at their spot outside the entrance.

Betsy always baked something for them—cookies or brownies, something sweet to keep them going—and she'd pass them around while they waited for the first car to come through. Those first few moments were his favorite. In a funny way, it reminded him of being in a locker room before a big game. He'd played football back in high school—made varsity his junior year—and he'd always gotten a rush the minute before they stepped out on the field, when he could hear the crowd cheering and picture the cheerleaders twirling, and the coach would bring them in for a huddle and he would feel the anticipation rising off him and his teammates like a thick steam. It was never as good as it was in that moment, even if they won, because in that moment they were shining and perfect, and as soon as they got on the field they would start to tarnish.

He had his job, sure, but it wasn't the same. There was the boss above him, who retreated into his office and closed the door, and there were the guys working the floor below him, who stopped dicking around when they caught sight of him and turned all straight-faced and diligent. His guys liked him—he was good to them, only busted their balls if he had to, always said yes to vacation requests—but he wasn't on their team.

The only person who'd been on his team was Bonnie. They'd been a team of two, him and her—they didn't need anybody else. People used to make comments about it, would say how it wasn't natural for two people to spend all their time together like that. "Don't you guys have any friends?" his sister asked once, and he and Bonnie just looked at each other and smiled. Why did he need friends when the only person he wanted to spend any time with was Bonnie?

Standing there on Saturday mornings, the air still carrying a chill, their breath coming out of them in little foggy puffs, one hand wrapped around a thermos of coffee, the other holding one of Betsy's brownies wrapped in a paper napkin, he felt like he was finally part of something bigger than him again, a team huddled together, steaming with anticipation and ready to fight.

He didn't think other people would understand, or, more accurately, he didn't think his sister would understand. After the blowout at her house, he didn't call her for a couple of days. She'd always been a hothead—when she was little, their mother used to stick her in the hall closet when she was having a tantrum because the coats would stop her from hurting herself when she started headbutting the wall—and he'd learned over the years that she took at least three days to return to orbit after a blastoff.

Him, he'd stopped being pissed off as soon as he walked through his front door. By then, his anger had dissolved like an Alka-Seltzer, and he was left with an empty stomach and a vague feeling of regret. He didn't like upsetting his sister. He didn't like upsetting anybody.

When he finally did call her, he could tell straightaway that he'd judged it right: she wasn't mad anymore. She launched into a long story about her dog getting sprayed by a skunk and her son trying to give the dog a bath in tomato juice and how the dog had shaken itself out and sprayed tomato juice all over the bathroom and how was she supposed to get tomato juice off the ceiling? And he told her that she should try vinegar next time and she said, "I should have called you in the first place, you always know this kind of stuff," and that was when he knew she'd forgiven him. That's why when they were getting off the phone and she asked if he'd been to any more bullshit protests, he told her no, he hadn't, and he wasn't planning to, even though he'd been up three nights in a row looking up some of the websites that Ken had suggested, and had already sent a text saying he'd be there next Saturday.

His sister had her team, you know? She had a whole goddamn football team between her husband and the kids and the dog and her friends from school and her friends from work and her friends from who knew where else. She made friends easily, his sister, which possibly explained why she had never felt the need to keep her temper in check: there was always somebody else in line waiting to tell her how great she was.

It wasn't like that for him. It was just the football team, and then Bonnie, and then nothing. Until Ken and Betsy and everybody who gathered outside the clinic on Saturday mornings opened their arms and invited him into their huddle and he felt some part of him that had been missing for he didn't know how long slot back into place.

OUTSKIRTS OF YESO, NEW MEXICO— 148 MILES TO ALBUQUERQUE

Cait saw a few squarish shapes rise from the horizon. Yeso was nothing more than a ghost town, all but abandoned and creepy as hell. Cait remembered it clearly from past trips. She also knew it marked the halfway point to Albuquerque.

She'd thought Rebecca was starting to open up a little. The way she'd laughed about the gas station attendant, the way she'd let her eyes close for a few miles. Cait had felt the knife sliding along the clamshell, loosening the muscle, just the way they'd taught her when she'd worked in the kitchen at the Catch back in high school. Gently, gently. You didn't want to crack the shell.

But then she'd mentioned the husband and Rebecca had seized back up.

She was running out of time.

It was ridiculous, this whole charade. Pretending like she didn't already know nearly everything there was to know about Rebecca, or everything the Internet would tell her. As if she didn't know that her husband was Patrick McRae. A man who was in a high-profile Senate race. A man who had been described by *The Washington Post* as "electric."

A man who had detonated an atomic bomb at the center of her life.

Cait woke up to the sound of her phone buzzing. She picked it up, squinting at it in the dim light, saw nine missed calls and thirteen text messages and God only knew how many WhatsApp notifications. All of them asking the same thing: "Have you seen the video?"

Alyssa had sent a link. Cait padded into the kitchen, put the kettle on the stove, and clicked play while she waited for it to boil.

It had been filmed on someone's phone in the audience. She could tell by the way the picture shook every time applause rang out, which was often. There was a man standing on a stage in a suit, his tie loosened around the throat, his hair darkened with sweat. When the video opened, he was mid-flow, his voice soaring as he hit the punch line. "We cannot accept anything less for our country!"

The crowd roared.

The kettle whistled.

Cait poured a stream of boiling water into the French press and started to wonder why the hell everyone was so keen on her watching this guy. She hit pause while she finished making her coffee. It was one of her little pleasures in life, sitting in her tiny egg-yolk-yellow kitchen in the morning and drinking a good cup of coffee. She wasn't about to rush it.

She took a sip and hit play. The man in the suit lurched back to life. A question from the audience. "Congressman McRae, what do you think about the Me Too movement?"

"Well, sir, I was lucky enough to be raised by a strong woman, and now I'm married to one." He took a moment to nod toward the pretty blonde standing behind him. "I believe that women deserve respect, and I believe that any man who rapes or sexually assaults a woman is lower than a dog." He paused for the applause. "That said, I think some people are taking things a little too far. I believe that everyone—man, woman, gay, straight, black, white—is responsible for their actions and the consequences of those actions. Too often I see the names of good, honest people being dragged through the mud on the Internet and on social media. These tools have made it all too easy to point a finger at someone and—boom!" His hands mimicked a mushroom cloud. "Their life goes up in smoke. If someone has done wrong, they should be punished, but here in America, we believe in innocent until proven guilty. We believe in civil discourse. We believe in hearing both sides of the story before destroying a person's reputation."

Cait put down her coffee. Her stomach had soured. She knew what was coming next, sure as if it were a freight train bearing down on her and she was tied to the tracks.

"Take what happened with that musician Jake Forsythe. I know Jake, I've been a big fan of his music for a long time, and I always try to catch one of his shows when I'm in Austin. Now, I'm not pretending to know what happened between him and that girl that night. Maybe he crossed a line. Maybe he made her uncomfortable. Maybe, God forbid, he even hurt her, though I honestly believe that if he did, it was unintentional. I don't know. None of us do, except for the two people who were in that bedroom that night. What I do know from speaking with Jake is that she never gave him a chance to explain himself or to apologize for what happened. She just ran out of his bed and went straight to tell her story on the Internet, where he was hanged, drawn, and quartered by the court of public opinion. What bothers me the most is that she did it anonymously, so she couldn't be questioned on her account of the evening, and her credibility couldn't be verified." He stopped, ran a hand through his hair, shook his head. "I'm not saying she's a liar, but to me, that doesn't sit right. To me, if you come out and accuse someone of wrongdoing, you should stand behind your words. Personally, I believe that—unless a crime has been committed—matters of the bedroom should be kept private between two consenting adults, rather than aired on the Internet for strangers to judge." He took a breath. "I believe in women, and I believe that men who have been proven to hurt women should be punished. But I also believe in responsibility, and civility, and the right to privacy in our homes and our bedrooms. Because if we lose that"—another shake of the head—"we lose the very principles that bind us together as a nation."

The applause was deafening. Whoever was filming was clapping so hard that he knocked the phone right out of his hand, and the video cut off abruptly.

She checked the tally at the corner. Seven hundred thousand views and climbing.

They passed a burnt-out shack, its blackened eyes staring back at them sightlessly, piles of curled-up rubber tubing stacked in front of the boarded-up front door. Low-slung brick bunkers crumbled by the side of the road, their metal doors bolted shut and rusted, faded graffiti sprayed across the fronts.

Rebecca's face was pale in the moonlight. "Where are we?"

"The village of the damned, basically. Don't worry, we'll be out of here soon enough."

They passed a derelict barn, its door hanging from the hinges, the timber frame bleached white in the headlights. Outside, a tractor lolled on its one remaining tire. "It's like the whole place got wiped out in a single day," Rebecca marveled as they rolled through. A factory loomed over them, its cement smokestack cracked and crooked. It looked abandoned, too. "I wonder if the factory shut down."

"Maybe. I've been through here a couple times and have never seen a single sign of life."

Rebecca shuddered.

They passed what once had been the post office, the painted sign rubbed to a dull smear on the bricks. There was nothing for them in a place like this, at least nothing they'd welcome. It felt like something was watching them. Something, not someone.

"Let's get out of here," Rebecca whispered.

Cait nudged the gas. She could see the edge of town up ahead. Just one last building, and then a return to the cold emptiness of the desert.

They passed a house, a clapboard Cape with a sagging front porch. A pair of rocking chairs slumped there, still in the breeze-less night. If you squinted, you could see what it looked like once: a dollhouse writ large, all lace curtains and painted woodwork and sweet, folksy charm. But now it was like the rest of the town: hollow-eyed and barely standing, the paint bleached away by the harsh desert sun, the wooden frame splintered and rotting. Forgotten and unloved.

In the window, a single candle flickered.

"You don't think anyone lives there, do you?"

Cait shook her head. "I don't know. But somebody must have lit that candle."

"Jesus."

A pair of headlights swung out from behind the house.

"Someone's awake," Cait said, her eyes locked on the rearview mirror.

Headlights lit the black tarmac a silvered gray.

"Who is it?" Rebecca's voice was tight with panic.

"I don't know."

Cait pressed down harder on the gas pedal. The little house soon disappeared from sight, but the headlights blazed steadily behind them.

"Maybe we woke them up," Cait said. Her heart was thudding at the base of her throat. She couldn't see the shape of the front end through the harsh glare of the headlights, but she knew in her bones what it was.

Rebecca's face was a mask of blank terror in the moonlight, and Cait could see that her hands had curled into tight fists. "Can you see?" Rebecca asked.

Cait glanced again into the rearview mirror. "No," she admitted. "Nothing."

The headlights never got any closer than a few hundred yards. Ten minutes passed, then fifteen. The lights behind them were constant, never wavering.

"Maybe whoever it is just decided to run an errand." Cait's voice sounded strange to her own ears, high and slightly strangled.

"At this time of night?"

"Maybe it's an emergency. It's not like there's anywhere in that town where they could go."

"How fast are you going?"

Cait looked at the speedometer. "Sixty." She felt the deep hum of the engine under her feet.

"If it was an emergency, don't you think they would have passed us by now? There's no one else out on the road—they could be doing eighty."

"I don't know," Cait snapped. "I have no idea what they're doing out here. I have no idea if they're following us, or going to the drugstore, or looking to murder us, or just decided that five a.m. is a fine time for a drive. I don't know, okay?" Cait shut her eyes, just for a second. "I'm sorry. I didn't mean—I'm just . . ."

"Scared."

Cait nodded.

"Me, too."

They let their eyes drift back to the mirrors. The headlights were still there, watching, waiting.

"How far do you think it is until the next town?" Rebecca asked.

Cait shook her head. "I'm not sure. Maybe a half hour." The

gas tank mysteriously emptying. The pickup truck trying to run them off the road. The creepy gas station attendant, the man from the diner . . . She should have gotten them off this road by now. They were sitting ducks out here, had been for hours, and she'd done nothing to protect them. She was supposed to be the one in charge here. She was anything but. "Do you have any signal on your phone?"

Rebecca pulled it out of her bag and looked at it. "Nothing."

Silence descended, just the sound of the two engines, the faint moan of the radio, and the throb of their hearts beating in their chests as they waited.

Rebecca knew she shouldn't have bought it.

She was in Target, picking up a few bags of Halloween candy just in case they had trick-or-treaters this year. That was unlikely—it seemed more organized now, parents only letting their kids go to the homes of people they knew rather than knocking on every door in the neighborhood like she had when she was a kid. Still, better to be safe than sorry. The last thing she wanted was someone turning up at the door and having to hand them a couple of wrinkled dollar bills or, worse, an apple as a consolation prize.

Secretly, she hoped she'd have tons of trick-or-treaters this year. She'd even bought a pumpkin and placed it on the doorstep, and she'd make sure to keep the lights on to let everyone know she was home. She wanted to open the door and find a whole gaggle of them waiting, plastic pumpkin pails outstretched, stiff-limbed and red-cheeked in their plush costumes, little unicorns and cowboys and fairy princesses and dinosaurs. She wanted to see the parents standing behind them, exhausted and sore-footed and already worrying about sugar highs and late bedtimes but delighted nonetheless, and she wanted to picture herself among them in a few years, her own little one dressed as a pea pod or a My Little Pony or whatever she wanted to be.

She was pregnant again. She'd taken the test earlier that week, crouched on the cold floor of the master en suite, watching the two blue lines take shape. She'd booked a doctor's appointment that day, and sure enough, the bloodwork had come back positive. "It's early," the doctor had said, "only a few weeks." He had been her doctor for the past two years. He didn't need to warn her about getting her hopes up.

She tossed a bag of Snickers into the cart before thinking twice—too many kids with peanut allergies these days—and swapping it for a bag of 3 Musketeers. She bought a new mug to replace the one she'd broken the other day, and a few rolls of paper towels, and a tube of toothpaste. She steered the cart as if on autopilot: she knew the aisles by heart.

She studiously avoided the baby section, but she'd forgotten about the dangerous no-man's-land displays leading up to the checkout. The Christmas decorations were already out, and there was a bin full of plush toys next to the register. Most of them were a strange, mildly sinister version of Santa Claus, but there were reindeer, too, and polar bears wearing little striped scarves.

It was the polar bear that got her in the end. She'd had a stuffed bear as a kid, brown with nubbly fur and black bead eyes, and she wanted her baby to have a bear, too. She grabbed one and tossed it onto the conveyor belt next to the paper towels. When she unpacked the bag at home, she held the little bear in her hand and stroked its soft white fur before tucking it away in a drawer in the spare room. The nursery room, as she secretly thought of it.

She didn't show it to Patrick when he got home from work. They were both holding their breath separately, tiptoeing around the tiny seed sprouting inside of her, worried that one move might suddenly change everything. Neither of them had so much as used the word "pregnant" yet for fear of jinxing it. Instead, they called it her "situation" or her "condition." The stuffed bear was tempting fate. She knew that, and she knew that's how Patrick would see it, too. So the bear stayed in the drawer.

Ever since that video went viral, he'd barely had time to take a breath. He was excited about the pregnancy, of course—he cried when she told him—but his attention was being pulled in a million directions. Just last night, he flew to New York for an interview on the *Today* show. Normally, she would have minded him being away so much, but she was happy for him. The truth was, she didn't feel like he was leaving her on her own. She had her baby with her. And she knew, deep in her bones, that this time her baby wasn't going to leave her.

Every morning, she would take the bear out of the drawer and hold it in her arms. She would imagine it nestled in the crook of her baby's neck or held tight in her fat little fingers. (She had decided the baby was a girl. She hadn't told Patrick that, either.) Her daughter would give the bear a name one day—something simple, like Snowy—and she would cry when it was lost and yelp with joy when Rebecca found it lodged underneath the sofa. She imagined rubbing a smudge of dirt out of its white fur before handing it to her daughter, and the little girl smiling up at her, her eyes the same cornflower blue as Patrick's.

After a few minutes of this, she would force herself to push the bear back in the drawer for the rest of the day. She had to mete out these moments of joy, in case they were stripped from her. They had been before. She told herself she was doing it to mitigate her own potential grief, as if grief were a river that could be dammed and contained and not a vast, wild, untamable ocean.

But deep down, she knew that this time the baby wouldn't be snatched from her like the others had been. This baby—her little girl—would be hers to keep.

"C'mon, baby," Cait muttered. Rebecca watched the needle on the speedometer climb. Soon they were up to seventy. The truck kept pace behind them, the headlights filling the cabin with a bright, harsh light. It caught every nick and groove on the windshield, turning it milky and opaque.

A sudden, sickening crunch of metal on metal. The truck made contact with their bumper, sending them fishtailing into the hard shoulder.

"Fuck!" Cait jerked the wheel into the spin. The tires skidded, sending up a hail of dust before finding a grip on the pavement. The truck's headlights dropped back. Cait floored it. The engine strained.

Rebecca glanced in the mirror again. Nothing but the pickup's haloed headlights, coming up again fast.

Another jolt as the truck hit them. The Jeep groaned as the wheels shuddered off the rumble strip.

Rebecca made a sound that was somewhere between a sob and a whimper. She scanned the horizon. Nothing but scrubland and the long flat ribbon of road and the vast black sky. No cars they could signal for help.

There was no way out.

Rebecca had known it as soon as the headlights appeared, though in the dark it was impossible to see its shape. Still, she'd known. It was the same pickup truck that had run them off the road a hundred miles back. And it had come back to claim her.

She'd thought she had more time than this. She hadn't thought the wheels would click into motion so soon. But looking back at the headlights bearing down on them, she couldn't deny it any longer: her time was up.

In that moment, she wished she could pray. She wished she could believe in something, anything, that would deliver them to safety.

But she couldn't. That's why she was out here on this road. Because she knew there was no miracle waiting for her, no matter how hard she prayed.

She imagined herself back in church, the smells of incense and wood polish, her mother kneeling next to her, her hands tightly clasped. Her mother had believed in miracles all the way through her illness, had bought into any quack theory she came across, filled the house with candles and crystals and tea that stank of sulfur and made her retch when she drank it. "I can feel it working!" she'd declare after each new cure, her eyes feverish and too big in her skull, but she didn't feel better, not really, and even if she did, she didn't get better. After she died, Rebecca's father gathered all of it up and threw it in the garbage without a word.

The truck nudged the bumper again. The crunch of glass as a taillight was punched out. The truck was toying with them. Taking its time. It was enjoying itself.

She peered through the windshield, trying to catch a glimpse of the driver's face. There was nothing but darkness beyond the glass.

The message from her editor was short and to the point: "We have a problem. Call me."

Cait dialed the number she'd left, already sick with dread. The editor picked up on the first ring.

"I've got some bad news."

Over the previous twenty-four hours, Patrick McRae's speech had gone viral. It now had over three million views and counting. People were describing it as a "star-making turn" and heralding him as a hero. "Patrick McRae's Powerful Response to the Me Too Era" was the headline in *The Wall Street Journal*, and Fox News pundits declared him a savior. "Finally," they sang, "somebody is willing to stand up and talk some common sense." Op-eds sprang up like dandelions: "Majority of Women Agree with McRae, Polls Show." They didn't need to add that the majority of men did, too. That was a given.

Cait had watched the explosion with something akin to awe. All this over something she'd written in twenty minutes for a website that mainly published articles about ten-step skincare routines? It was a national news story, the launch pad for a man's entire political career, and she was still pouring dollar drafts during happy hour. There was a part of her that thought it was funny. The whole thing was absurd, really. Like something out of a farce.

She knew from the tone of her editor's voice, though, that she was about to lose her sense of humor.

"We've been hacked."

"What do you mean?" She already knew what it meant.

"They know your name, Cait. I'm so sorry."

And just like that, Cait's world as she knew it came to an end.

She shut down her Twitter and Instagram accounts immediately, but not soon enough that they weren't already flooded with messages. Her Twitter feed was full of trolls telling her to drop dead, but somehow the Instagram comments cut her more deeply. Strangers posted comments on old vacation photos, calling her fat and ugly. "I can't believe Jake Forsythe had sex with THIS," one of them said. "He must have been blind drunk." "No wonder she made up all of those LIES. How else would a dog like her get any attention?"

She felt the same familiar emotions flood through her. Shame. Anger. Shame. Despair.

There was already a 4chan subthread dedicated to her. 4chan /Caitlyn_Monaghan. She scrolled down to the comments, trying to conjure up some of the anger she'd felt the last time around, but seeing her name splashed across the page, all she felt was fear. Tens of thousands of strangers, baying for her blood. There were people asking where she lived, where she worked. "Let's find this bitch and make her pay."

She knew then that this would be different from the first time around. The article she'd written was no longer just some stupid clickbait to be hate-read and forgotten. They knew who she was now, and they hated her more than ever.

This was big-time. This was dangerous.

OUTSKIRTS OF VAUGHN, NEW MEXICO—
128 MILES TO ALBUQUERQUE

Cait's eyes were locked on the rearview mirror. The pickup was a few lengths behind them now, still close enough to pick up the glint of the Jeep's rear end in the headlights. They needed to get some distance between them, fast.

The fork in the road was getting closer. Cait's mind whirred. If the driver was after them specifically—and she was sure now that he was—he might know the route she took to get to Albuquerque, in which case he would expect her to stay on 60 and head through the center of Vaughn. She remembered the place, a decent-size town, a couple of motels, a few gas stations.

She might be able to pull into one of those gas stations and call for help, but if the guy in the pickup was carrying, she wasn't sure she'd be able to get inside quick enough to save them from getting shot. She flicked her eyes back to the mirror. He was dropping back, waiting to see what she would do.

There might be side streets in Vaughn that she could hide down, though from what she could recall, the place was pretty sprawling, and flat, too, the buildings mainly single-story concrete boxes hugging tight to the ground. Hiding the Jeep would be a tall order, even in the middle of the night.

She could drop south onto 285 or 54. She could head north on 54 toward Santa Rosa. She could stop and swing around and play a nasty game of chicken with him, use the Jeep's steel frame as a weapon, catch him at his own game.

She glanced over at Rebecca. No, she couldn't do that. She couldn't risk this woman's life. Not when Cait knew that whoever was driving that truck was after her, and her alone. She'd thought she would be safe. They couldn't trace the plates to her, and she'd been careful to check that no one was tailing her when she left Austin. But they had tracked her down just the same, and now they were hunting her like a dog.

She had only one option. She had to make them disappear.

"Do you trust me?"

Rebecca looked at her. "What do you mean?"

"Do you trust me?" Cait asked again, and this time Rebecca nodded, just once.

Cait killed the lights and punched the gas. The road in front of them went black, just a faint outline in the dark that Cait had to squint to see. The taillights were out, too, but the brake lights would come on if she used them. Which meant she couldn't use them.

"What are you doing?"

Cait's eyes were locked on the mirror. He was dropping back a little farther. She'd confused him, at least for a second. Good.

"Hold on."

She took the turn onto 54 hard, leaning into the curve without touching the brakes. Gravity pushed her against the door before the road straightened out, and she floored it.

Just like that, he was gone.

4chan/Caitlyn_Monaghan

Anonymous: Love that the bitch is getting the attention she deserves. She is a national discgrace.

Cucks_Suck: Patrick McRae should be President after calling her out for the trash she is.

TruePatriot368: she should be in jail for trying to ruin an innocent man's life. I swear to god one day that girl is going to pay for what she did, just like all the little lying bitchs should pay.

Anonymous: I know where she lives. Maybe somebody should pay her a visit.

Underneath was a screengrab with her home address.

"No phones behind the bar." Cait swallowed the bile that had risen in her throat and looked up to see Stacy scowling at her from the manager's office. She raised a hand in apology and slipped her phone in her back pocket.

Since her name had been leaked by the hackers, her life had gone berserk. She'd been hounded by the national media—*The*

New York Times, *The Washington Post*, *Time*—and invited on the *Today* show and *The View*. She turned them all down, and when they kept calling, she changed her phone number. Her editor got back in touch to say that her piece had gotten another wave of traction, this one bigger. "Our server crashed, twice!" she had written, unable to hide her delight, though she had tossed in a half-hearted "Thinking of you" at the end.

The editor asked if Cait would write another piece for the website, and she wasn't alone. Editors who had ignored her emails from a few months back suddenly flooded into her inbox. They all feigned interest in the pitches she'd sent, but really, they wanted to know one thing: would she write a response to Patrick McRae, and could they publish it? Cait could imagine the ad revenue signs flashing in their eyes, like a cartoon dog's at a slot machine. "No, thank you," she typed out, over and over. "I'm focusing on other work."

The only people who didn't want a piece of her were the Sisters of Service. "I think it might be good if you lay low for a couple weeks," Lisa said to her. "It's too dangerous to have you out in the lot right now."

Cait had begged her to reconsider, even though she had known deep down that Lisa was right: she was a liability. But her work with the Sisters of Service was the only thing of value she did in her life, and it felt in darker moments like the only thing keeping her tethered to reality. She didn't know what she would do if she lost it. Eventually, Lisa took pity on her and gave her a desk job back at the office. "We could use your writing skills in our communications department," she said, making it sound like a promotion rather than a banishment.

And so, for a few days, the situation felt manageable. The calls stopped. Her work at Sisters of Service continued. She kept turning up to the bar and slinging beers, and when her shift finished, she went back to her apartment and locked the doors and felt a moment of something approaching calm, or maybe it was just exhaustion.

But now all of that was gone. They knew where she lived. They could be at her apartment right now, breaking down the door and trashing the place. Or worse, slipping in unnoticed and hiding. They would wait until she went to sleep and then they'd slither out from under the bed and murder her. Or worse.

"I need to go on break." She didn't wait for the other bartenders to answer, just pushed past them and ran through the staff door and out the back entrance into the muggy night air. It was late October, but Austin was under the spell of an Indian summer, and temperatures had been in the nineties all week. She pulled her phone out of her pocket and sent a text to Alyssa: "Can I crash at your place tonight?"

She smoked a cigarette while she waited for a response.

"My sister's in town so she's already claimed the couch but you can bunk with me if you want? Are you okay????"

Cait closed her eyes against the response. She saw herself arriving at Alyssa's apartment after her shift, sweaty and tired and smelling of stale booze, and the two sisters looking at her with pitying eyes. She couldn't face it. "Don't worry, everything's fine—but I'll just stay at mine tonight. Have fun with your sister!"

"Let me know if you change your mind! Drinks next week?"

"Def xx"

She shoved the phone back in her pocket and made her way back to the bar. Stacy was waiting for her, arms folded, mouth turned down into a deep frown. "You need to ask permission before you go on break. You can't just leave the bar like that."

"I know, I'm sorry. It was kind of an emergency."

Stacy didn't soften. "I don't care if it was an *actual* emergency. You still need to ask permission. I know you think your shit doesn't stink because you took in the most money last week, but there are a dozen girls who would kill to have your place behind that bar." She reached up and tapped the brim of Cait's Stetson hat. "Use that pretty little head of yours, will you?"

Cait had to shove her hands in her pockets to keep from punching Stacy. It was moments like this when she wished the boss had never caught JB pleasuring himself in the manager's office. He was a creep, sure, but a lazy one, and she'd take being managed by a lazy creep over being micromanaged by Stacy any day.

She risked one more look at her phone. Three missed calls, none of them from known numbers. They could be robocalls, she told herself, but she knew better than that. Robocalls stopped after nine p.m., and it was close to ten. The post had gone up on 4chan an hour ago, which experience had taught her was more than enough time for them to find her new number. She'd have a lot more calls coming her way before the night was over.

"Cheer up, maybe it'll never happen." She looked up to see Ken grinning at her. He stopped when he saw the look on her face. "Hey, you okay? You don't look so hot."

"I'm fine," she said, grabbing his empty glass and pouring out a fresh draft.

He nudged Nick with an elbow. "What do you think? Boy trouble?"

Nick grunted. His eyes stayed fixed on the TV.

Cait pushed down a flash of anger. "I'm just having a bad day, that's all."

"And what's this 'bad day' called? Joe? Fred?"

"Fuck off, Ken." She saw the slapped look on his face and instantly regretted it. She'd just broken one of the cardinal rules of bartending: she'd stopped getting the joke. "Sorry, I didn't mean . . . I'm just having a really shitty day, that's all."

He waved her away, but she could tell he was hurt.

She nodded toward his draft. "You want a chaser with that? On the house."

"Nah, you're okay. The wife'll smell it on me."

"I didn't know you were married."

"Yeah, well." He took a long swig from his beer and turned his eyes to the TV above her head. He had a strange smile on his face, like he knew something nobody else did, and he found it particularly funny. "I guess there's a lot we don't know about each other." His eyes flicked to hers. "Hey, I heard you got yourself into a little trouble," he said quietly. Nick's eyes had unpeeled themselves from the screen, and he was watching her, waiting.

Dread ran through her like a hot knife. So far, nobody at the bar had connected her to the Jake article, though she knew it was probably just a matter of time. She knew Stacy wouldn't be happy about it. It was the wrong kind of attention to be bringing to the place, and she'd been looking for a reason to fire Cait since the minute she stepped through the door. The last thing she needed was Ken flapping his big mouth about it. "Oh yeah?" She turned her back to him and started straightening out the bottles on the top shelf. "What kind of trouble is that?"

He paused for a minute and locked eyes with hers. There was something there she hadn't seen before, a reckless kind of malice. He knew he was putting her on edge, and he was enjoying it. But it was gone as quickly as it had come, replaced by his familiar good-natured bluster. "Came in last week and Stacy told me you'd blown off your shift. Said you had some excuse about having some kind of dental emergency." He winked at her. "I think you were playing hooky."

"I lost a crown," she said. "I was eating a Bullseye and it came straight out." This was true, though the dentist who'd fitted the temporary crown had told her it was probably from grinding her teeth at night. She'd been doing that a lot these past few days, waking up in a cold sweat with a sore jaw and a free-floating sense of dread.

He blew out his cheeks in a pantomimed version of disbelief. "Sounds like some dog-ate-my-homework shit to me, pardon my French."

"Have a look yourself." She leaned over the bar and opened her mouth wide. She pointed to a back molar that was too white and slightly lumpy. "I've got to go back to make it permanent next week."

Ken looked impressed. "Well, I apologize. It seems we were slandering your good name for nothing."

She wagged a finger at him. "It wouldn't be the first time. You want another?"

"Yes, ma'am," he said, pushing the glass toward her. Nick did the same, eyes already fixed back on the screen.

She hoped they didn't notice how her hands were shaking when she poured out another round.

Cait rubbed at the spot on her collarbone where the seat belt had bitten into the flesh. She couldn't bring herself to look at the road, or what had been the road a minute ago but was now just an endless sea of black.

"I—I think we've lost him."

She looked over at Rebecca, who was squinting into the side mirror, a pained look on her face. Cait's eyes followed. There was nothing there now, no sign of the truck's headlights or the silver gleam of its grille. Just darkness, everywhere, enveloping and terrifying in equal measure.

Cait nodded. "I saw him take 60. He's heading to Vaughn now." Just like that, it was over. They'd been spared, at least for now. She turned to Rebecca. "Are you okay?"

"I think so. Are you?"

Cait didn't answer. How could she possibly be okay? A man had tried to kill them. Again. They may have lost him for now, but chances were good that he'd be back. And deep down, she knew she was the one who was responsible for the whole sorry mess.

"I think I need to pull over for a minute." She was already easing over onto the shoulder.

Rebecca flinched. "I don't think that's a good idea. We should keep going. He could come back . . ."

"I just need a break, just for a second." Cait pulled the Jeep to a stop.

The two sat in silence. The radio found a signal, and Van Morrison came on, the car suddenly filled with him singing about marvelous nights. Outside, it was pitch black. Cait flicked the headlights back on, and the scarred tarmac reemerged. "I'm going to get out and check the damage," she said, already tugging on the handle. She was desperate for some air.

Rebecca reached out and grabbed her wrist. "I don't think you should get out of the car." In the moonlight, her face looked pale and stricken. "Please."

Cait shook her off. "I need to see if it's serious before we get back on the road. What if the fuel line is nicked?"

"He didn't hit us hard. There'll be a dent on the bumper, nothing worse. We should keep driving until we get to the next town. It's too dangerous out here."

"I just need to get out, okay?" Cait opened the door, trying to hide how badly her hands were shaking. "I need a fucking cigarette."

"Fine." Rebecca scrambled for the door handle. "I'm coming, too."

Cait opened her mouth to protest but closed it again. There was no point in fighting her on it. She probably needed the air, too.

The night air was icy-sharp. Cait tapped out a cigarette and offered her the pack. Rebecca shook her head before changing her mind and taking one for herself. She took a drag and felt something loosen at the back of her skull, just before her stomach turned and she started to cough.

Cait watched her, bemused. "Not a natural smoker."

"I haven't done it in years," Rebecca spluttered.

The two of them smoked in silence, cigarette smoke mixing with the white fog of their hot breath.

Rebecca turned to her. The tip of her cigarette flared red in the dark. "I couldn't see his face. Could you?"

"No. It was too dark." Cait took a long drag. "I'm pretty sure it was the same truck from before."

"Me, too."

Cait took another drag and tossed the butt. The red ember flared in the dirt. It was time to pull the plug. She'd pushed it too far now, had taken too many risks with their lives. She may have broken every rule in the book to get here, but she was still part of the Sisters of Service. She had a duty of care to this woman, regardless of who her husband was, or how much of a hypocrite she might be, or how good the story would have been if Cait had been able to tell it. It was time to fix this mess. "We need to call the police."

Rebecca looked as if she'd been slapped. "We can't do that."

"Somebody tried to run us off the road. We have to tell the police." She took a breath. "We should probably turn back, too. If he's come after us twice already, there's no guarantee he won't do it again, especially if he knows my route."

"But you're off the route now. We can go another way to Albuquerque, one he won't be expecting. We can—"

She held up a hand. "I'm sorry, but we can't risk it."

Cait felt bad about calling off the trip, but things had gotten out of hand. The guy in the truck, whoever he was—he had scared the shit out of her. She might not like Rebecca, and she sure as hell didn't want to turn back now, but she didn't see that she had much of a choice. Their lives were in danger. The protocol was spelled out in the training manual: "Sisters of Service holds the right to terminate a drive at any point if the client's safety or the driver's safety is in immediate danger."

She should have turned back a long time ago. She had held out hope that the dangers and setbacks they'd faced might still somehow end up just a series of misunderstandings, or unfortunate coincidences, and the trip would go back to normal, or as normal as any of these trips could be.

Cait was as upset about calling off the trip as Rebecca. The truth was, if she turned back now, she'd have nothing. She'd end up back on shift at the Dark Horse on Tuesday, slinging Bud drafts to Ken and Nick and a bunch of drunk college guys wearing backward baseball caps and popped collars, and maybe she'd finally ask about management, now that Stacy had moved on to that wine bar on Second Street. Finally stop wearing those dumb Daisy Dukes. She was going to be twenty-six next year. How long could she keep pretending this wasn't her real life?

Ten hours back the way they came and she'd be back in her apartment in Austin. Back in her tiny yellow kitchen, making herself a good cup of coffee and watching Adam tug the garbage bins onto the street. Back wondering if today was the day someone was going to slip a death threat under her door, or sneak up behind her while she was pumping gas, or lie in wait for her in a darkened parking lot. Back searching her name on the Internet and seeing strangers say the worst things imaginable about her, all because she happened to write an article and a politician she'd never met had turned her into a national symbol worthy of being hated and reviled.

Rebecca shook her head. "Please. If the police get involved, they'll have to make a formal report, and those reports are searchable. If my name gets out there—"

Cait looked at her. This was it. This was the revelation she'd been waiting for. "You're scared of your husband."

Rebecca reeled back, shocked. "No! God, no. It's just . . . it's complicated. Please. I'm begging you. No police. I have to get to

Albuquerque by the morning. If I don't . . ." She shook her head and began to cry.

Cait had never seen her look this upset, not even when a homicidal maniac was threatening to run them off the road. There was something going on here, something Cait wasn't seeing.

Something, Cait realized, that was bigger than any story she could ever hope to write. "Rebecca," she said gently. "What's really going on here?"

The woman shook her head and wiped her eyes. "It's just . . . I need to get there, that's all. You have to take me there. Please. I know I'm asking a lot from you—I *know* I am—but . . . I don't have a choice. You have to help me. You have to get me to Albuquerque tomorrow. It's my only chance."

For the first time, Cait saw Rebecca not as some stuck-up politician's wife, or the subject of an explosive story, or even a client she was ferrying around. She saw her for what she was: a scared, desperate woman who needed her help. She took a deep breath. "Fine. No police. We'll keep going to Albuquerque."

The doctor's face was carefully arranged. "I'm afraid we've had some bad news," he said, perching on the edge of the stool.

Rebecca sat up and pulled the paper dressing gown around her. She wished they'd let her get dressed after the scan. She felt exposed sitting on the table half naked, her stomach still slicked with gel, her socked feet dangling over the edge. Like a child.

"The scan shows that the fetus has some . . . abnormalities."

Her head snapped up, alert. He'd been calling it a baby before. Now it was a fetus. Something inside her wrenched and soured. "What kind of abnormalities?"

He looked at her over tented fingers. "Rebecca, are you familiar with a condition called anencephaly?"

She shook her head. She should know this. She should know everything that could possibly happen to her baby. Why didn't she know?

His frown deepened. "It's when the brain of the fetus fails to develop properly in utero."

"What does that mean? Will the baby be okay?"

His eyebrows collapsed. "I'm afraid it's very serious. If brought to full term, there's a seventy-five percent chance the baby will be stillborn. For those that do survive the birth, they will likely only survive for a few days, perhaps weeks." He shook his head. "There's no cure."

The world telescoped away from her, the walls of the examination room collapsing like a house of cards. She heard a great rush in her ears, as if she were standing at the edge of a waterfall, and then she felt herself plummet into the dark. When she opened her eyes, the doctor was standing above her, his eyebrows knitted together, the careful mask stripped away, leaving only a sad, helpless man behind. "I'll get you something to drink, and then we can discuss next steps," he said quietly, once she was able to sit up again, and the door shut behind him with a soft click.

In the silence, all she could hear was the soft whir of the air conditioner and the far-off beeping of machinery in an adjacent room. She pulled her knees to her chest and hugged them tight. If she made herself small enough, she could protect her baby. She could heal it just by the force of her will. She pictured the little bean swimming around inside her, the clusters of fingers and toes and the tiny swooping nose and the soft curve of eyes. She had seen it just minutes ago, watched it hovering on the screen. A miracle. A ghost. The nurse's breath had caught in her throat when she'd seen it, but Rebecca had thought that was a natural reaction to seeing her baby swimming inside her body. How could anyone not be awed by it? But now she could see it clearly: the way the nurse had avoided her eyes when she'd moved the wand across her swollen stomach, her smile disappearing like quicksand. She had known the baby was doomed.

Rebecca dressed quickly, her fingers fumbling with the buttons on her shirt, her shoes feeling heavy and leaden as she laced them. The paper crinkled as she stood up from the table. She didn't want to be there when the doctor returned. Maybe, if she didn't see him again, what he'd said to her would be made untrue. She grabbed her bag and ran out of the office, ignoring the reception-ist's calls to book another appointment. She would never go back, she decided as she unlocked her car door and slid into the driver's seat. She would go home and stay there until the baby was ready to come, and then she would bring it into the world herself and cradle it in her arms, and she knew—she knew!—that she would be able to protect it. She would be able to make the baby okay.

She turned the key in the ignition but couldn't bring herself to drive. Instead, she sat there idling in the parking lot, watching other expectant mothers trail in and out of the doctor's office, faces flushed with excitement or pale with nausea but all of them happy. None of them looked like the face she saw now in the rear-view mirror, ashen and devastated.

She pulled her phone out of her bag and Googled it. Anen-cephaly. Reams and reams of photos came up, babies with heads shrunken and deformed, eyes closed, mouths open. She knew she should stop but she couldn't, she looked and looked until her eyes felt gritty and sore. She didn't know how long she sat there. An hour? Two? There was a knock on the window and she jumped, her phone skittering out of her hand and under the passenger seat. When she looked up, she saw the face of the nurse who'd done the ultrasound peering down at her. The woman mimed rolling down the window, and Rebecca pressed the button without thinking. The window whirred down.

"Are you okay?" the nurse asked, though she could see for her-self clear as day that Rebecca was not okay, nowhere near it, and she knew exactly why.

Rebecca was silent. Something dark and heavy had lodged in her throat. This grief would live with her now, deep inside her, quietly choking the life out of her. She knew she should cry, but she was beyond tears.

The nurse opened the door and crouched down next to her.

"Do you want to come back inside?" she asked. Her eyes were filled with such kindness that Rebecca couldn't bear to look at them. She shook her head. "Okay, then," the nurse said, taking Rebecca's hand in hers. "I'll sit with you out here for a while, okay? And then maybe, once you're feeling up to it, we can talk a little. But only if you want to."

Rebecca nodded and let her hand be held by the woman. She didn't feel like she was inside her body anymore, she felt like she was floating above it, watching, waiting for whatever this was to end because she knew deep in her soul that it couldn't be real. It couldn't. In the real world, her baby was growing inside of her, healthy and strong, wiggling its little broad-bean feet and waving its little hands, and soon, in just a few short months, the baby would emerge from her in a flood of blood and pain and love and it would open her eyes and look up at her and she would know her better than she had ever known anyone in her life, including herself. Her baby was not one of those monsters on the screen. Her baby was perfect.

At some point, the nurse reached over and switched off the car engine, and later still she called a colleague and asked that they phone Patrick. When he arrived, Rebecca allowed him to gather her in his arms and then walk her back into the doctor's office, where she was seated in a hard plastic chair and made to wait while he went inside to talk to the doctor. The nurses kept bringing her cups of sweetened tea that went cold, untouched on the table next to her. When Patrick emerged, he looked older somehow, the lines around his mouth suddenly deeper, the skin under his eyes pouched and dark. He took her hand and led her back to his car, and together, they drove home in silence.

"We're going to find you a new doctor," he said as he tucked her into bed. "That one doesn't know what he's talking about.

Don't worry, Becca." He leaned down to kiss her on the forehead. "It's going to be all right."

But Rebecca knew with a shocking, shrill clarity that it wasn't going to be all right, that she was going to lose her baby, and after that, nothing would be the same again.

Rebecca didn't know what had made Cait change her mind, and right now she didn't care. She was too worn out with exhaustion and fear and relief to feel anything other than numb.

It had been nearly half an hour, and the pickup hadn't reappeared. Maybe Cait really had lost him with that headlight trick. Maybe they'd never know who was behind the wheel. She didn't care. All that mattered was that they were on their way to Albuquerque. By this time tomorrow, she'd be back in her bed in Lubbock, this whole nightmare would be over, and she could begin the long, impossible work of piecing her shattered heart back together.

Patrick's voice pushed into her head. *Just believe, baby. Just believe.*

"Do you believe in miracles?" She hadn't realized she was going to ask the question until it came out of her mouth.

Cait looked at her for a moment and finally shook her head. "No, but my mom does. When I was a kid, she used to find signs from God everywhere: a rainbow after a storm, or a single flower blooming in the middle of winter. She'd point them out to me and tell me that they were God's way of telling us that He was looking out for us. My grandma used to do that, too, only with feathers. She thought they were signs from her own mother. Every time she came across one, she'd pick it up and turn her eyes to the sky and say, 'Hi, Momma. Hope you're doing fine.'" Cait smiled at the memory. "What about you?" she asked.

"My mother did, too." Rebecca took a breath. "She died when I was eighteen."

"Oh, God. I'm sorry."

"Have you ever seen someone die of cancer?"

Cait shook her head.

"I hope you never do. It eats them from the inside until there's nothing left of them. Cancer ate my mother slowly at first, over the course of a year, and then suddenly, all at once, in two weeks. By the end of it, she looked like a skeleton lying in that bed. Her hair was gone, and her lips bled all the time, and she was in constant, constant pain." Rebecca closed her eyes against the memory. "All through it, she kept telling me that a miracle would save her. The priest came and blessed her with holy water, and she bought stuff online—special teas and oils and salves that were supposedly infused with some kind of magical healing powers but were really just a bunch of junk. She prayed all the time for salvation, and she held out hope until the very last day that God was going to save her." Rebecca's face was wet with tears, and Cait fought the urge to reach out and wipe them away. "She died thinking that she'd been abandoned by her God. She didn't find peace. She fought it the whole way down, and when it finally claimed her, you know what she thought?"

"What?" Cait whispered.

"She thought it was her own fault. That if she'd just prayed a little harder, or believed a little bit more, that she would have been saved." Rebecca shook her head. "Of course, nothing could save her. She died just shy of her forty-fifth birthday."

"That's awful. I'm so sorry." Cait was silent for a minute. "I've never believed in miracles."

"Neither do I." Rebecca stared at her reflection in the window. "The baby's sick," she said finally. "She has a condition that means she won't survive, at least not for more than a few days, and those days that she could live . . ." She closed her eyes. "It wouldn't be any kind of life I'd wish for her. That's why I'm doing this."

Cait's face crumpled. "Oh, God. I'm—I'm so sorry."

Rebecca smiled sadly. "Me, too."

She could see Cait working to piece things together. "So your husband doesn't know that the baby is sick?"

"He knows." Rebecca shook her head. "He's a great believer in miracles, my husband, and he believes our baby will be a miracle."

"And you don't?"

She shook her head again. "I know better."

Patrick knelt next to the bed and wrapped his arms around Rebecca. "Baby, please. You just have to have faith."

Three doctors' visits in three days, and all of them said the same thing: there was no hope for their baby. She would die, either before she was born or during childbirth. If she did manage to survive the birth—which would be a "miracle," one doctor said, though Rebecca wished he hadn't used that word—the baby's life would be short. A few hours, maybe a day. And then she would be taken from them.

"There was a child," Patrick was saying now, "in France. I read about him online. He had the same condition, and he lived until he was three years old." He squeezed her hands. "We could have three years, Becs. Maybe more."

She had read that same article and countless others. Women who had carried their babies to term, tugged down on their foreheads the little woolen hats they'd knitted, kissed them and held them until they died. She couldn't do this. She knew that it would break her, even more than she was already broken. She knew that she would never recover.

"I can't do it," she said, and Patrick sank his head into his hands.

So maybe she was a coward.

No, that wasn't it. Or wasn't all of it. She knew that this loss would break her either way, that she would never be able to gather together the splintered pieces of her heart and make them whole again. As soon as her doctor had said those words—"I'm sorry"—she'd known that she was being banished to a shadow world.

If she believed that her child would be able to experience even a moment of happiness on this earth, she would give it to her. Her baby wouldn't be able to hear her, or see her, even feel her touch. She would be born into a cold, blank world, kept apart from her love, and then she would die.

At least for now, she could keep her baby safe and warm. And at least for now, she could decide the kind of death she wanted for her baby. One that kept her warm and safe inside of her up until the last possible moment.

Patrick believed in miracles, and he believed in his ability to conjure them into being. He had faith, her husband. In God. In fate. In himself. It was one of the things she loved about him.

But she had no use for faith right now, or God, or miracles. None of that mattered. None of that was real. What was real was the child growing inside of her, as irreparably broken as her own heart.

And it was up to her, her mother, to be merciful, and to deliver her into grace.

ARABELLA, NEW MEXICO—
125 MILES TO ALBUQUERQUE

Cait sneaked a glance at Rebecca. Her eyes were closed, her face turned toward the window. She looked so small in the Jeep's seat, so frail . . .

Cait's eyes trailed to the tape recorder under the dash. If she listened hard enough, she would swear she heard the gears whirring. What sort of person would plan something like that? An awful one. One who deserved all the shit life had thrown at her and then some. She was the traitor, not Rebecca. She'd misled this woman, maybe even put her in harm's way. How could she know for certain that the man in the pickup truck wasn't coming for Rebecca? There were enough people in this world who wanted to see her dead. More than enough.

She tried to imagine the moment when Lisa realized that Cait had picked up Rebecca for the drive, not Pat. She would be furious, rightfully so. Cait had let her down, badly, and had betrayed the trust that was central to the Sisters of Service. She had thought she'd been so clever, too. That was always her downfall. When would she realize that?

She'd been in the office with Lisa when the call had come in. She could tell right away that something was up by the way Lisa pivoted her body away as she bent over the phone. "Of course," Lisa had said soothingly. "We guarantee anonymity." Cait watched her scribble something down on a notepad and underline it twice. "We'll be in touch as soon as we've made arrangements," Lisa said, and hung up the phone.

Cait's journalism professor had stressed the importance of learning how to read upside down—"An invaluable way to glean information from unsuspecting subjects"—so she'd nearly had a heart attack when she read the name Rebecca McRae in Lisa's precise writing. "Is that *the* Rebecca McRae?" she asked, but Lisa just shook her head and closed the notebook.

"Forget about it," she said. "You know the rules."

Of course she did. Drivers were prohibited from having personal connections with the clients. And her connection to Rebecca . . . well, it could definitely be described as personal in Cait's eyes. Which was why, after Lisa returned Rebecca's call to confirm that Pat would be driving her to the clinic in Albuquerque in a week's time, she knew she had to act fast. When she first asked Pat to swap clients, Pat balked at the idea, but once Cait pointed out that her own drive was much shorter—just a routine one from the Austin suburbs to the clinic—and that Pat's would be overnight . . . well, it didn't take much more convincing. Cait promised she'd tell Lisa about the schedule change, but it conveniently slipped her memory.

Yes, her days with the Sisters of Service were definitely over.

She hated herself sometimes. She really did.

Rebecca's eyes stuttered open. "How long have I been asleep?"

"Not long," Cait said, glancing at the clock. "Maybe ten minutes or so."

"Any sign of him?"

She shook her head. "Plain sailing so far. I think we'll be in Santa Rosa pretty soon. We can figure out the route to Albuquerque then."

"I really appreciate you doing this," Rebecca said quietly. "I know I'm asking a lot of you to keep going. I honestly can't thank you enough."

"It's the least I can do," Cait said, flushing with shame. She didn't deserve this woman's gratitude, not after what she had planned.

"Well, I mean it. Thank you." Rebecca stretched her arms above her head and let out a yawn. "Do you have any gum? I thought I had some in my bag, but I can't seem to find it."

"Sure, there should be some in that little cubbyhole under the dashboard." As soon as she said it, a flash of white-hot terror. What happened next seemed to unfold in slow motion. Rebecca's hand reaching for the pack of gum in the cubbyhole. Her fingers brushing against the tape recorder affixed to the top of it. The look of confusion on her face as she pulled it free, and then the fear, and then the rage.

"Are you"—she shook her head, disbelieving—"are you recording us?"

Cait's mind raced. There must be something she could say, some excuse, some story . . . but there was nothing. Just a blank, howling silence and a roiling deep in her guts.

She watched, frozen, as Rebecca hit the rewind button on the recorder and then hit play. The two women's voices filled the cabin. "Oh my God." Rebecca dropped the recorder in her lap as if it were on fire. "You've been taping us this whole time." She turned toward Cait, eyes wide and shining. "Why would you do that?"

"It's not what you think." Only that was a lie. It was exactly what she thought. "Look, Rebecca—"

"Who *are* you?"

She hated how scared the woman looked, and hated that it was her fault. "I'm Cait! I'm exactly who I said I was!"

"Let me out of this car right now."

"We're in the middle of nowhere—"

"I don't care!" Rebecca's face was paper-pale. "I need you to pull over right now."

"It's not safe."

"Don't you dare tell me what's safe," Rebecca hissed. "Pull over."

Cait steered the Jeep to the side of the road and cut the engine. "Look, Rebecca, let me explain—"

But the passenger door had already swung open, and Rebecca was already striding away from her across the desert, her blond hair silver in the moonlight.

Cait unclipped her seat belt but didn't move to follow her. Her heart was pounding in her chest, her stomach churning. She squeezed her eyes shut, but the guilt kept coming, wave after sickening wave. She had fucked up. There was no getting away from that. Rebecca was right to hate her—she deserved her disgust. Her mother's voice popped into her head. "Do good," she would say as she waved her off to school in the morning. "Make yourself proud."

Shame burned through her. Cait couldn't remember the last time she'd made anyone proud, not least herself.

She glanced out the window and saw Rebecca's silhouette pacing across the desert. There was no way to erase what had happened, but she could try to make up for it going forward. At the very least, she could get Rebecca out of the cold and back in the Jeep and see her safely to Albuquerque. She could do that much, surely. It wasn't much, but it was a start.

The only way she could do that was by coming clean.

Her footsteps rang out across the desert as she ran to catch Rebecca, who was standing still by then, arms wrapped tightly across her chest, shoulders shaking, either from the cold or from silent tears. She didn't turn around when Cait reached out and touched her arm.

"Rebecca . . ." What came next? How could she explain herself to this woman whose life she'd set out to intentionally ruin? She took a deep breath. "I'm a writer."

Rebecca's head dropped an inch. "You said you were a bartender."

Cait took a step forward. "That part was true. But I'm also a writer, and I was planning on writing a piece about you. About this," she said, gesturing around vaguely.

"You were going to write about me. About this." Rebecca's voice was flat. Deadened. As if she'd expected something like this to happen. As if she wasn't surprised at all.

Cait felt another stab of guilt. She struggled to find the words to explain herself. Suddenly, her whole carefully constructed reasoning seemed flimsy and pathetic. What was wrong with her? She had exploited the trust of a woman at her most vulnerable, betrayed the organization that had given her back a sense of purpose in life, and for what? Some misplaced revenge fantasy. Anyway, hadn't this been all her fault, right from the beginning? Hadn't she known what she was doing when she wrote that article? What did she think was going to happen when she went home with Jake that night, anyway? Maybe Patrick had been right to call her a coward. She'd been punishing other people for her own mistakes. Wasn't that the very definition?

"I know who you are, and I know that you're married to Patrick McRae."

Rebecca let out a little mewl of pain. "What do you want? Money?"

"I don't want money."

"Are you even with that organization? Sisters of Service? Or was that a lie, too?"

"I'm with them."

"They told me that it would be anonymous. They *promised*." Rebecca's shoulders shook harder, and Cait knew then that she was sobbing. "You're going to ruin my life."

Cait shook her head. "No, that's not—I just thought—"

Rebecca laughed bitterly. "You know what? Go ahead. Write the damn article. It's too late, anyway. My life is already fucked."

"Rebecca, stop. I'm not going to write about you. I'm going to get you to Albuquerque and back to Lubbock like the Sisters said I would, and I swear to God I will never breathe a word of this to another soul. Okay?"

Rebecca was silent. In the moonlight, her hair was almost silver. Cait couldn't take talking to the back of her head anymore, and she reached out and spun her around. Rebecca's face was streaked with tears, and her eyes were pink and swollen. She looked . . . desolate. "What do you want from me?" she cried, her voice thickened with grief. "My baby is dying. Isn't that enough for you? Why are you doing this?"

Cait ducked her head. "It's not because of you. It's because of your husband."

Rebecca's lips were white and stretched tight across her teeth. "Oh, I figured that out already. A quick buck writing about the famous Patrick McRae's wife having an abortion? I can see the headline now: 'Politician's Wife Murders Own Baby.' I bet that would get you enough money to stop pouring drinks for a while, huh?" She shook her head and spat into the dirt. "You make me sick."

Cait felt a surge of anger. That was the truth, wasn't it? People like Cait had been making people like Rebecca sick for as long as there'd been stars in the sky. Okay, so she'd screwed up. Royally. Okay, so she'd intended on exploiting this woman, but hadn't her husband done exactly that while this woman stood behind him, smiling that pretty smile of hers? Cait tightened her grip on

Rebecca's arm. "That speech he made, the one where he talked about Me Too and Jake Forsythe, the one that went viral? I was the one who wrote that article. After your husband said that about me, someone hacked into the website's server and released my name. They found my home address, too, and they made it a point to terrorize me. I got death threats in the mail, people calling my phone at all hours, coming to my apartment . . . Every single day, I live in fear, and it's your husband's fault. I thought that you were just some hypocritical politician's wife looking to sweep a scandal under the carpet. I didn't know about your baby's . . . condition. If I had known, I never would have planned it." She took a breath. "So I'm sorry if I acted like an asshole, and I'm sorry that I recorded you without your knowing about it, and I'm sorry that I was going to write that article, but you have to understand that Patrick McRae *ruined my life*. You have to understand that."

For a few moments, the only sounds were the distant cries of a bobcat and the two women's thundering breath.

"I'm sorry that happened to you," Rebecca said stiffly. "I'm sure Patrick didn't do it intentionally."

Cait forced herself to let this go. "I'm sorry I betrayed your trust." She shoved the recorder toward her. "Here. Take it. I don't need it."

Rebecca stared at her for a hard minute. "Are you still going to write the article?"

Cait shook her head. "God, no. Of course not."

"And you'll still drive me to Albuquerque?"

Cait nodded. "If you'll let me."

Rebecca took the tape recorder, tossed it on the ground, and stamped on it until it broke, and then she wiped her eyes with the backs of her hands and started walking back toward the Jeep. Cait hurried to catch up with her. "I really am sorry, Rebecca. I swear, if I'd known—"

Rebecca held up a hand to stop her. "Let's just get back on the road, okay? We've already lost too much time tonight. I can't afford any more delays."

The two women climbed into the Jeep without another word and were soon back on the road, heading west.

PATRICK

Patrick sat in the greenroom of a local TV station, waiting for the man with the clipboard to wave him through to the set. It was his third interview in as many days, and he had reached the point where he'd become his own mimic. He felt disembodied from the sound of his own voice, and the words that came out of his mouth felt foreign and strange, like he was listening to them on the radio rather than speaking them himself.

It had been a week since they'd learned the baby was sick, and he hadn't slept longer than a couple of hours.

He hadn't slept the previous night or the night before that. Instead, he had lain awake in the bed he shared with Rebecca, listening to her lying awake next to him like a pillar of stone, and he'd silently prayed to God. *Give me strength*, he pleaded. *Show me the way.*

He knew that if he prayed hard enough, He would give him what he needed. He always had.

There were so many ways in which he was blessed, even if sometimes he found it hard to remember. There were days when, striding across a mud-soaked field to address a half-dozen bored-looking farmers, or preparing for an interview—because he still had to do his day job, at least for the time being—he felt God's warm light wane a little. But then he remembered all the ways in which he'd been shown grace, and the light shone on him again.

It had always shone on him, though he hadn't always been able to identify it for what it was. When he was a kid, his mother had taken him to church every Sunday, but his palms would itch as soon as he set foot inside the building, all the way through the pastor's sermon until the service was over and he was allowed to go play in the parking lot with the other kids while his mother socialized. She'd always tsk when she came to tell him it was time to leave, taking in his rumpled shirt and grass-stained pants. "You have no respect," she'd tell him as he buckled himself into the backseat. She didn't like him to ride up front with her, didn't think it was proper. He'd lower his eyes and apologize, but he never really meant it because he knew that as soon as they got home, she'd make him a cold glass of chocolate milk and sit him down in front of the television and the whole thing would be forgotten until next Sunday.

He hadn't known what it was during school, either, when his teachers used words like "gifted" and "brilliant" to describe him. He hadn't needed to work hard: his brain was like some kind of low-maintenance, well-oiled machine living inside his skull. After he aced the SATs, one of his teachers suggested that he might be able to get a scholarship, and helped him apply to colleges with glossy brochures featuring pictures of lush green spaces and smiling, white-toothed students clutching notebooks. After the acceptance letters came in the mail, his mother had been proud but distant, and had treated him more like a visiting dignitary who happened to be staying with her than her own son. He'd understood, in a way. He was the first person from his family to go to college, and the first person to leave his hometown since they'd settled there four generations ago. He didn't belong to her anymore: he belonged to something bigger that she didn't understand, a world she respected and feared in equal measure.

He'd chosen to move to the West Coast, thinking it would somehow be more familiar and forgiving than the East Coast, but as soon as he clapped eyes on the great swelling Pacific and the mountains cut from dark green felt and the women with their long blond hair and easy smiles, he knew it was nothing like what he'd known in Texas. Still, he slotted himself into his new surroundings without a second thought. He'd let his hair grow a little, styled it so it curled over his eyes in a way that girls seemed to find charming, checked his accent, learned to surf. It was all so easy for him, college included. A few classes a day and then nothing but time. How could anyone consider it difficult?

Of course, he thought, smiling fondly back on his younger self, that was just arrogance talking. He'd been a puffed-up son of a bitch, there was no denying that, but how could his head not swell when everything he wanted in life seemed to fall right into his lap? Even Rebecca.

His moment of epiphany came late in life, but when it came, it engulfed every cell of his being. It was simple, really: he surrendered. With that surrender came even more blessing. A move back home to Texas. A shot at the Senate. A baby on the way.

Now God had sent him the greatest test he had ever faced.

If his wife went through with this, he would lose everything. His child. His political career. The pure, unadulterated love he felt when he looked at Rebecca. Worst of all, he knew that if he allowed it to happen, he would be stripped of God's grace.

This was his forty days in the desert. This was his fight against the darkness. This was his faith being held to the fire and his will being forged in the flames.

This was his moment to rise above.

Cait heard something crack in her neck as she climbed out of the Jeep. She'd spent the past ten hours slinging Natty Ices and over-fried cheese sticks at college kids watching the Longhorns get the tar beaten out of them. The football shifts were always rough— people got too drunk too early, and there was always at least one asshole to cut off and at least one smear of vomit to mop up— but it was particularly bad when the hometown team was losing. People got mean drunk, the kind of drunk that made them take a swing at a guy for looking at somebody funny or call the girl at the table next to them a bitch. It made people stop tipping their friendly neighborhood bartender, too. Cait had walked out that evening with a measly forty-three dollars in tips and a throbbing lower back.

So her heart sank a little when she saw her neighbor open his door and wave for her to stop. Adam was a nice enough guy— dragged her empty garbage bin back from the curb, reminded her to move the Jeep on the days the street sweepers were due—but he had a tendency to appear at exactly the wrong moment. This was a perfect example. "Hey," she called as she strode toward her front door. "I'm kind of in a rush, so—"

"Somebody was looking for you."

Her heart seized. "What do you mean?"

"A guy came by the apartment earlier. I saw him drive by a couple of times, and he kept slowing down when he got to your house. I thought maybe he was lost or something, but then he pulled up to the curb and just sat there with the engine running. He was there for like twenty minutes."

"How do you know he was looking for me?" *Of course he was looking for me*, Cait thought.

"I went up to the truck and asked him if he needed anything."

"You did?" Cait felt a clutch of fear. "You shouldn't have done that. He could have been a nutcase." Of course he was a nutcase. The question was: which nutcase? There were so many of them at the moment, spilling out bile on 4chan and onto her phone, sending threats in the mail. One of them had even sent her a pig's head. There was no note attached, which somehow made it worse. Most nights, she crashed at friends' apartments or stayed late at the Dark Horse, sinking free beers with the barbacks and waiting for the sun to come up. If she had to sleep in her own bed, she kept a knife under her pillow, one hand resting on the hilt.

"It wasn't a big deal." Adam shrugged, oblivious. "I didn't like him hanging around like that."

"Did the guy say anything?"

"He asked when you'd be home."

"What did you say?"

"I told him it was none of his business."

"Did he leave after that?"

"Yeah, after a while. I watched out the window until he drove away."

Cait thought she was going to be sick right there on the sidewalk. "Thanks, Adam. Look, if that happens again, call the police. Have you got my number?"

He shook his head. She wrote it down on an old receipt and handed it to him. "I'm serious, okay? Don't try to talk to the guy. He could be dangerous."

He nodded. "Are you okay? Do you want to sit down or something?"

Cait shook her head. "I'm fine, thanks. I'm going to head inside now. Have a good night, and thanks for scaring off whoever that guy was." She worked up a smile. "My hero."

She closed the door behind her and double-checked the locks.

OUTSKIRTS OF SANTA ROSA, NEW MEXICO— 120 MILES TO ALBUQUERQUE

The atmosphere in the Jeep was flayed and red-raw. Neither woman had said much since the confrontation out in the desert, both of them locked tight in their own thoughts, stewing.

Ten miles, fifteen. Twenty. And then suddenly, a billboard rising up from the side of the road, announcing a BBQ joint up ahead. Cait thought it was a mirage at first, it had been so long since she'd seen one. She guessed there wasn't much call for advertising on these highways. Too few eyes, not worth the marketing spend.

"We're almost in Santa Rosa," she said. "I'm going to need to stop for directions."

"Do you think there'll be something open?"

Cait shrugged. "It looks like a decent-size town to me." On the horizon, buildings started to emerge and coalesce. They passed a couple of concrete boxes that looked like office buildings, a corrugated-iron-clad barn, even what looked like a suburban road lined with houses, cars parked neatly out front. "I think there are actual people living here."

"Are you sure we should stop? Won't there be road signs we can follow?"

"I don't want to risk us getting lost in the desert and running out of gas again. We should have bought an extra can back at the

189

station, but I didn't think of it at the time." More houses, a middle school, a couple of sheds. "There's enough civilization around. We should be safe."

A sign for an RV park, an old military tank parked in the middle of a stretch of brittle, frost-tipped grass, a motel. "There should be a night receptionist on duty there," Cait said, pointing to the motel sign. "I'll run in and ask for directions."

America's Best Value Inn turned out to be a bust: it was closed for renovations until February. They climbed back in the car and took a right on Route 66. There was a Food Mart directly after the turn, and Cait pulled in and parked at the pump. "I'll just be a second," she said as she unbuckled her seatbelt.

"Take your time," Rebecca said, already halfway out the passenger door. "I need a little air."

Cait swiped her credit card through the reader and watched Rebecca pace around the parking lot as the tank filled up. She looked washed out and anxious; her eyes were still puffy from crying. The gas pump clicked off, and Cait placed the nozzle back in the holder and screwed the cap back on the tank. "I'm going to go inside and ask for directions," she called. Rebecca raised a hand but didn't look at her.

The gas station took its location literally: the walls of the shop were painted in racing checkerboard and lined with Chevy and Ford decals. Behind the register, someone had painted a reasonable approximation of the classic Route 66 sign, the words AMERICA'S ROAD OF FREEDOM written underneath. The attendant looked up and smiled. "You get your gas okay?"

Cait nodded. "I paid at the pump. Can you tell me the best way to get to Albuquerque from here?"

The man scratched at his beard. "I reckon the fastest route would be to head west on 66. You'll see it marked as 40 sometimes, too—don't worry about that, you're still on the right track. That'll take you straight into the city, I believe."

Cait thanked him and bought a pack of gum and a Diet Coke for his trouble. No stealing this time, not from this guy. She was about to stick her head out the door to ask if Rebecca wanted anything when a scream shattered the air. Cait dropped the Coke on a shelf and ran, the attendant fast behind her.

Outside, Rebecca was still screaming as a skinny kid in baggy sweatpants and a wifebeater took off down the street. He had Rebecca's bag in his hands.

Cait didn't think. She ran after the kid, sneakers slapping against the concrete, arms pumping, lungs screaming. He was quick, but he didn't have the stamina she did, and after a couple of blocks, his pace started to drop. She saw her opening. She opened up her stride until she was nipping at his heels, and then she launched herself onto his back, bringing him down to the pavement heavily. She started pummeling him with her fists. "Who the fuck are you?" she screamed, her voice raw in her ears. "What the fuck do you want?" There was a smell coming off him, something animal and damp, and it made Cait's stomach heave. In that moment, she was convinced it was him.

A hand grabbed Cait's shoulder and lifted her off him. Cait kicked at the air. "Leave him be, now," the attendant said, pulling her back. "That's enough. He didn't mean no harm, did you, Billy? He can't help that he's a goddamn jackass."

The kid—and he was a kid, she saw that now, no older than fifteen—raised his bruised head off the pavement and shook it solemnly. He held out Rebecca's bag to her. "I'm sorry, miss."

"Wait till I tell your mother about this," the attendant said, tugging the boy to his feet and giving the side of his head a swift smack. "She'll tan your hide the color of molasses."

The kid started blubbering. "Please, Jeff, don't tell my ma. Please."

Cait left the two of them to sort it out between them and headed back to the gas station, where Rebecca stood, pale as milk and clutching her sides. Cait held out the bag without a word.

Rebecca took it with shaking hands. "Was it him? The man in the truck?"

Cait shook her head. "Just some punk kid."

"I didn't see his face. He just ran up and grabbed my bag and I thought—I thought—"

Cait reached out and touched her arm. "I know, but it's okay. You're okay now."

Rebecca nodded. "Thanks for chasing after him like that." She held up her bag. "You're fast."

"I ran track in high school, and I still run a few times a week, just to keep myself sane."

"I could tell." Rebecca glanced over at where the boy and the gas station attendant were locked in a heated argument. "Do you think I should say something?"

Cait raised an eyebrow. "Like what?"

She shrugged. "I don't know . . . like 'Don't go around stealing bags, you little shit'?"

Cait laughed. "Our friend over there has it covered. I don't think that kid's going to be stealing anything any time soon."

Rebecca looked at her. "I mean it, Cait. Thank you."

The air between them suddenly cleared, like the air after a thunderstorm. Cait took a deep breath and nodded. "No problem."

The two women got back in the Jeep and headed west without another word.

"Can I get you anything? A cup of coffee? Water?"

Rich held up his hand. "I'm fine, thanks."

Rebecca lowered herself gingerly onto the love seat. Rich was already sitting down—he'd walked straight into her house and made himself comfortable in one of the living room armchairs—but Rebecca had hovered in the doorway for ages, trying to think up an excuse to escape. She'd never been alone with her husband's campaign manager, and so far, she wasn't enjoying the experience. He'd always made her slightly nervous, and now, after he'd turned up at the house when Patrick was at work without so much as a phone call to warn her, she had to actively fight the urge to run.

"Thanks for seeing me like this," Rich said, as if she'd had a choice in the matter. "I know you're very busy." He said this poker-faced, but Rebecca caught something dancing behind his eyes, a little private joke to himself.

He didn't like her much. She'd known that from the first time they met, when he'd given her a too-firm handshake and a once-over that seemed to conclude in a single glance that she was both definitely fuckable and completely unsuitable to be a politician's wife. Rebecca hadn't liked him, either. He had the oily look of a salesman who worked on commission, and all the charm, too. Patrick had told her over and over how lucky he was that Rich had agreed to work with him. Looking at him that first time, Rebecca sensed that Rich was the lucky one to have hitched his wagon to Patrick's particular star.

Now his eyebrows tented together in a vague imitation of concern. "How are you feeling?" he asked, leaning forward on his elbows.

Rebecca realized then why he was there. She kicked herself for being slow: she should have known as soon as she'd spotted his car (an Audi TT, what else) pulling up the drive. Patrick had told him what she was planning on doing, and he was here to stop her.

"I'm fine, thank you," she said tightly. She wouldn't give him the satisfaction of acknowledging her pain. "How are *you* feeling?"

"Oh, you know. Can't complain. But I'm not here to talk about myself. I'm here to talk about you." His eyebrows knitted farther together. Rebecca had to marvel at them: they were like a pair of caterpillars being pulled on strings. "Patrick told me your . . . news."

Rebecca dug her fingernails into the flesh of her palms. "What news would that be?"

"About the baby's"—a nod toward her stomach—"illness."

She didn't say anything. *Fuck him. He'll have to work for this.*

"He told me that you're thinking about terminating the pregnancy. Is that right?"

Rebecca stood up. "I think we're done here."

Rich stood, too. "I wish we were, but I'm afraid we're not. You see, I think you're being a little rash about your decision. I know Patrick thinks so, too."

"What my husband thinks about this is none of your business."

"It's exactly my business."

"Not when it comes to our private life."

He shook his head sadly, like she was the silliest little girl in the whole wide world. "There is no 'private' for Patrick now and, by extension, you. He's running for public office. That means he's public property, and his family is public property." Rich sat back down and gestured for her to sit, too, which she did, because her legs could no longer hold her up. "If you go through with this abortion, you'll kill Patrick's chances of ever being elected. I'm not just talking about the Senate seat, either. I'm talking any public office, ever. His whole career will be shot dead, just like that." He punctuated this remark by making a gun with his thumb and forefinger and pointing it squarely at her. "You don't want to be responsible for killing your husband's dream, do you?"

"Our baby's condition is fatal. Did he tell you that? If I go through with the pregnancy, it"—she didn't want to tell him that the baby was a girl, she didn't want to give him a single precious inch—"will die in a matter of hours after I give birth. Days, maybe, if we're particularly unlucky. It will be born specifically to die, and it will suffer horribly."

He spread his hands wide. "Aren't we all born just to die? Isn't that what life is, when you drill right down to it?"

"So you think I should carry a baby that is destined to suffer and die so my husband can win an election."

"It's what Patrick wants."

"Patrick wants to believe that the baby will be okay. *That's* what Patrick wants. If he could snap his fingers and change this baby into a healthy, thriving child, he would do it, even if that meant giving up politics forever."

"Rebecca, why do you think I'm here?"

"Because you're an asshole?"

He allowed himself a small smile. "Apart from that."

"Because you care about winning the election above everything else. Why else would you be here?"

He leaned forward in his chair. "Why do you think Patrick told me about your pregnancy?"

"He knew that it had the potential to have political fallout. Presumably, he wanted to get your advice."

"He wanted more than my advice, Rebecca. He wanted me to do something about it." Rich tilted his head as he looked at her. "You're in a delicate position, sweetheart. I have friends in high places, friends who would be more than happy to do me a favor."

"Are you threatening me?"

He held out his hands, supplicant. "Now, let's not toss such a nasty word around. I would never want you to feel *threatened*. I just want you to know the reality of the situation you're facing. All around the country, the winds are changing. New laws are coming into effect every day, and it's only a matter of time before what you're planning is finally made a crime in this country." He smiled nastily. "I wouldn't want you to fall foul of those changing winds, Rebecca. You never know how hard they might blow."

SANTA ROSA, NEW MEXICO— 120 MILES TO ALBUQUERQUE

They were a couple miles away from the gas station when Cait remembered her Diet Coke. "Shit."

Rebecca looked at her, eyes full of worry. "What's wrong? Is it the gas tank again?"

Cait waved it away. "Nothing like that. I left my Coke back at the gas station, that's all."

"Oh." Rebecca twisted the gold ring on her finger. "I thought it was him back there, you know. The driver. When he grabbed me, I thought he'd found us. I thought he was going to kill us."

Cait nodded. "Me, too."

"Do you think he's out there looking for us?"

"Probably." There was no point in lying to her. No point in lying about anything. They were in this together, for better or worse, until the bitter end. "But so far, he hasn't found us. Hopefully our luck will hold."

She heard Rebecca take a breath and braced herself for what was coming. "You said that people had been threatening you. Do you think . . . ?"

Did Cait think they were coming after her? "I don't know. I didn't see anyone follow me out of Austin, and I was looking. They can't trace the plates to me, either, so there's no way to track me out here." She glanced over at Rebecca. "Are you sure your husband doesn't know where you are?"

"I'm sure," Rebecca said, a little too quickly.

"Would he come looking for you if he did?"

"No." A pause. "Not personally, at least."

Cait shot her a look.

"His campaign manager," Rebecca said. "He's connected. He could get things done if he wanted to."

"Do you think he wants to?"

Another pause. Finally, Rebecca nodded.

Cait blew out her breath. "Why would your husband let him do something like that?"

Rebecca looked at her, her eyes hollow. "Remember what I said about miracles?"

Cait nodded.

"He thinks if we just have faith, we can save our baby. He wants me to carry her to term so he can be proven right. And, of course, all his campaign manager cares about is how it will affect his poll numbers. Apparently, bringing a child into this world who is destined to suffer and die has better optics than a woman choosing to have an abortion." She shook her head. "I didn't want her to be used as a political pawn or as proof of faith. She deserves better than that."

"You do, too."

Rebecca shrugged. "It doesn't matter what I deserve. I would give anything in this world to make my child healthy, but that's not possible. Trust me, if I thought there was even the slimmest chance . . ."

Cait nodded. "What are you going to tell him?"

"I'm going to tell him that I had a miscarriage while he was away."

"Do you think he'll believe you?"

"I don't know." Rebecca paused. "I hope so."

"So you still want to be married to him. After everything." Cait tried to keep her voice neutral.

"I love him," she said simply. And then, "He's a good man. I have to believe that."

Cait had to stifle her disbelief. *No more judgment*, she reminded herself. *You're standing in a house made of glass.* "Do you think he'll win?"

Rebecca looked at her. "What?"

"Your husband. Do you think he'll win the election?"

"Oh. I don't know. Maybe. The poll numbers are good."

"I think he will."

"You do?"

Cait nodded. "He's the type of guy who wins. You can tell by looking at him." She paused. "Will you vote for him?"

Rebecca had never been asked the question before, had never even considered it. "Will I vote for him?" she repeated, stalling for time.

Cait didn't bother to hide her smile. "Yeah. Will you go into that voting booth on March whatever-the-day-is and fill in the little bubble next to your husband's name?"

Rebecca opened her mouth. Hesitated. "No."

Cait's eyebrows went into her hairline. "You won't?"

Rebecca shook her head.

"Will you tell him you voted for him?"

"Honestly? I don't think he'll ask."

"You'll have to do that photo op, probably, of the two of you walking up to the voting place together, holding hands and smiling for the camera."

"He tends to keep me out of the politics stuff. I've done a few rallies, but no press yet."

199

"That'll change when he gets elected. You'll be a senator's wife. Public property."

Rebecca winced. "Don't say that."

"Well, it's true."

"I'm sorry about what happened to you, with that speech . . . I don't think he had any idea that it would blow up in the way it did."

Even as Rebecca said this, she wasn't entirely sure it was true. There were a lot of things she'd thought he was incapable of doing that now felt all too possible.

"I'm afraid I won't be voting for him, either," Cait said. "Though I don't think my vote's going to be the one that stops him."

Rebecca turned her face toward the window. "You're right. I don't think anything will."

Cait was sure someone was following her. It was a sunny Monday afternoon, and she watched the black Dodge Durango snake its way through Windsor Park, staying a few car lengths behind the Jeep but always there when she looked in the rearview mirror. Eventually, she punched her way through a yellow light on Manor Road and pulled around back of the Dairy Queen and waited until she saw the Durango drive past.

It had been two days since Adam had told her that someone had come looking for her. Two whole days, and still nothing had happened. Not only that, but the message boards had quieted down, or at least the ones she could access. She kept the knife tucked under her pillow, but she'd managed to grab a few hours of sleep last night, before a stray animal scurrying in the bushes outside sent her flying out of bed.

Maybe people were starting to forget about her again. They had found—like they always did—someone else to hate. She allowed herself to think that she might be safe.

But then that Dodge Durango appeared in her rearview mirror, the windshield tinted black, and she knew that had been a lie.

She waited in the DQ parking lot for ten minutes, watching a pair of pigtailed girls suck Blizzards through straws, before she edged the Jeep's nose back out on the road. She drove home slowly, carefully, diving down back streets and doubling back, but she didn't catch another glimpse of the truck. Whoever it was, he must have given up. For now, at least.

Adam was raking leaves when she pulled up in front of the house. He raised a hand to wave hello, but when he saw the look on her face, he dropped the rake and strode over to the Jeep, where she was still sitting in the driver's seat, her belt still clipped in, her hands still tight on the steering wheel.

"Everything okay?" he asked.

"Yep, thanks!" She was trying for a bright bluster, but she could hear the tremble in her voice. She reached for the buckle and found that her hands were shaking too badly to unfasten it.

He was watching her through the window. "You need some help?"

She shook her head. If she could just get her hands to work, she could get out of the car and walk across the lawn and open the door to her little apartment and lock it behind her. She could check all the windows and pull down the shades and she could crawl into bed and pull the covers over her head and she could— what? Wait for them to come?

She'd been a fool to think this was over. It would never be over, she knew that now. They would always try to find her.

Adam pulled open the driver's-side door and reached in to unbuckle her seat belt. "Come on," he said, holding out a hand and helping her down from the seat.

He led her into his apartment and sat her down at his kitchen table while he poured a few fingers of vodka into a tumbler. "Sorry," he said, watching her wince as she tipped it down. "It's all I have."

They sat in silence for a minute as she let the liquor do its work. "Thank you," she said finally. "Sorry I went all weird like that."

"Don't worry about it. You want another?" She shook her head and he took her empty glass, rinsed it out in the sink, and sat down across from her. "What happened?"

"It was nothing. I thought I saw someone following me, but . . ." She was embarrassed now, by her shaking hands and her paper-thin nerves and her overactive imagination. She should be tougher than this. Stronger. "It was stupid. I was just being paranoid."

He was watching her carefully. "Is this about the guy who came looking for you a couple days ago?"

She suddenly felt the walls closing in on her, too tight. "I should go," she said, scraping her chair back from the table. "Thanks again for the help, and the vodka. Sorry if I—" She didn't finish her sentence. There were so many things she was sorry for at this point, she didn't know where to begin. "I owe you a drink," she said, forcing a smile, and she rushed to the door as fast as she could without breaking into a full run.

Her front door was unlocked. Had she left it like that? She didn't have time to think about it. She slammed the door shut and locked it behind her. Across the lawn, she saw Adam's silhouette in the window, watching to make sure she got in safely. She raised a hand to signal that she was okay, and he disappeared.

She spent the rest of the day in her darkened living room, waiting to hear something scratching at the door, hoping to get inside.

OUTSKIRTS OF SANTA ROSA, NEW MEXICO—
110 MILES TO ALBUQUERQUE

The desert had started to undulate, rising into soft, sloping hills fringed with shrubs and prickly pear. It felt like, after a long, blank sleep, the land around them was finally waking up.

There were a few more cars on the road, too, mainly eighteen-wheelers whose drivers had emerged from wherever they'd parked overnight and were looking to get a jump on the morning traffic.

It was morning now, or nearly, the clock ticking past five-thirty even though the sky remained stubbornly black. At this time of year, Rebecca knew it would be another couple of hours before the sun made an appearance. She'd been waking up in the pitch black for weeks, fingers fumbling toward Patrick's side of the bed and finding only cold sheets. He liked to get up early and head to the gym before work. He used to kiss her goodbye before he left, but now he just slipped out of bed and disappeared.

She thought about what Cait had said, about Patrick being one of life's winners. It was true: that was one of the things she'd loved most about him. It wasn't that he was arrogant, though he could be at times. It was more that he believed so completely that life would turn out the way he wanted it to, if he just tried hard enough. When she first met him, she found that kind of confidence intoxicating. He took up space in this world without apology, and encouraged her to do the same. That is, until his vision for what their life should be like started to diverge from hers.

She didn't remember him being particularly religious when they were younger. He talked about having faith sometimes, and he would go to the Baptist church in Hamilton Square on Ash Wednesday and spend the rest of the day with soot smudged between his eyes. Their first Christmas together, they'd gone to midnight Mass in Alameda, leaving her father dozing on the couch while they held hands in the darkened church and breathed in the incense and the fresh pine of the tree beside the altar. She'd thought that it was tradition for him more than belief, but then he'd started working at the DA's office, and talk over dinner turned decidedly more biblical.

After they moved to Texas, his faith deepened further. He started to go to church every Sunday and encouraged her to come along. She agreed to go once, just to see what it was like. Patrick had joined one of the huge megachurches that seemed to populate every second street in Lubbock, though he said proudly that this was one of the most popular in the city. "It's like a big party," he told her, eyes shining. "You'll love it."

When she'd first walked through the double doors into the vast atrium filled with thousands of people singing and praying and holding their hands up to God, and heard the swell of music coming from the loudspeakers, she'd felt something stir inside. It was nothing like the Catholic Masses she'd attended as a kid, with their endless, droning hymns and the stifling incense and the priest peacocking in his gold-embroidered vestments.

Here, the pastor was a young guy in jeans and a button-down, and he threw around words like "buddy" and "chill." He talked about how we all failed, and how that made us human, and beautiful, and still loved by God. "God doesn't want perfection," he said at one point, as behind him a man holding an electric guitar twanged out a few opening chords. "He wants love, just like the rest of us."

Rebecca had thought about that idea as the lite-rock version of "How Great Thou Art" swelled and the crowd began to sway. She had let her body sway along with the music and had held on to Patrick's hand as he lifted it up in devotion, and for a second, she'd sensed what it would feel like to be loved the way Patrick knew he was loved: infinitely and without judgment.

But the feeling didn't last. The next time she went, all she could see was the cheap nylon carpet and the plastic folding chairs and the look of desperation on the faces of the people as they raised their hands up to this man with his jeans and his "hey, buddy," and the whole thing filled her with such deep sadness that she had to close her eyes to stop the tears from coming. Of course, Patrick had seen this and assumed she was having a moment of conversion. She'd never forget the look of sheer joy on his face when she opened her eyes and saw him watching her. Like she was a long-lost dog who'd finally found its way back to the warmth of its home.

At night, after he'd gone to sleep, she'd lain awake staring at the ceiling and conjured up the paintings that hung on the walls of her Sunday school classroom. Jesus, head haloed in gold, heart laid bare for all to see, a mass of red wreathed in thorns. She willed her own chest to crack open, ribs split down the middle and splayed, the muscle of her heart waiting to be filled with God's love.

"You just have to believe." That's what Patrick told her when he placed his hands on her swollen stomach and prayed, lips moving silently, eyes shut tight against the evil swarming around them. She would sit there, numb, and wait for him to finish. Even after the scan, when every cell in her body wanted to believe in the miracle he promised, her soul stayed stubbornly unmoved. "All you need is faith," he said, cradling her face in his hands. "Please, baby. Just make the leap."

Nothing. Her heart was faulty, an iron weight sitting heavy in her chest, and no amount of effort could make it flesh.

"Do you believe in God?" Rebecca hadn't realized she was going to ask the question until it came out of her mouth.

She felt Cait's eyes on her, watchful and worried. "What you're doing isn't wrong."

"That's not what I'm asking. Do you believe in God?"

Cait hesitated. "I went to church a lot as a kid. Texas, you know," she added with a smirk. "I went to Bible study, Christian camp, the whole thing. I even wore one of those chastity promise rings in high school." She caught Rebecca's eye. "Only because all the cool kids were doing it, not because I actually thought I was married to Jesus."

"Do you still go?"

Cait shook her head. "I stopped when I went to college. It was more a community thing than a faith thing for me, I guess. My parents aren't too happy about it, but they've sort of accepted it. Anyway, they have my brothers and their families. They go to church still."

"Do you see them a lot? Your family?"

Cait shook her head. "Not really. My hours at the bar make it tough, and I don't have all that much in common with them anymore. Don't get me wrong, I love the shit out of all of them. We're just . . . different."

Rebecca thought about Patrick kneeling by the bed every night to say his prayers. "I know what you mean," she said. "You still haven't answered my question, though. Do you believe in God?"

There was a long pause. "I think there's something more than this," Cait said eventually, nodding toward the desert road. "I don't know if it's God or whatever, but I don't think we just evaporate after we die. I think we have souls that live on somehow." She shot Rebecca a nervous glance. "Are you worried about your baby? I don't believe any of that bullshit about limbo or whatever. I don't think that God is out to punish children for not being baptized, or that babies are born unclean, or any of that. Don't even let that thought cross your mind."

Rebecca shook her head. She knew what would happen to her daughter after this was over. She'd made her peace with it. Still, there was a part of her that wanted someone to finally give her an answer that she could cling to, a rope tossed out to the middle of a very cold sea. "Where do you think we go when we die?" she asked, knowing before the words left her mouth that it was hopeless. She knew the truth; she was drowning in it.

"I don't know. Somewhere better than this, I hope." Cait looked at her. "What about you? Do you believe in God?"

Rebecca thought of her mother's face lying in silk, the blank eyes of the fox lying by the side of the road, the soft, limp body of her pet bunny cradled in her small hands.

She reached into her purse and touched the soft fur of the polar bear hidden inside. She'd grabbed it out of the drawer just as Cait had pulled up to her house. She'd wanted her daughter to have it with her for a little while longer.

"No," she said quietly. "But sometimes I wish I did."

Rebecca went to the library to do the research, because it was the only place she could be sure no one she knew would see her. She sat on a too-hard plastic chair and typed out search terms on an ancient computer while the air conditioner whirred in the background. Her heart sank as she scanned the results. The closest clinic was a near-five-hour drive away, in Dallas, and she'd need to stay over for a couple nights to wait out the mandated twenty-four-hour "consideration period." There was no way she could do it.

After Rich came by the house, she made the decision. Even though she hated him, she knew that Rich was right: if news got out that Patrick's wife had terminated a pregnancy—regardless of the reason—his political career would be finished. She would go through with the abortion, but she would do it in secret. It was the only way she knew how to protect her baby from suffering and Patrick from a truth that had the power to destroy him. She would do this on her own, and she would keep that secret until she was dead and buried.

But as she stared at the map on the screen and the red pins signifying Texas clinics spread out so sparsely, she wasn't sure she would be able to do it on her own. The logistics were too complicated, and she was being watched too closely. She had to find another way.

When she saw the flyer stuck to the community message board, it felt like a bolt of lightning coming from the sky.

TRUST WOMEN. TRUST US.

WE ARE A NONPROFIT ORGANIZATION OF WOMEN DEDICATED TO HELPING WOMEN. NO QUESTIONS ASKED. ANONYMITY GUARANTEED.

There was a phone number listed underneath. Rebecca didn't know if they would be able to help her, but it felt like a lifeline. She pulled a tab off the flyer and shoved it in the back of her wallet.

She waited until Patrick went to work one morning and then drove herself to Walmart, where she bought one of those prepaid cell phones, the cheapest she could find. She went through the checkout with it and then circled back inside with a shopping cart and stocked up on cleaning supplies and Christmas decorations and whatever else she could think they needed. She wanted to make sure she had a valid receipt in case somebody started asking questions.

The woman she spoke to on the phone was kind, gentle, considerate. She told Rebecca that providing someone to drive her to the clinic in Albuquerque wouldn't be a problem. There was a pause on the line when Rebecca told her the address, but it was so quick she almost didn't notice. The woman made the appointment for her, too, and told her what to bring with her, and what to expect. When Rebecca got off the phone, she walked over to the liquor cabinet, poured herself a glass of whiskey, and winced it down.

There was a date set for just over a week. It was real now, and she knew there was no going back.

RICH

The polished brass bar gleamed as Rich swept his hand across it. "The way I see it, I'm half artist, half soldier. It takes a certain finesse to do what I do, but you've got to be willing to sacrifice the blood, sweat, and tears for it, too." The music—piano-heavy innocuous jazz pumped from speakers embedded in the dark, wood-paneled walls—wasn't so loud that he needed to raise his voice, but it was loud enough for him to know that he wouldn't be overheard. It was one of the things he liked about the place. That and the fact that it reminded him vaguely of his club back in D.C., albeit a very poor imitation.

He nudged his empty rocks glass toward the bartender with a nod, and the bartender pulled a bottle of whiskey off the shelf and poured another double. "It's long hours and sleepless nights and shitty hotel rooms in shitty towns, and at the end of the day, even if your guy wins, you're not gonna be the one who's up there on the stage in front of your adoring fans, if you see what I mean. What I mean is, you can't do it if you're looking for glory. Nobody's ever gonna slap you on the back and tell you that you're The Man, because The Man is the guy you're trying to get elected. You can't forget that. Not for a second."

He picked up his glass, sniffed it, and frowned. "They call this top-shelf? This is rail shit," he muttered, raising it to his lips and tipping it down his throat anyway.

"Some people say to me, they say, 'Rich, why aren't you the one up there on that stage? You could run for anything—you could run for a bus and win.' And you know, I'd be lying if I said I hadn't thought about it. Back when I was in college—I went to school in New Haven—back in college, I was VP of the student council. I won the highest proportion of votes in the history of the YCC: it was an absolute landslide. So I could do it, you know. I had the secret sauce. But you know what I realized? The day-to-day business of government is a grind. It is! It's goddamn boring!" He picked up his drink and finished it off. "Do you want another one?"

Rich raised his hand and signaled the bartender for a refresh without waiting for an answer. The bartender poured straight into his empty glass.

"The fun is all in the running. It's all in the strategy, in the chase, in the kill. You know when the people love a politician the most? The night he gets elected. After that, it's all downhill. You're looking at me like I'm crazy right now, but I'm telling you, it's true! They never love you more than they do the night they call your name." He looked down at the glass, swirled the whiskey, smiled. "That night, for the guy who got him up on that stage, for the guy who won him that election? It's the best feeling in the world. Better than sex, better than drugs, better than this shithouse whiskey. It's like"—he opened his eyes wide—"BOOM! A shot of adrenaline straight to the heart. You feel invincible that night, you really do. And then your guy gets up on the stage to give his acceptance speech, and he opens his mouth, and you hear your words coming out. It's like being a ventriloquist, only you don't have to stick your hand up the guy's ass." He smirked. "I had one or two of them ask me to do that, but that's another story. So yeah, it's hard work and you'll never sleep and you'll never have a family and if you do you'll lose them, but goddamn if it isn't the best job in the world. At least that's what I think."

He took a sip of whiskey, thought for a minute.

"My guy, now—maybe our guy, we'll see—he's got everything. He's got looks, he's got brains, he can talk, he can do the crinkly-eyed bullshit that makes all the housewives love him, he can do the down-home-good-ol'-boy-cowboy shit that makes the men love him, he works hard, he goes to church, he doesn't complain, and goddamn if he isn't the most charming motherfucker I've ever met. I'm telling you, I've been doing this for ten years and I've never seen a candidate like him. He's got what it takes to go all the way, and I mean that. I know it sounds crazy, me saying that to you while we're sitting here in this shitty bar in this shitty hotel"—his eyes flicked to the bartender—"no offense. But I'm dead serious. The guy could make it to the top, and I plan on being the one to take him there."

He shook his head as if weighing something up. "Only problem is the wife. She looks the part—pretty face, blond hair, straight white teeth, the whole package—but she's not exactly the touchy-feely type, if you know what I mean. Got a little bit of Hillary in her. Worse, her heart's not in it, you can tell. She's done a couple of events and she just stands there, like"—he stretched his face into a rictus grin—"and I mean, you can see people just not buying it. They think she thinks she's better than them, and that's because she *does* think she's better than them. Hell, you should see the way she looks at me: like something she scraped off the bottom of her shoe. She's from California, you know. San Francisco. Has a master's in basket weaving or something. She used to work as a teacher, which you'd think would work for us, but when she talks about it, she sounds like a hippie or something. It's all 'integrated classrooms' and 'emotional intelligence,' all that kind of mumbo-jumbo shit that frankly does not fly with voters who are worried about their kids being stuffed into classrooms with a whole bunch of Mexicans who don't speak any English. *Comprende? No comprende!*"

He chuckled to himself, sighed, grew serious.

"Anyway, I've got a real shitshow on my hands at the minute. We're talking a class-A weapons-grade plutonium nightmare that has the potential to torpedo the whole election, and she's smack bang in the middle of it. I told him when I came on board that she was a liability, but this." He shook his head in disbelief. "This is something else."

He finished his drink, checked his wristwatch. "I gotta get going. I'm meeting the boss in twenty to go over strategy for next week's event. The polls have him up by seven points. Look, I'm sure you've figured it out by now, but I didn't invite you here just so you could watch me drink subpar whiskey and shoot the shit. This situation I'm talking about, in the hands of lesser men, it would ruin a candidate's political career. But in my hands"—he stretched his fingers out wide and grinned—"I'm about to spin this shit into gold, and I want you to be in on it. This is a once-in-a-lifetime opportunity to cement your name in history."

He signaled the bartender for the bill, slapped his credit card on top.

"What I'm about to propose is going to sound like political suicide, and sure, the wife will be collateral damage, but trust me: if we play this right, he's going to be in the Senate next year, and after that it's straight on to 1600 Pennsylvania Avenue. And you know what that means for you? I'm not just talking about the circuits. I'm talking all the way to the top. So, what do you say: can I count on you to help make history?"

OUTSKIRTS OF SANTA ROSA, NEW MEXICO— 83 MILES TO ALBUQUERQUE

Cait felt the nerves starting to build again, thrumming in her chest, making her fingers and toes itch. They'd just passed another sign for Albuquerque: eighty-three miles. Just a little over an hour at this rate.

They passed a single house at the end of a long dirt track. She squinted into the dark. There was a light on above the front door and a beat-up old Cadillac parked up out front. Someone was home.

She waited for the sweep of headlights, the growl of the pickup's engine, but there was just darkness and silence and the endless stretch of road.

He was close, though. She could sense it. She knew that Rebecca did, too.

Cait kept an eye on the door, half expecting to see someone stride into the bar and blow her away with a single shot. She'd slept like shit the night before, getting up every ten minutes to check the locks, peering out into the dark for a pair of eyes to appear on the other side of the glass, convinced that the guy who'd followed her in his Durango was out there waiting for her. Every creak and groan that the old apartment gave out sent her skittering off the bed, knife clutched in both hands. Like she would actually know what to do with it if someone did break in. Like she wouldn't already be dead.

She finally drifted off when the sun came up, only to be woken up by her alarm a couple of hours later. She was on a double shift at the Dark Horse. The new manager had changed the usual schedule "to mix things up," as he'd said during the introductory meeting he'd called at nine a.m. on a Monday, but they all knew that he was really doing a little dick-waving to show he'd arrived. She'd managed to hold on to her Saturday-night shift, but the rest of her schedule was dogshit. Normally, she would have thrown a fit—she was one of their longest-serving bartenders and definitely one of the best—but she was happy to have the quiet, even if it meant eating ramen noodles for the next month. If the bar was empty, she'd be able to see whoever was coming through the door. Maybe in time to hide or at least duck.

The door swung open, and her heart clenched in her throat, but it was just Ken. He gave her a wave, but instead of making a beeline for his usual seat at the bar, he slid into a booth at the back and signaled one of the waitresses for a menu. Cait had already started pouring his drink, but now she cut off the tap and left the glass half full on the drip mat.

It was a slow shift, deep in the midweek doldrums, so there was a small part of her that was sad to lose the company (and the tip), but mainly, she was grateful she wouldn't have to make small talk about UT's football prospects or smile through jokes she'd already heard a thousand times. Still, she kept an eye on Ken as he placed his order with the waitress, and she felt a little sag of relief when the drink ticket came in and she was proved right about his drink order after all. The new manager had made a big deal about wastage. She filled the rest of his glass and placed it on the service station for the waitress to collect.

The door opened again. She didn't recognize the guy: middle-aged, dark hair, chinos and a green polo shirt with an embroidered logo she couldn't make out. He was wearing a pair of sunglasses and had his hands buried deep in his pockets. Did Adam say if the man who'd turned up at her apartment had dark hair? She should have asked him what he looked like, made him sketch it out. She hadn't been able to see who was driving the Durango yesterday. Was this him?

He stared straight at her, his mouth curling up in a sneer. He pulled his hands out of his pockets. She saw the glint of something metal and felt her legs go weak. She gripped the side of the bar. Her eyes darted toward the back entrance. Could she make it in time?

He looked down at the cell phone in his hand before sliding

it back in his pocket. He turned and saw Ken sitting in the back booth, waved, and slid in at the same table. She watched as Ken pushed a menu toward him.

He wasn't coming for her.

She was so relieved she barely had time to register the fact that Ken was drinking with someone other than Nick. Three years and she'd never seen him in the bar with anyone else. It was clear they knew each other, though: as soon as the guy had ordered his drink from the waitress, their heads were bent together, deep in conversation.

Cait spent the rest of the shift trying to control her nerves. The bar stayed quiet. A couple in their sixties came in, nursed two glasses of house white with their dinner, complained about the music being too loud, and left her two bucks on a thirty-dollar tab. A group of red-faced Englishmen stumbled in wearing matching soccer jerseys, sank three beers each in under an hour, and stumbled back out into the night. A woman in a business suit ordered a double Scotch straight up, drank it in two swallows, and left without saying a word. By the end of the night, Cait had made eleven dollars in tips, and Ken and his mystery friend were the only ones left in the place. The waitress chucked their bill on the table unceremoniously and stalked out back for a cigarette. They hadn't drunk much—just a couple of beers each—and they hadn't eaten, either, so the tab wasn't worth the waitress's effort. She knew, same as Cait, that the night was a bust.

Ken didn't wait for the waitress to come back from her smoke break. He brought the bill up to the bar, handed it to Cait with a twenty, and told her to keep the change, which came to a princely sum of four dollars. A generous tip, but not enough to make a difference in the waitress's night.

"No Nick tonight?" Cait asked as she tucked his change back into the billfold for the waitress.

Ken shook his head. "Not tonight. Hey, Mike." He waved to his friend, still sitting in the booth. "I want you to meet a friend of mine."

The man got up from the booth and came toward the bar. He wasn't a big man, but he moved slowly and deliberately, like his clothes were sopping wet and too heavy. He had removed his sunglasses, and she saw that he had eyes the color of the bluebonnets that grew outside her parents' house in Waco, and that they were filled with sadness.

"Nice to meet you," he said, but he didn't put out his hand to shake hers, and she didn't offer. She had the feeling that she already knew him.

"You're from Austin?" she asked, already knowing he wasn't.

"Mike here's from Columbus," Ken said, as if that were some particular achievement.

"I know Columbus," she said. "My family is from Waco, so I drive through it whenever I go to visit them."

Mike nodded once but didn't offer anything more. They stared at each other for a few silent seconds, and then Ken slapped the counter so hard it made all three of them jump. "Well, Caity, I know you'll be anxious to close up, so we'll get out of your hair."

"See you soon, Ken."

"I'm sure you will. Keep my seat warm and the beer cold while I'm gone."

"Will do. Nice to meet you, Mike." She walked them to the door so she could lock it behind them. "Have a good night," she said, holding the door open for them.

"You, too. And be careful getting home," Ken added, a funny little smile playing on his lips. "It's a wild world out there."

The two men exchanged a look and laughed. She watched them cross the parking lot before closing the door behind them and sliding the dead bolt into the lock.

She didn't sleep that night, either.

4chan/Caitlyn_Monaghan

TruePatriot368: why hasn't someone snuffed that bitch out??? I thought we were soldiers here

Cucks_Suck: Big talk no action,.

Cucks_Suck: if you want it done so bad why don't you do it yourself. instead of whining here like a little bitch.

TruePatriot368: If someone wants to spot me a plane ticket to TX i'm there.

TruePatriot368: this is straight up bullshit that she's still breathing after all she did. Chicks like her should be pinushed so the rest of them know what happens when they step out of the kichenn.

Anonymous: Mission accepted, brothers. Keep your eye on the weather. A storm's coming straight toward her.

OUTSKIRTS OF CLINES CORNERS, NEW MEXICO—70 MILES TO ALBUQUERQUE

When the headlights appeared again, Rebecca couldn't say she was surprised. She'd known something was coming for a long time, long before the pickup truck rammed them a hundred miles back, long before she set foot in the Jeep and breathed its musty, stale air. She'd known it ever since she'd stared at the scan of her baby and made the decision not to bring it into this world. A part of her had known then that it would be the end of her, in one way or another.

The pickup was coming up fast now, two spotlights hurtling toward them in the dark, blinding and inescapable.

"Do you think it's the same truck?" Cait asked, eyes trained on the mirror.

"Of course it is," Rebecca said, and closed her eyes.

The scream of metal on metal was louder than she'd thought possible. It seemed to emanate from the inside of her skull. They'd been sideswiped. The Jeep jerked onto the shoulder, gravel spitting at the windshield, before Cait wrenched the wheel and corrected. Her face was ghost-white in the glare of the headlights, a pale sheen of sweat clinging to her forehead and the fine hairs on her upper lip, her jaw locked tight.

They shuddered back onto the tarmac. Rebecca scanned the

horizon. There was no one else on the road with them. The early-morning traffic had melted away.

Cait gripped her arm with one hand, keeping the other on the wheel. "Are you okay?"

"I'm okay," Rebecca said. "Are you?"

Cait touched the side of her head and nodded. "I think so."

The truck dropped back a few lengths. They both felt it behind them, waiting. Cait punched the gas and the engine whined.

"What about the Jeep? Do you think it'll make it?" Rebecca was watching her face, looking for clues.

Cait frowned. "She's okay, too, I think." But her voice lacked conviction. They dropped in speed a little, and she could feel the Jeep's power slackening.

"What are we going to do?" Rebecca heard the tremble in her own voice and worked to steady it. *Think*. Her hands fumbled for her phone. No signal.

Cait was watching her. "Any luck?"

She shook her head.

"Doesn't matter anyway," Cait said. "By the time anyone got to us . . ."

She didn't need to finish the sentence. They both knew how it ended. In a slick of blood and glass and twisted metal scraped against the tarmac as the desert looked on, cold and impassive.

"It's nearly six o'clock in the morning. The sun will be up soon. He can't just run us off the road in broad daylight."

Cait shook her head. "It won't be light for at least another hour."

"There'll be more cars on the road. There already were, a few minutes ago. We'll have witnesses. He can't—" But even as she said it, Rebecca knew that he could. He had tracked them all the way across this ravaged place. He could do anything.

"He's coming again," Cait said, eyes tight on the rearview. "Get ready."

Rebecca placed her hands across her stomach and squeezed her eyes shut. *This wasn't supposed to be how it ended, baby girl.* Rebecca was going to die, and so was Cait, and so was her baby, but not in the way she'd wanted. It would be brutal and painful. Rebecca imagined her head colliding with the dashboard, her body sailing through the windshield, the flinch of glass as it made a thousand pinprick cuts, the scrape of her skin across the tarmac, bone and blood and metal mixing. There would be fire, too— the sharp smell of gasoline followed by a plume of smoke rising blindly into the dark sky.

The man would get out of his pickup truck and stand over her while she died and his eyes—his dead black eyes—would be the last thing she saw in this world before the lights went out and she stopped existing, just like that rabbit she'd held in her hands as a child and her mother taking her last breath. She would become nothing. And deep inside of her, for a few seconds or maybe whole endless minutes, she didn't know, her baby would keep on living, and the baby would know—even with her condition—she would know that her mother was gone. She would be all alone and scared and floating untethered in her mother's body and then she would die, too, starved of all the things her mother's body gave her to survive.

Or worse: Rebecca wouldn't die, at least not right away. Her spinal cord would be severed and her brain starved of oxygen, but they would be able to save her body (not her mind, but her mind wouldn't matter, not here) and they would hook her up to machines that would breathe for her and feed her and pump her heart for her and they would wait until the baby had grown inside her belly and then they would cut her open and bring that baby into this cruel world, and the cold would shock her thin skin and she would die, shivering and alone, surrounded by masked strangers and beeping machines and cold metal.

Rebecca braced for impact and waited, but the pickup truck just kept revving its engine and dropping back.

"What is he doing?" she gasped. The terror was making it hard to breathe. "Why is he doing this to us?"

Rebecca felt Cait's hand in hers. "It's going to be okay," Cait said. Her voice was strangely calm. "We're going to get through this." She twined her fingers through Rebecca's and squeezed, and something in Rebecca's chest loosened, just a little, just for a moment.

The Jeep was solid. Rebecca touched the door with her free hand and felt its cold strength. She pictured herself inside it, a seed within its protective shell.

She closed her eyes and waited.

Cait's training had not prepared her for this.

It had prepared her for some things, sure: extracting the women from the house if an abusive partner was there, guiding the women through the chanting crowds when they arrived at the clinic, knowing the post-op signs that a woman needed further medical treatment.

They hadn't discussed this particular scenario over grayish cups of coffee and stale Pepperidge Farm cookies: that she might end up in the middle of goddamn nowhere with a terrified woman in her car and a lunatic trying to run them off the road.

The truck was idling behind them. She could see only the outline of the driver, but she could picture the smile on his face. He liked keeping them waiting.

She looked over at Rebecca, whose face was tilted away, toward the window, and all she could see were the tips of her mascaraed eyelashes and the soft curve of her cheek. Her hand was still resting on her stomach, cradling it. Cait wanted to reach out and place her hand on top of hers, tell her it would be okay, that they would make it to Albuquerque in time and that everything would go smoothly and that she would be back home in Lubbock before she knew it. The words were like sawdust in her mouth. She couldn't promise anything. She had no idea what was waiting for them up ahead.

She took a deep breath and exhaled slowly. "I'm sorry if this is my fault," she said quietly.

Rebecca nodded. "I'm sorry if it's mine."

They watched the headlights coming toward them again.

Cait fixed her eyes on the road and gripped the wheel tight. She heard the trainer's voice in her head, clear as the night sky: "The patient's safety is our first priority." "I'm going to do my best to get us through this alive," she said. "Now hold on tight."

The pickup surged again, the headlights bright in the mirror, lighting up the inside of the Jeep a brilliant, blinding white.

"I can't see him," Cait said, squinting into the mirror. "Can you?"

Rebecca looked back. All she could see was the chrome grille of the truck and the darkened windshield. Nothing inside. "No, nothing."

Cait pressed down farther on the gas and the Jeep lurched forward. Rebecca could hear the engine struggling, feel the hesitation in the acceleration. There was no way they could outrun him, not in this condition.

"What are we going to do?"

Cait shook her head. "I don't know."

Rebecca scanned the road. There was a pair of headlights coming toward them across the divide. She pointed. "Can you signal him somehow? Flash your lights, maybe?"

"They'll just think we're warning them about a cop up ahead."

"The horn, then. If you honk, maybe the driver will look over and see what's going on."

Cait nodded, but she didn't look convinced. "It's worth a shot."

The sound of the horn shattered the night's silence. The truck dropped back a length and they watched as the window of the on-coming truck—an eighteen-wheeler carrying farm equipment—rolled down and a man's face appeared, ghostly white. Cait kept leaning on the horn and they both started pounding at the windows, but the man shook his head and retreated back into the cab. He must have thought they were drunk, Rebecca realized, or crazy.

The taillights of the eighteen-wheeler disappeared in the rear-view mirror just as the pickup's headlights advanced. Soon he was close enough to nudge their bumper. Once. Twice. A third time, harder.

Cait gripped the steering wheel and cursed. "There's no way out," she muttered.

Rebecca's eyes followed hers. There was nothing in front of them but flat road and desert. Nowhere to hide.

The pickup pressed forward again, edging into the left lane and nestling itself close to their side.

"What is he doing?" Rebecca asked.

Cait looked to her left. The passenger window of the pickup was nearly parallel with her window. She pressed closer to the glass, hoping to get a glimpse of the driver. The windows were tinted, though, and all she saw was her own reflection staring back, white-faced and terrified.

Think. Think. You need a plan.

She had the pedal pushed all the way to the floor, and the Jeep was still struggling to hit eighty. It was sick. She could hear it in the grinding of the gears, feel it in the engine's vibrations. The transmission was slipping. It must have been damaged when he rear-ended them.

C'mon, girl, she coaxed. *Don't give up on me now.*

The truck stayed tucked against the Jeep's side. It was a newer-model Chevy four-by-four, with a double-wide cab and a growling, powerful engine. There was no way she could outrun him.

She'd have to outsmart him.

"Hold on."

She slammed on the brakes, hard. The rear end fishtailed and Cait struggled to keep the wheels straight. The tires screeched as they gripped the pavement, and the air filled with the sulfuric tang of burnt rubber. The pickup was ten yards in front of them, twenty, fifty. The seat belt bit into the flesh around Cait's collarbone.

They came to a juddering halt in the middle of the highway, the only sound their breath as it rattled through their throats.

"What the hell?" Rebecca looked at Cait, wild-eyed. "What are you doing?"

Cait didn't take the time to explain. She flicked off the headlights and the road went black. If it worked once, she figured, it might work again. She threw the car into reverse, backed onto the shoulder, accelerated into a U-turn, and floored it.

"We're going the wrong way."

Cait's eyes didn't waver. "I know."

Cait's heart was pounding so fast, she could feel it pulsing in her skull. She was driving seventy miles an hour, with no headlights, the wrong way down the highway. It would have seemed like she had a death wish if she hadn't been trying so hard to save their lives.

So far, nothing was coming in either direction. At least out here, she'd have a fair amount of warning, though she knew they would scare the ever-loving shit out of another driver once she flicked on the headlights. All they needed was a little time. If they could make it back to that travel center back in Clines Corners, maybe she could flag down help. She couldn't worry about Rebecca and the police anymore. They needed help, whatever it took, whatever the sacrifice. Better than ending up dead.

She checked the rearview. Still clear. She didn't think he'd let her get away that easily. He would have seen her turn around, would have watched her taillights extinguished in the dark. Why hadn't he followed?

They were heading east now, and for the first time she saw that the edge of the horizon had turned a burnished gold. She glanced at the clock: 6:34 a.m. The sun would be up in another half hour. She no longer knew if that was a blessing or a curse.

"I see something."

Cait looked over to see Rebecca hunched over in her seat, peering at the side mirror. "What is it?"

"Someone's coming in the other lane."

Cait's eyes went to the mirror. She caught a glimpse of the headlights at the edge. "Is it him?" In the gloaming, the light bounced off the chrome grille of a pickup truck.

She knew the answer before Rebecca nodded and began to cry.

The pickup cut across the divide and landed behind them with a bounce. The growl of the engine filled the air, and Rebecca could hear the urgency in it, and the anger. Whoever was driving that truck was going to get them, no matter what.

She let her eyes close. Fine. Let them come.

The pickup pulled alongside them again, but this time it hugged the rear wheel. Cait squinted into the wing mirror. "I can't see what he's doing back there."

The answer came quickly. The truck punched into the side of the Jeep, its front end biting and sending them spinning off the road. The wheels hit the edge of the curb and suddenly the Jeep was airborne. It flipped, the windshield suddenly a funhouse mirror reflecting an upside-down world. It bounced hard on the driver's side, shattering the windows and caving in the roof, before hurtling through the air again and tilting back onto its wheels.

The engine let out a long, painful hiss before falling silent.

There were no airbags to deploy, and Rebecca's seat belt had slackened at some point during the crash. Her face had smashed against the dashboard, and her neck had snapped back against the seat when the Jeep landed. She reached her hand to her mouth. Her fingers came back bloodied.

The world tilted again. She'd never been good with blood.

She pawed at her own body, searching for injuries. Her neck sang with pain every time she moved it, and her right shoulder was bruised and tender to the touch. She moved her legs gingerly; her ankle screamed. She must have twisted it in the footwell. She touched the soft swell of her stomach last. It was still for a few heartbeats, and then she felt it: the slightest movement, butterfly wings brushing inside her. She sagged back in her seat.

Maybe it would have been a blessing if she'd miscarried during the crash. But she didn't want to give whatever monster was driving that truck the satisfaction of knowing he'd won. It would be on her own terms. No one else's.

She turned her attention toward Cait. She was slumped over in the driver's seat, limp as a rag doll, her dark hair matted, her face streaked with blood. Shards of glass glittered across her skin like diamonds.

Rebecca reached out and shook her. "Cait, can you hear me? Cait?" Nothing. A bubble of pink spit rose from the woman's mouth and burst. Rebecca shook her harder. "Cait, if you can hear me, you have to wake up." She peered out of the shattered window into the gloaming. No sign of the truck, but she knew that he was out there.

She knew he was coming to finish the job.

Cait's eyes stuttered open. She blinked out at the splintered windshield, the desert shattered into a thousand refracted segments. It was quiet, the only sound the gentle roar of the blood rushing in her ears. For a moment, it was almost peaceful.

And then the pain came.

Her face felt as if it had been bathed in acid, each nerve set alight and burning. Her tongue was swollen and bloodied in her mouth, and when she looked down, she saw that her left arm was hanging at a strange angle.

She felt someone's hands on her, shaking her, and heard her name called over and over. She opened her mouth to speak but couldn't find the words. She closed her eyes again. She wanted to sleep now. She wanted this nightmare to be over.

"Cait!" Her eyes flickered open and she saw Rebecca's face hovering above. Her chin was dripping with blood, and her mouth was swollen and painful-looking. It was her eyes that scared Cait the most, though. They were feverish, burning into hers. They were terrified.

"We have to go." Rebecca was fumbling with something at her side. "I'm going to move you so I can get in the driver's seat, okay? I'm going to get us out of here."

The seat belt released and Cait sagged forward against the wheel. Her whole body was lit up with pain. "Cait, can you hear me?" She managed a grunt. "Can you put your arms around my neck?" Cait tried but couldn't lift them. She fell back against the seat. "It's okay," Rebecca murmured. "Don't worry." Hands tugged at her shoulders. Cait yelped as a bolt of pain shot through her left arm. "Okay, it's okay," Rebecca soothed. "I think your arm is broken. I'll try to be careful, but we don't have much time." Arms around her waist, tugging, pulling. Her body shifted. Pain shot through Cait like an arrow.

She must have passed out from it, because when she opened her eyes, she was half in the passenger seat and Rebecca was climbing over her to the driver's side. Cait watched her lower herself into the seat and fumble at the keys.

Rebecca turned the key in the ignition. The engine stuttered. She tried again. *Stutter, stutter, cough.* Cait could hear the death rattle in the Jeep's throat. The engine had flooded. She reached a finger toward Rebecca. "The gas . . ." she whispered. "Push the gas pedal . . ."

Her words were drowned by a long, shivering scrape of metal on metal. The two women froze. They heard soft footsteps on the ground outside, a hand rattling at the door handle, another long scrape along the Jeep's battered body.

Rebecca fixed her wide, terrified eyes on Cait.

"It's him," she whispered.

The door wrenched open and the silhouette of a man filled the frame.

Rebecca looked up at the man blocking the doorway. She had never seen him in her life.

She watched as confusion filled his dark eyes, followed by anger. "Who the fuck are you?" he asked, and he punched her square in the face before she had the chance to answer.

Her head snapped back against the seat. Stars swam in her vision. She covered her face with her hands just in time to block the next blow, this one a firm backhand to the side of her head. Her skull seemed to swell. She closed her eyes and let out a whimper. "Get the fuck out," the stranger said, and he reached in and started dragging her out of the Jeep.

She swung her arms out wildly, hands scrabbling for purchase, fingers probing for weakness. She jabbed a thumb in his eye, and he reared back before reaching for her neck and tightening his grip until she felt her trachea crack. He let go just before she passed out, then watched as she bent over the wheel and retched.

"Get out," he said again, wrenching at her arm, and she felt herself begin to slide out of the seat.

She swung her legs out to kick him. She caught him square in the chest and he stumbled back. "Cait," she shouted, pulling at the girl's arm. "You have to wake up! You have to get out!"

The man caught Rebecca's bad ankle in his hands. His palms were cold and slicked with sweat. She thrashed like a fish snagged on the hook, but he held on and pulled her body out the door. She landed hard on the ground, and the back of her head scraped against the edge of the doorframe, sending a shock of pain down her spine.

Her fingernails scraped along the dirt as he dragged her into the scrub.

"Who are you?" she screamed, just before he kicked her in the stomach and the world went black.

The air was cold on Cait's face, and she tried to tilt her head away from it. She was cold all over now, her whole body shivering, every nerve raw.

From somewhere far away, she heard the sounds of a struggle, followed by a series of dull, heavy thuds. She kept her eyes closed and turned away from it. She just wanted to sleep now. Deep, endless oblivion.

A scream pierced the night. Cait's eyes snapped open. Her face was tilted upward, and through the shattered windshield, she could see the navy velvet of the sky shot through with tendrils of purple and fuchsia. It was the most perfect thing she'd ever seen.

The scream again, cut short. Silence. Heavy footsteps coming closer. Her fingers twitched. Something deep inside her animal brain telling her to go, move, run. Her body wouldn't comply.

The door next to her opening. More cold air whipping at her skin. A voice, murmuring. Hands on her body, pulling, lifting. A familiar smell filling her lungs. She tried to focus her eyes, but all she could see was the vast expanse of painted sky staring down at her, beautiful and heartless.

The scrape of her heels dragging across the dirt.

A door opening. Leather seat slippery-soft underneath. Another door slamming shut. The click of a key in the ignition. An engine growling to life.

OUTSKIRTS OF MORIARTY, NEW MEXICO—
54 MILES TO ALBUQUERQUE

He hadn't said a word since he'd pulled her into his car, but she could smell him: oranges undercut with cologne, spicy and sweet. Her head felt like a balloon filled with glue.

Time was skittering; she couldn't manage to grab hold of it. She closed one eye and let the other settle on the dashboard. Eventually, the green numbers came into focus: 6:46. Numbers circled in her mind. Her mind tugged something up to the surface. "Rebecca." She fought off the rising tide of panic. "Rebecca. Where's Rebecca?"

She'd seen his face most days for the past two years, but here, in this light, he looked different. Younger, maybe. The moonlight caught the faint scarring on his cheek, a souvenir from teenage acne.

"How did you find us?"

He scratched at the back of his neck. She could hear his nails scraping at the flesh, too hard. "You need to be quiet."

Silence, thicker now.

She looked over at him. His profile was eerie-white in the darkness, and she could see the outline of the soft flesh underneath his chin. He looked sweet, innocent.

Now, though. Now she had to relearn him. He was a man who had followed her for hundreds of miles. He was a man who had intentionally driven them off the road, had nearly killed them in the process. He was a man who had pulled Rebecca out of the Jeep and beaten her, maybe to death.

Her stomach lurched.

Rebecca. Where is Rebecca?

And now he was a man who was driving her God only knew where, and who held her life in his hands.

The shaking returned with a vengeance, and she pulled her good arm tightly to her chest. How long had he been following her? Was it just tonight? Or had he been following her for months?

Those times when she'd gotten home after a late shift and crossed the yard, certain that someone was watching her. She'd clutched her keys between her fingers, tensed to fight, until she'd locked the front door behind her and laughed at herself for being so hysterical. The long nights spent staring into the darkness, waiting for the sound of footsteps outside her window. The knowledge that she wasn't safe, even in her own home.

And him standing at his front door, waving at her, smiling, telling her to have a nice day. Being all fucking neighborly.

A shudder ran through her. It had been him all along.

ADAM

How long had he spent out in the cold? Long years when he had been nothing more than a worm wriggling through the dirt, disgusting and despised. They had hated him at school, even from the first day when he'd spilled milk on his shirt during snack and one of the other boys had mocked him for smelling like sour milk. He knew now that it wasn't possible for the milk to have soured that quickly. The boy had smelled something else on him, something rotten at his very core, ingrained in his skin and bones and soul.

When he was eight, his mother insisted that he have a birthday party and invite everyone from his class. They booked space at Roller Kingdom, and his mom took him to Party City and let him choose whatever decorations and favors he wanted. He passed out the invitations himself—red and blue, Superman-themed—and watched as the kids shoved them in backpacks and cubbies without a word. When the day arrived, nobody came. Not a single person. He could still remember feeding quarters into the claw machine while his mom stood behind him, pretending not to cry.

After that, he kept to himself as much as he could, creeping around the perimeters of playgrounds and lunchrooms, slinking up the stairs to his bedroom after school each afternoon.

They always found him, though. No matter how hard he tried to be invisible, they always sought him out. It wasn't enough for them to hate him. They wanted to hurt him, too.

Puberty was particularly cruel. Days spent seeing revulsion reflected in the eyes of every popular girl in school, and most of the unpopular girls, too. Meathead jocks laughing at him, shoving him into lockers, spitting in his lunch. He spent his nights locked in his room, ignoring his mom shouting for him to come down to dinner. He filled whole notebooks with poems for girls who would never love him, and torturous diary entries in which he described every excruciating detail of his rejections.

He used to spend hours staring at his reflection in the mirror, trying to figure out what it was that made him so repulsive. Okay, so he was skinny. When he took his shirt off, which he did only when he showered, he could count his ribs like piano keys. His mother used to give him weight gainer when he was a kid, thick, gloopy shakes that tasted like sweetened sidewalk chalk, but he stayed resolutely thin. His face was thin, too, and long, and his eyes looked like they were too big for his skull. Once, one of the jocks called him Auschwitz because he looked like a victim of a concentration camp, and the nickname stuck.

It got a little easier in college. People seemed to hate him less. He even made a couple of friends. But no matter what he tried, he couldn't get a date. All he wanted was to hold a girl's hand at the movies, kiss her good night, take care of her. He was a nice guy. Why wouldn't they give him a chance?

One night a couple of years ago, a girl at a bar laughed in his face when he asked if he could buy her a drink. He'd thought about killing himself that night—had even gotten so far as running a bath and finding a razor—but he'd pussied out in the end.

Instead, he typed "why won't girls sleep with me?" into a search engine and ended up in a subthread called braincels. At first he was kind of weirded out by the stuff they were saying about women, but the more he read, the more he found himself agreeing. How many times had a girl rejected him and gone home with some 'roided-up asshole? He stayed on the thread for hours, and when the sun was coming up, he finally worked up the courage to write something himself. He described what had happened that night and how it had been the same night he'd been having over and over since high school.

"Might as well swallow the black pill," one of the commenters wrote underneath his post. "Come on in, the water's fucking freezing."

He looked up the definition on Urban Dictionary: "A concept derived from the notion that romantic success is more determined by genetic signs of good health, prosperity and intelligence (physical attraction, strength, symmetry) than by any esoteric personal quality like kindness or strength of character."

He felt like he'd been struck by a lightning bolt. Suddenly, it all made sense: the rejection, the loneliness, the helplessness. They had been born this way, every one of them. They would never get a girl to like them, because genetics had determined that they were physically inferior and therefore repulsive. The only guys who got to have sex were muscled-up Chads who would treat them like shit, or beta guys for whom girls were willing to settle as long as they had money.

Here was a community of people who understood that unfairness and shared in it. He finally felt like he belonged.

And when he found out that he was living next door to that stupid feminazi bitch, he finally felt like he had a purpose.

He would be the one who killed her.

CLINES CORNERS, NEW MEXICO—
58 MILES TO ALBUQUERQUE

Cait closed her eyes and pretended to be asleep. She needed time to think. Time to plan.

What did he want from her?

Rebecca, lying in the dirt, covered in blood. Oh God oh God she was dead. And it was all her fault.

She never should have let her set foot inside the Jeep. She should have turned back as soon as the truck ran into them that first time, she should have insisted on calling the police. She should have taken better care of her. Now she was dead.

And soon she would be, too.

Calm. Just stay calm.

The desert swept past, endless empty road. No cars to flag down, though how she'd manage even if there were, she wasn't sure. A billboard for a junkyard: YOU TRASH, WE SMASH. A deserted rest stop.

She couldn't tell if they were heading east or west. Had she passed through here before? She tried to remember landmarks, but of course there weren't any. There was nothing out here in this godforsaken place.

Where was he taking her?

She risked a look. He was staring straight ahead, eyes focused on the road. His face was inscrutable. How many times had she let her gaze slide right past him? She could still remember the day she moved in, the way he'd loped out onto the lawn and waved to her, asked if she needed any help. Together, they'd lugged her mattress into her apartment, and she'd offered him a beer as a reward. She remembered thinking that night that she was lucky to have a decent neighbor next door, one she didn't have to worry about. One she could trust.

Who was he, really?

More important: what did he want from her, and how could she give it to him without giving him her life?

ADAM

At first it had been like a movie. He felt powerful behind the wheel of the pickup truck, tall and strong. He could have had her all the way back in Texas, but he'd waited, taken his time. He liked the feeling of hunting her down, the little green dot from the tracker moving across the screen, staring up at him, urging him on. He liked the feeling of knowing something she didn't, of casting an invisible noose around her neck that he could tighten at any minute.

That first time, after the IHOP—he'd planned to finish it then. It was just as he imagined: the blind terror on her face, the surge of adrenaline as he plowed the truck into the side of the Jeep, the beautiful screech of metal on metal. It was intoxicating, like a drug. He hadn't wanted it to stop. So he'd teased it out as long as he could, dropping back, letting her think she'd lost him, that she was safe. When she'd played that trick with the headlights, he'd laughed. He was happy to let her have that little victory. They were playing a game, one he would ultimately win. But victory would taste that much sweeter after the chase.

After a while, the chase wasn't enough. He wanted to hear that shriek of metal again, wanted to see the fear on her face up close, wanted to feel the power flowing through his veins. Wanted to see that power reflected in her eyes.

So he went in for the kill.

That moment when the Jeep flipped over . . . he'd never experienced anything like it. It was like that scene in *Pulp Fiction* when Travolta jabbed the girl in the heart with adrenaline, only he felt like both Travolta and the girl at the same time. Just pure, pure power.

He hadn't expected the other girl to be there. He didn't know how he'd missed her before—a trick of the light, maybe, or he'd been so focused on Cait, it had been to the exclusion of everything else. When he wrenched open that door and saw the blonde staring up at him from the driver's seat, all he could think was that she looked just like this girl in high school, Jenny, who'd laughed in his face when he said hello to her in the hall this one time, and after that . . . God, he hadn't known he was so strong. How hadn't he known? He'd heard soldiers talk about the veil of rage, and that was how he felt in that moment. Overcome.

Now, staring at his hands gripping the steering wheel, he could see that his knuckles were bloodied and bruised, but he still couldn't feel any pain. Was this what it felt like to be alive? Was this what he had been missing for all of these years?

Now that he had a taste of it, he only wanted more.

OUTSKIRTS OF MORIARTY, NEW MEXICO—
49 MILES TO ALBUQUERQUE

Rebecca knew her eyes were open, but the world remained stubbornly dark. She reached a hand to her face. Her eyes were swollen to slits, and her eyelashes were crusted together with dried blood. She rubbed them, scraping at the blood with her fingernails until she could at last see the deep purple light of the dawn and the scarred wasteland of the desert.

The Jeep sat squat and silent in the dirt. The truck was gone. Rebecca scanned the horizon and caught the last glimpse of taillights heading east just before they disappeared.

She struggled onto her hands and knees and dry-retched onto the cold ground. Her knuckles were bruised and bloodied, and she couldn't put much weight on her right arm. Pain radiated through every cell of her body.

A gentle breeze carried through the desert, ruffling the soft hairs on the back of her neck. She shivered. She was cold, she realized. Freezing. She needed to get somewhere warm, fast. She needed water and bandages and medicine.

She needed to know what had happened.

"Cait?" Her voice came out as a hoarse whisper. Her throat was raw from the man choking her. When she tried to swallow, it felt like a knife cutting straight through. "Cait?" Louder this time, but still nothing.

She took a few deep breaths, engine oil and Cait's shampoo and the strange sweet smell the man had left behind. She listened hard, ears straining, waiting for the sound of the engine to reappear, but the silence had settled like a fresh blanket of snow.

She couldn't say how long she stayed like that, her senses heightened and alert, breath caught tight in her throat like a small, trapped bird, waiting for something to break.

A whiptail scurried across the dirt. It saw her and froze, eye trained on hers, black and unblinking. She could sense the workings of its mind, feel the febrile patter of its heart beneath its skin, before she blinked and the spell was broken. The lizard skittered into the brush.

She struggled to her feet and limped over to the Jeep. She moved slowly. She knew what she would find, and she knew she didn't want to see it: Cait's body bloodied and mangled, her dark hair thick with blood, her eyes the dull flat black of the dead.

She bent double, retched onto the sand.

"Please no, please no."

Dread built in her like a wall, each step another brick. She reached the driver's side, placed a careful hand on the jagged edge of the window, leaned forward.

The Jeep was empty.

Rebecca scanned the horizon, looking for any trace of her. The road stared back, blank and empty. She moved over to the passenger side—Cait's side. The door was hanging open, and there were drag marks in the dirt leading to the truck's tire marks. She followed the tracks out onto the road, saw where they crossed back over the median and headed east.

He had taken Cait.

Was she still alive?

Why had he left Rebecca?

She was a witness. She had seen his face.

Maybe he'd thought she was dead.

She remembered the look on his face when he'd opened the door and seen her in the driver's seat. Pure, undiluted rage.

She wished she'd fought harder.

She cupped her stomach with her hands. When he had kicked her, she had tried to curl herself up and shield her baby from the blows, but she knew that his foot had connected at least once. She lifted her shirt and saw the pale pink bloom of a bruise beginning to form. Her baby.

Who was that monster?

And now he had Cait.

Would he come back for her?

She remembered the taillights heading east. She turned her eyes to where the Jeep was languishing in the dust. One of the headlights was dangling by a wire, and there was a long, vicious scrape along the driver's side, the shattered window dark and gaping like a missing tooth. She peered inside. The keys were still in the ignition.

She glanced to the east, half expecting to see the truck's headlights bearing down on her again, but the road stayed dark. She wasn't sure how long she'd been out—it could have been a few seconds or an hour. Even if he stayed on the same road, there was no guarantee she'd be able to catch him. And if she did—then what? What was she supposed to do about it?

Cait was the one he had been after all along—not her. This wasn't her responsibility. She wasn't even supposed to be out here with Cait—the girl had admitted that herself. She had lied to get Rebecca in the car with her, and lied about her motives, and all the while she'd been planning to betray her. Sure, she'd owned up to it eventually, but was that really enough? Cait had set out to destroy her life, and she'd put them both in danger in the process. Rebecca didn't owe her anything.

This was her only chance. She was eighteen weeks pregnant. The window was closing. She touched her fingertips to her stomach.

She remembered the knock on the door, the man thrusting the summons at her, the thin smile on his face before he turned and ran back to his car. The hearing was scheduled for eleven a.m. at Lubbock County Courthouse, and she wouldn't be there for it. Failing to appear in court was a criminal offense. It was a risk she had known she was taking when she climbed into Cait's Jeep, and now she had to make that count.

She had come so far already. If she didn't make it to Albuquerque, she would be sacrificing all of it.

She didn't owe the girl anything. Cait had made the choices that led her to this point, just like Rebecca had made her own. It was Cait who knew the man in the truck, it was Cait he was after. It was her fault, not Rebecca's.

Even as she thought this, she knew it was wrong. Cait was no more at fault than Rebecca was. Wasn't living under the constant threat of danger just a part of being a woman in this world? Keys clutched between fingers, earphones out when walking home at night, always waiting for a hand to reach out and grab you, always waiting for the moment that would end it all. Always wondering who it would be: a man you already knew or a man you didn't. Hadn't she been certain up until the moment the man wrenched open the door of the Jeep that he had come to kill her, not Cait? Hadn't she been convinced that it was all her own fault and that somehow she deserved it?

Who could possibly deserve this kind of life?

No more apologies. No more blame. From now on, only action. There wasn't much time.

The seats of the Jeep were covered in glass and stained dark with blood; she carefully brushed the glass off the upholstery and pressed a scarf she'd kept in her bag across the seat before sliding in. Shards still crunched under her weight.

She turned the key in the ignition. That same cough-stutter.

"Shit."

What had Cait been trying to tell her? Rebecca's eyes went to the gauge. It was showing nearly a full tank, so that wasn't the issue. There was a good chance that the Jeep was just broken. It had flipped over twice: it would be a miracle if it was still drivable. Most likely, it had given up the ghost.

She turned the key again. Nothing. Just a sad cough and then silence.

She was about to give up hope when she remembered something. The gas. Hadn't Cait said something about the gas pedal?

Rebecca pressed down gently on the gas pedal and tried again. The engine still stuttered but sounded a little more robust. She floored the gas and turned the key, and after a few tentative, spluttering seconds, the engine roared to life.

Rebecca shifted the Jeep into drive and pulled back onto Highway 40. Heading east, following the taillights that had disappeared from sight.

CLINES CORNERS, NEW MEXICO—
58 MILES TO ALBUQUERQUE

First Cait tried bargaining.

"You don't have to do this," she said. "If you just stop the truck right now and let me out, I promise I won't say anything about what happened."

His face twisted in anger. "Don't tell me what I need to do."

Wrong move. Time to backtrack. "I'm sorry. I didn't mean—"

"Yes, you did. Don't pretend like you don't think you can control me. That's what all you women think, isn't it?"

Cait silently recalibrated her approach. She thought about how Rebecca had handled Scott back in the eighteen-wheeler, stroking his ego, letting him talk. Appeasing him.

"I would never tell you what to do," she said, making her voice soft and gentle. "I don't want to control you. I just want to help you."

"I don't need your help."

Shit. Wrong move again. "I know you don't need my help. I just want to make things right between us. I thought we were friends."

He laughed bitterly. "We were never friends."

"Okay, well, I want to be your friend now. Just tell me what

I've done wrong and I'll try to make it right. Is it about money? I don't have much, but—"

"Of *course* you would think it's about money. That's all you women think about, isn't it? Well, *Cait*, some things can't be bought. Things like respect, and dignity, and honor. You know what women like you are? You're leeches. You suck the blood out of everything around you."

"Adam, please, if you'll just tell me—"

"Stop telling me what to do!" He squeezed his eyes shut. The truck veered across the road. "I told you," he said through clenched teeth, "to shut your mouth." He raised his hand from the steering wheel and slapped her, hard, with the back of his hand. Her head snapped back against the seat, and her ears rang from the pain. She cradled her jaw in her hand and tried not to cry.

He was going to kill her, that much was obvious, and there was nothing she could say that could stop him.

She needed to make a new plan.

ADAM

He hadn't planned on hitting her, but every time she opened her mouth, another lie came slithering out like a thick black snake, coiled and ready to strike. He couldn't think when she talked like that. It clouded things in his brain, made him foggy and slow and confused.

There was a smell coming off her—blood and sweat undercut with something else, something animal. He didn't like the fact that he was breathing it in, taking her smell into his lungs, pushing it deep into his cells.

He didn't like the fact that she kept talking, either. He'd told her to shut up, but she wouldn't listen. Of course she wouldn't listen. He had to teach her a lesson.

Hitting her had made every nerve in his body sing.

At first he'd figured he would just kill her. Shoot her straight between the eyes and put her down like the dog she was. Now he wanted to drag the moment out, really savor it, now that she was next to him, so close that if he reached out he could touch her, feel her warm blood racing underneath her skin, touch the soft dark curls on her head . . .

He had been locked away in his own dark prison for so long. Now that he had been released, he wanted to revel in his freedom. He wanted to look into her eyes and see his own power reflected there. To see that he was a god and that she was nothing in the face of him.

This is your purpose on this earth, and you are fulfilling it.

CLINES CORNERS, NEW MEXICO—
60 MILES TO ALBUQUERQUE

The sun edged up over the horizon, a single blinding point of white light that turned the sky and the desert floor a burnished orange, as if the whole world had gone up in flames and she was driving straight into the center of the inferno. The kind of sunrise meant to inspire awe at the extraordinary beauty of our world.

Rebecca flipped the visor down and squinted out of the splintered windshield. The Jeep was hurting pretty bad, but she pushed it as fast as it would go, the engine rumbling, the speedometer clocking over eighty, her eyes locked on the highway, searching for the pickup's taillights.

She saw the crest of the Clines Corners Travel Center at the intersection of 40 and 285. Four directions, four choices, no sign of the taillights. She punched the gas and the engine groaned. It wouldn't hold like this forever. She had to find them, fast, before it broke down for good. It was close to seven a.m. There were a few big rigs sharing the road with her now, and she weaved past them, ignoring the spark of fear she felt every time she got near one. She wanted it to be just her and the road and the wink of the truck's taillights.

She hit the junction and slowed. Nothing in front of her but an eighteen-wheeler hauling a pair of tractors. Nothing in the rear-view, and it wouldn't make sense for him to double back on himself. Route 285 South stretched out to her right, empty except for a radio tower far off in the distance.

She caught a set of taillights heading north on 285. She couldn't be sure they were his, but it was the best chance she had. She clicked her turn signal on and peeled left.

I'm coming for you, she thought, fixing her gaze on the taillights and gunning the engine. *I'm coming.*

He'd taken a left turn at the junction, and they were heading north on an unfamiliar road. Cait's heart sank. Even if by some miracle people were looking for her, the chances of them finding her were even slimmer. Surely the first thing they'd do would be retrace her steps, though how they'd do that, she didn't know. She tried to think of the people they'd seen along the drive, anyone who might act as a witness. The waitress back in the diner. Scott the trucker, though he would be long gone by now. The gas station attendant.

There was no one, really. She was in uncharted territory, alone.

She thought about her parents, how they would feel when a policeman showed up at their door and told them that their only daughter was dead. Her father would crumple like a tissue—he'd always been the soft one of the two—and her mother would stand there stone-faced and pale, as if this were a burden she was destined to carry.

It had been months since she'd been back to Waco, and she'd never thought to call them, even when all that stuff about her came out in the news. Her mother had called the day after her name had been revealed to the press. Cait had seen the missed call after her shift, but she'd never returned it. What could she possibly say? Her parents were good people, had worked hard to keep their family afloat, had taught her and her brothers right from wrong, had raised them right, and what had she done to thank them? Left for the city and never looked back, then dragged the family name through the mud. She knew the way that people at church would have looked at them afterward, the whispers and the pitying looks. And she hadn't even had the courage to let her mother say that she was disappointed in her.

She had let them down, and now she was going to break their hearts. The policemen would hold their hats in their hands, would stand respectfully on the threshold of the little house on Pine Street, and her father would weep and her mother would nod and thank them for their time and then she would call Cait's brothers and tell them the news that their sister had been killed.

That's if they found her body. They were out in the middle of nowhere, and from the look of it, Adam seemed determined to drive them even deeper into it. In the distance, she could see the faint crest of a distant mesa. A good place to hide a body, in the canyon below. Was that what he had planned?

She had to get away. Like Rebecca had said when she chased after that kid at the gas station, she was a good runner. He would have to stop the truck sometime. She would get out and run as fast as she could. Her legs started tingling at the thought. Yes, that's what she would do. She would run and run until her lungs gave out on her, run until she could no longer see him, and then she would keep running. As soon as her feet hit the ground, she would never stop running again.

Her ankle, though. She'd twisted it pretty bad when they flipped. Her ribs ached, too—one of them might even be cracked. She wouldn't know what kind of shape she was in until she got out of the truck, and by then it might be too late. If she was too weak, or too slow, he would be able to catch her. And then he would kill her for sure.

Who was she kidding? She'd been a dead woman as soon as that truck appeared on the road behind her. It was just a matter of time now.

Cait's eyes trailed to the rearview mirror. In the distance, about a half mile back, a cloud of dust gathered on the road, a boxy shape lurking behind it. At first she thought her eyes were playing tricks on her—a mirage in the desert, pretty fitting—but then she saw the glint of metal off the grille and she knew it was real.

She would know that Jeep anywhere.

ADAM

He didn't know what she was smiling about. Just trying to make him feel small, probably, like the rest of them. He could feel her worming her way into his head, burrowing into the soft tissue of his brain. She was laughing at him. After everything he'd done, she was still laughing at him.

He was still that little boy standing in Roller Kingdom, watching his mother hide her tears because she knew her son was a loser. He was that pimply teenager getting chased through the parking lot by a bunch of jocks. He was that guy in the bar whom women turned their backs on when he approached them. He was one of life's rejects. Pathetic. A maggot.

Then he saw that Jeep in the rearview mirror, and the power surged through him again.

Remember the mission, he told himself. This was a war they were fighting, and he was their soldier.

He and his brothers had spent a lifetime being told that they weren't good enough, tall enough, rich enough, handsome enough. They had been rejected over and over by a society that favored the female every single time.

No more. Now they were rising up, and he was leading the charge.

He remembered the words one of his brothers had posted: "Resist. Stand tall. Live for you. Go your own way."

Never give up, he thought, gunning the engine. *Never surrender. Make them pay.*

The pickup took a right onto a single-track road marked by a Dead End sign, and Rebecca followed suit, heading deeper into the desert. The Jeep kicked up a cloud of dust and she struggled to see the road through the cracked windshield, but she could just make out the Texas plate on the rear bumper. It was definitely him.

She didn't like leaving the main road behind. Out here, on this thinly paved road, there were no cars to be seen, or billboards, or any sign of life except the occasional flash of movement she caught out of the corner of her eye of a jackrabbit or a lizard skittering across the desert floor.

This was wild country.

Where was he going? What did he have planned?

She needed a plan.

The land stayed flat, but now she could see a ridge of blue-tinged mesas in the distance.

She couldn't track him forever. Sooner or later, he was going to clock that he was being followed, if he hadn't already. Out here, there was nowhere for her to hide.

She had to make the first move.

The paved road ended, replaced by a dirt track that cut up into the mountains. The land changed quickly, the flat sand replaced by packed, craggy earth, the scrub turning a deeper green and then to forest. She watched carefully, committing each terrain change to memory. She would need it when it was time for them to run. She would need it if they had to hide.

The mesas loomed above, blunt and brutal.

The engine was whining continuously now, a high-pitched buzz that set off her tinnitus and suggested that something was deeply wrong and would only get worse. There was no time to lose. She had to act.

She waited until the pickup followed a bend in the track up ahead that momentarily took her out of its sight line, and she floored the gas. The Jeep lurched forward, gears grinding in complaint. When she caught sight of the truck again, it was only a few lengths ahead of her. She peered through the broken windshield. All she could see was the top of his head peeking over the driver's seat. An invitation.

Her plan was simple: do to him what he'd done to them, and hope the Jeep was up to one final challenge.

First she needed to make sure Cait was inside that truck.

C'mon, Cait.

She hit the engine with a little more gas. The wheels skidded on the gravel.

They were climbing now, the slope gentle at first, trees leaning toward them from the brush, the roadway blurring and reforming every few feet.

The speedometer climbed past seventy. The Jeep skidded into a turn. A tree skimmed past her window, its branches scraping at the door.

The truck kept climbing. His eyes were in the rearview mirror now, fixed on hers, dark and wild. Their gazes stayed locked together as they climbed up the mesa.

And then, for just a split second, his eyes flicked to his right. Someone was in the truck with him.

The engine was stuttering. She couldn't keep this pace much longer.

She didn't want to hurt Cait in the process. She wanted her to be prepared.

She leaned hard on the horn. A flock of flycatchers rose from the trees and took off through the sky.

A hand appeared above the passenger-side headrest of the truck. Slim fingers curled together. A thumbs-up.

Rebecca floored the gas pedal. She pulled the Jeep's nose level with the rear end of the truck and wrenched the steering wheel, hard.

Cait watched Rebecca's face in the wing mirror. All traces of softness had been erased. She was a bullet aimed squarely for the truck.

When the horn blared, Cait checked the clasp on her seat belt and raised her hand above the seat. She wanted Rebecca to know that she should do whatever it took to stop him. She wanted her to know that if Cait died because of this, it wouldn't be her fault. She wanted Rebecca to know that she was grateful for her coming when she could have saved herself. She wanted her to know that she deserved more than this hand she'd been dealt, and she hoped that, when this was all over, she'd seek it out.

The front end of the Jeep bit into the truck's rear tire, sending it skidding into the dirt. He corrected and spun back onto the road. There was a long scrape on the left side of the truck, but it looked superficial. She hadn't gone in hard enough.

She caught his face in the mirror, a smirk playing on his lips. The truck began to pull away. She sank the pedal to the floor.

They thundered up the road together, her bumper just a few inches away from his but unable to connect. The Jeep was struggling to keep pace. The road worsened again, not much more than loose dirt and rubble. The shock absorbers weren't up for the challenge, and her body rattled in the seat like a Tic Tac.

She didn't have much time.

There was a steep bank up ahead, ringed in thick fencing. If she could squeeze him onto it, the truck might just be unstable enough for her to flip it. She needed him to be distracted enough to drop his pace, even for a split second.

Cait had gripped the edges of the seat and readied herself for impact as the Jeep approached, but when it came, she barely felt it. The truck was solid, and Adam was a surprisingly good driver, leaning into the skid without flinching before steering them back on the road. There was a steely calm in his eyes she'd never seen before, and it scared her.

Now the Jeep seemed to be fading. The engine sounded sick, like maybe the transmission was shot, and there was a high-pitched whine that she'd never heard before. Rebecca didn't have much time to give it another try. Neither did Cait.

She glanced over at Adam. His eyes were fixed on the road, his mouth hard. Her jaw still stung from where he'd backhanded her, but pain was irrelevant now, when death felt so certain. She had to help Rebecca.

Her eyes searched the cab of the truck, looking for something she could use. Her eyes lit on a pen shoved into the cupholder between them. Her fingers twitched. Could she get to it quickly enough? If he caught her, things would only get worse for her.

Fuck it. She had nothing to lose.

She snatched the pen and plunged it as hard as she could into the top of his thigh.

The truck swerved sharply. Its pace dropped quickly so that Rebecca nearly plowed square into the back of it, but she managed to jerk the wheel at the last second to avoid the collision. She pulled level with the truck, sandwiching it between the Jeep and the steep bank. It was now or never. She caught Cait's eyes through the window and nodded at her, once. She saw the shadow of a smile play across Cait's lips right before she turned the wheel sharply and slammed into the side of the truck.

The shriek of metal filled the air. Rebecca watched as the truck tilted up the side of the bank and over, cutting down several fence posts, back end fishtailing wildly as he tried to correct. She saw Cait's head snap back against the seat, her good hand braces against the dash, the dark swing of her hair as the truck began to spin.

Rebecca thought the truck might tip, but it held steady, and soon he had the wheels steering straight. But he didn't manage in time to avoid the tree.

The piñon pine knifed the front end of the truck, metal buckling around it, the back wheels spinning momentarily in the air before crashing down to earth with a sickening bang.

Rebecca stayed frozen. She'd braked hard as soon as the truck started skidding, and now she was fifty feet behind, stopped short in the middle of the dirt track.

She cut the engine and climbed out onto the road.

The quiet was what hit her first. After the rage of the engines and the blood rushing to her ears, the sudden silence felt deafening. She could hear the soft hiss of the truck's engine, the soft rustle of the breeze through the pines, the distant call of a circling hawk. The sharp tang of gasoline hit the back of her throat, followed by the acrid smell of smoke.

Cait's side of the truck was scraped raw; the window had blown out in the impact, leaving behind an angry, gaping maw. Inside the truck, nothing was moving.

Please be okay, please be okay.

Rebecca came level with the window and peered inside. Adam's body was angled toward the driver's-side window, the airbag pressed tight against his chest, his head lolling against the doorframe. She could see an angry gash on his forehead, and his face was pale and still.

Cait was slumped over the airbag, her dark curls stark against the white. Her eyes were closed. She looked peaceful, almost. Like she was sleeping. Rebecca reached a hand in and touched her, gently. "Cait? Can you hear me?"

Please don't be dead.

Cait's eyes opened and locked on Rebecca's. A mewling sound escaped her mouth.

Rebecca's knees almost gave out. "Thank God. Are you hurt?"

Cait shook her head gently. "I don't think so." She coughed, winced. "Nothing too bad." The chemicals from the airbag clung to her clothes and her skin like a fine dust.

"Do you think he's—" Rebecca didn't want to say the rest, didn't dare jinx it.

Cait looked over at Adam and nodded. "I think so."

"Let's get you out." Rebecca wrenched at the crumpled door, but the handle was jammed. "I can't open it." She tugged on it again. "You're going to have to climb out through the window."

Cait nodded and began the slow, careful work of disentangling herself, one eye always trained on Adam's slumped, still body. When she was free of the airbag and the seat belt, Rebecca reached inside and helped pull her through the shattered window. "Come on," she said, shouldering Cait's weight. Her eyes were trained on the dark smoke billowing out of the truck's hood, thicker by the second. "We have to get clear."

The two women limped toward the Jeep. Rebecca was reaching for the handle when she looked over to see the truck's door swing open and a pair of boots hit the ground.

She saw then that the gash on Adam's head was bleeding badly against the pale white of his skin and that one leg of his jeans was stained dark with blood and that he tensed when he put weight on it, but still he raised the gun he held in his hand and aimed it squarely at her chest, and in the split second before he pulled the trigger, she saw that he was smiling.

Cait heard the creak of metal from the door's hinge and turned just in time to see Adam emerge from the truck. She caught the look in his eye and the glint of metal in his hand and pulled Rebecca down to the ground right before the gun went off. The bullet lodged in the Jeep's side, just to the right of where Rebecca's body had been a half second ago.

Next time, Cait knew, he wouldn't miss.

They scrambled through the dirt, another bullet ricocheting off the rear door as they dove behind the bumper. "I didn't know he had a gun," Rebecca whispered.

Cait shook her head. "Neither did I."

Footsteps in the dirt. He was limping, they could hear that in the way one of his steps was heavier than the other. Cait was glad she'd plunged that pen into the meat of his thigh when she had the chance.

He was hurt. They were hurt, too, but the fact that he was

hurt was something. An advantage, maybe, if they played it right. First they had to get the hell out of there. They were sitting ducks behind the Jeep. And the footsteps were getting closer.

Cait saw her moment. Rebecca had risked her own life to save her. Now it was her turn to return the favor. Besides, she'd always liked a grand gesture. "Listen," she whispered, "I'm going to go for his legs. You run as fast as you can. No matter what happens, you keep running."

Rebecca shook her head. "We both go for his legs, and then we both run."

"Let me do this for you. Please." Cait heard the desperation in her own voice. "This is your chance."

Rebecca held her eye. "Our chances are better if we stay together."

Step, drag. Step, drag. Cait could see the edge of his boots and his shadow in the dust. He was so close, she could almost smell him.

Rebecca was right. If Cait went for him and missed . . . well, neither of them stood a chance. Together, though . . .

She nodded, held up her hand. Started ticking off fingers. One. Two. Three. They would go on five.

BOOM.

The explosion tore through the desert, the noise deafening, the heat rippling out in waves, scorching their skin and sending debris from the pickup high into the air.

It took Rebecca a second to figure out what had happened, but Cait was already tugging at her arm, urging her to run.

The fire had finally reached the truck's gas tank, and it had detonated like a bomb.

They could only hope that it had taken Adam with it.

They took off through the brush, darting between trees, stumbling over rocks, brambles snagging into flesh, sand slipping underfoot, the only sound that of their hot breath in their throats, the air filled with black acrid smoke, never daring to look back.

Adam's hair was singed from the heat of the explosion and his lips were blistered and he could feel the melted fibers from his shirt clinging to his skin but he didn't feel the pain. He felt nothing now but pure, beautiful rage, and it flowed through his veins like ice water.

He watched the two women run.

He wouldn't rush. He knew they wouldn't get far.

There was no plan. There was only the pounding of their hearts and the rush of blood and the feverish will to survive.

He followed them into the brush, his bad leg dragging in the dirt. He still couldn't believe that bitch had stabbed him.

He'd make her pay. He'd make them both pay. He was a soldier. He was a warrior. He would march and fight until the battle was won.

They were fifty feet ahead of him now, but they were injured, too, and the pain was starting to catch up with them. He couldn't feel his own pain. There was a power surging through his veins that made him feel invincible. He gripped the gun harder. He saw Cait stumble and fall, then the other one pulling her up and pushing her on.

He aimed the gun and stared through the sight. There she was, her pretty little face smeared with blood and dirt, her pretty little mouth twisted in pain.

He put the gun down. He was too far away. He wanted to look straight in her eyes when he pulled the trigger. He wanted her to feel how powerful he was, and how merciless.

Cait turned around and saw a flash of movement through the trees below.

He was coming for them.

They were climbing, knees and hands scraping against jagged rocks. There were places to hide up there, craggy inlets to tuck themselves behind, and they would be able to see him coming. They needed an advantage. This was the only one she could think of.

"There," she said, nodding toward a gash in the rock above.

They kept climbing.

He watched them climb and smiled to himself. Stupid, stupid girls. Didn't they know there was no escape?

They reached the bottom of the caprock. It was too steep for them to go any farther.

Rebecca looked at Cait. "We're trapped."

He took his time. He could see them watching him. He pulled out the gun and aimed toward them. Saw them flinch.

Rebecca pressed her back against the rock. The air smelled like burnt rubber and gasoline. "What are we going to do?"

Cait shook her head. "I don't know." She had led them up there. It was her fault. She had to come up with a plan. He was getting closer.

Step, drag. Step, drag.

She could see his face, and the outline of a smile playing across his lips. Who was he? She had thought he was just the guy who lived next door. Sweet. Harmless. But no. He was a monster.

She looked over at Rebecca, who was clinging to the rock, one hand on her stomach, lips moving silently.

Seven hours ago, she'd been a stranger, but she'd risked her life to save Cait.

Cait couldn't let her die. Not here. Not like this.

There was no plan.

Sometimes, though, plans were unnecessary.

Sometimes you just had to act.

She turned toward Rebecca. "Whatever happens, run."

Cait hurtled down the slope, picking up speed as she went. She pictured herself as a bullet slicing through the air, impenetrable and unstoppable.

She was twenty feet away when he lifted the gun.

Ten when she saw his finger twitch.

She waited for the crack of gunshot, though she knew she'd be dead before she registered the sound.

She waited for hot metal to enter her chest or her skull or her abdomen, tearing through flesh and cartilage and bone.

Her eyes locked on his.

She saw his finger squeeze the trigger.

She waited for oblivion.

The bullet grazed her left temple. She felt its whispered promise as it passed.

She heard him cock the gun.

She launched herself at his body, the air whistling past her ears as she flew. She hit him square in the chest and knocked him to the ground, sending the gun skittering out of his hand into the brush.

Their two bodies were locked together, fingers clawing, elbows gouging, knees pinning each other tight. She sank her teeth into the soft flesh of his forearm and he screamed. He grabbed a handful of her hair and pulled until she felt it tear from the roots. Her thumbs searched for his eye sockets. She wanted to hurt him as much as she could. She wanted him to suffer.

He was strong, though. Stronger than he looked. His hands found her neck and started to squeeze. When she tried to pry his fingers away, he smashed her head against the ground, hard. The blue sky began to darken. She heard her breath in her ears, too loud, gasping. He squeezed harder.

"How does it feel to suffer?" he hissed, eyes burning into hers. "How does it feel to die?"

Her hands and feet went numb. All of the struggle drained out of her, and she lay there, limp, as he bore down on her and the world began to fade. She closed her eyes as a strange warmth spread through her body. This was a place beyond pain.

She didn't hear the gun go off. She felt his weight collapse onto her heavily and the wet warmth of his blood as it poured through the hole in his neck and the muffled rasp of his breath as it left his body for the last time. But she never heard the gun.

She opened her eyes to see Rebecca standing above her, the sun haloed around her face.

It was morning, and they were alive.

They left Adam's body on the mountainside for the police or the vultures to find. If it was the latter, in a few weeks, there would be nothing left but bleached bones. The desert was a hungry scavenger, and it wouldn't waste time.

They left his truck there, too, its charred body wrapped around the scorched remains of the pine tree. Cait had never seen him drive a pickup—he had an old Corolla with a Longhorns decal on the window—so she wasn't sure it was even his. Probably a rental, which meant that someone would miss it eventually. They might even come looking for it. It wouldn't matter. She and Rebecca would be long gone. She had already decided that if the police came knocking at her apartment door, asking about her missing neighbor, she'd tell them she didn't know anything about him. In a way, it would be the truth. He was more of a mystery to her now than he ever had been.

The Jeep's engine took a couple of tries to turn over, but it managed in the end, and together they wound their way down the dirt track and back onto the main road.

Cait didn't look back. Her ribs were bruised and her face bloodied and swollen and her left arm throbbed, but what had happened back in the desert already felt like a dream. She knew she'd left part of herself back there on the mesa, too, next to the body and the burnt-out truck. She didn't think she would miss it.

They found an auto body shop attached to a gas station just shy of Moriarty and pulled in. Just in time: the Jeep was limping hard, and Cait could feel it was about to give up. She parked around back and they went straight to the ladies' room to clean themselves up as best they could. Cait's mouth was swollen and sore, and Rebecca had a nasty-looking gash above her eye, but the rest of their injuries could be hidden. Cait had a couple of changes of clothes in the backseat: leggings and baggy sweatshirts that made them look like a pair of sorority sisters on their way to a cleansing retreat. They stashed their bloodied clothes under the seat for Cait to get rid of later, once they were back in Texas.

They'd fixed their story on the way. If anyone asked—and the mechanic did, as soon as Cait pointed to the Jeep parked in the back of the lot—they would say that a fox had run in front of them and she'd swerved off the road trying to avoid it. The best stories are always the ones rooted in the truth: sure enough, there was a tuft of fur lodged in the grille, and a faint spray of blood. Enough to make the mechanic stop asking questions and start talking numbers for the repairs.

"She's pretty beat up," he said, shaking his head. "We're probably talking a new front axle, maybe some engine damage, too. It's gonna take some time, and it's gonna cost."

Rebecca already had her bag open and was rummaging for her wallet. "That's fine. I'm happy to pay whatever it costs to get back on the road."

Cait stepped forward. "Do me a favor," she said, walking around the Jeep. "Put it up on the jack and let's have a look together."

The mechanic shook his head. "I'm not sure—"

"Please." She shot him a winning smile. "Just humor me."

The mechanic winched it up onto the jack, and together the two of them slid underneath its belly. After a few minutes, Cait scooted out gingerly.

"Looks like a cracked pan gasket to me," she said, easing herself to her feet and wiping the grease from her hands with a rag.

"Me, too," the mechanic agreed begrudgingly. "I guess she's made of tougher stuff than I thought. It'll be ready in an hour or so."

Cait bought a bunch of snacks from the gas station—powdered doughnuts, a tray of tortilla chips covered in nacho cheese from a pump, jumbo-size coffees with cream and sugar—and laid them out on the picnic table at the back of the parking lot, though neither woman ate anything. The sun was full in the sky, the heat warming the plastic tabletop.

It was nine o'clock, and they were still a full hour away from Albuquerque.

"I'm sorry we didn't make the appointment," Cait said quietly. "I could call them, ask if they can reschedule for later in the day . . ."

Rebecca shook her head. "It's too late."

Cait didn't understand. Rebecca was only eighteen weeks pregnant, according to her file, which gave her plenty of time, and Cait was sure the clinic in Albuquerque would do whatever they could to accommodate them. "Are you sure you don't want me to make a phone call, or—"

But Rebecca just smiled that sad smile of hers and tilted her chin up toward the sun, and after a few minutes Cait did the same, feeling the warmth of the rays on her skin, breathing in the crisp air. Something inside her loosened and unspooled.

It would be Christmas soon. She would go home to Waco this year, give away her shifts at the bar even though Christmas Eve was one of her biggest nights, tips-wise. She might even spend a few weeks there afterward, tucked up in her childhood bed-room, staring up at the posters she'd tacked to her wall as a teen-ager, photographs of New York and London and Paris, all the places she'd dreamed of visiting one day, and all the people she'd dreamed she might become.

They took a different route home, south on 25 and then 380
through Roswell, where cars with "I Believe" decals lined the
parking lots of the UFO Museum and the Alien Zone gift shop.
Neither of them could face going back the way they'd come, even
if this route took them a little longer.

They had a lot of time to talk during the drive back to Texas.
Enough time for Cait to explain to Rebecca who Adam had been
to her, but not enough time to explain why he'd decided to come
after her—after them—the way he had. She said she'd always
sensed that he was lonely, as if that might be a justifiable reason
for trying to kill her. Rebecca wished she could absolve Cait of the
guilt she was carrying. What had happened to them couldn't be
explained or rationalized. Blame couldn't be apportioned. Whoever Adam was, whatever had driven him to try to kill them . . .
they would never understand it, because evil like that couldn't
be understood. It could be withstood, and resisted, and survived.
But it couldn't be understood.

So no, Cait shouldn't blame herself. Yes, she'd written the article about Jake, but that hadn't been justification for what had
followed, just like it hadn't been Rebecca's fault that Patrick had

made that stupid speech. You could only be responsible for your own actions in this life. There was nothing else.

They passed a road sign: WELCOME TO TEXAS. DRIVE FRIENDLY, THE TEXAS WAY.

There were moments when Rebecca had thought she might never again cross the state line back to Texas. Back home.

Was it home? This great wide empty place, where the skies were bigger and bluer than she'd ever imagined, where, on a spring morning in April, she could open her doors wide and let in the sweetest air she'd ever smelled. She tried to picture the house she'd left not even twenty-four hours before. Was that really still her home? Could she walk through those doors and sit at that kitchen table and climb into bed between the soft sheets and feel that she belonged?

She was suddenly aware of Cait's eyes on her, watching. "What are you going to do?"

It was unnerving, the way the girl could read her mind sometimes. "I don't know," she admitted.

"We could keep going, you know. Straight to Austin. There's a clinic there, I know the women who work there. You could stay with me."

Rebecca let the possibility hang in the air in front of her, glittering like a mirage. "That's a very sweet offer," she said eventually, which she knew wasn't an answer. It was close to five o'clock in the evening. The summons stashed at the bottom of her bag had demanded that she appear in court at eleven a.m., which meant the hearing would have happened in her absence hours ago, and while she couldn't know for sure what the judge's decision would have been, she had a pretty clear inkling. It was just as Cait had said on the road all those miles ago: Patrick was one of life's winners. As soon as she'd read the charges filed against her, she'd known she would be on the losing side. That was why she'd had to go to New Mexico. The summons had started the clock ticking, and she couldn't afford the twenty-four-hour waiting period mandated in Texas. So she'd had to risk crossing state lines, and she'd had to do it before the hearing took place. After that, the police would be watching her, waiting for her to make a move. She figured they were already watching, but until the judge banged his gavel, she'd had to hope they wouldn't stop her. And they hadn't. She'd made it to New Mexico. She just hadn't made it to Albuquerque.

All of which meant now that she was back in Texas, they'd be looking for her. She wondered if it had been a mistake to turn down Cait's offer to stay in New Mexico a little while longer, but she didn't want the girl to get in any more trouble than she already had, and she was pretty sure that if Cait helped her get an abortion once the hearing had occurred, she'd be considered an accomplice. This way, it would be just Rebecca's neck on the line.

Cait steered the Jeep into the Allsup's parking lot. "Last fill-up until we get back," she said, swinging open the door. "Do you want anything from inside?"

"No, thanks." The idea of the fluorescent-orange snack foods that Cait seemed to favor made Rebecca's stomach heave.

She watched Cait's back retreat into the store. The cloudless sky had turned a deep slate blue. It would be dark soon.

Rebecca shifted in her seat, a futile attempt to get more comfortable. It was dark inside the Jeep thanks to the temporary plastic sheeting the mechanic had taped to the windows. The windshield would have to be replaced, too, thanks to the spidery crack in the top left corner. She'd give Cait some money to help pay for it. Her stomach roiled after so many hours without food, though the thought of eating felt impossible. She wondered how long it would be until she regained her appetite. She wondered if she would feel this sick for the rest of her life.

She put a hand on her stomach. *I tried, baby girl. I tried every-thing I could, but it wasn't enough, and now I've failed you.* She closed her eyes against the thought.

A knock on the windshield, too loud.

She looked up to see a man in a dark blue uniform standing in front of the Jeep. Square jaw. Cap pulled low. The glint of a badge. Hand resting on his holster.

She opened the door a crack. "Can I help you?"

"Rebecca McRae?"

She nodded.

"Ma'am. Please step out of the vehicle."

Judge Proctor swept into the room and perched behind his bench like a shrewd-eyed crow who'd just spotted his next meal. He had a stack of papers in front of him, and he straightened them on the bench as he told the courtroom to be seated.

Rich noticed the scrape on the judge's left knuckle, fresh from his fall during their squash game that morning. He should send a bottle of champagne to apologize, he thought, even though the shot he'd taken had been fair and it wasn't his fault that the judge wasn't as steady on his feet as he should have been. Really, the judge should be the one sending *him* champagne, not just because he'd let him win the match. This case was a peach, enough to make the judge's name, maybe even get him on the short list for the circuit. He could already hear the solemn tones of the nightly newscaster: "A remarkable breakthrough for antiabortion activists in Texas today as Lubbock County judge Anthony Proctor ruled that an unborn fetus deserves the same rights and legal protections as a person."

Of course, he hadn't made the ruling yet, but Rich knew he would. There was a reason he'd told his lawyer to go for Judge

Proctor. He knew which side his bread was buttered on. Rich had made sure of that.

Patrick's knee started to judder under the desk next to him, and Rich nudged him to stop. He knew the guy was nervous, but he needed to hide it. There were cameras waiting for them on the other side of those double doors. He needed his candidate looking calm and assured as soon as they started snapping.

The judge cleared his throat. "Thank you for coming this morning. I've had the chance to consider both sides of the argument and am ready to give my ruling. On the matter of *McRae v. McRae*, with the defendant Rebecca McRae understood to be in absentia, the court sides with the prosecution and hereby agrees to a temporary injunction preventing the defendant from taking her unborn child, hereby referred to as 'Baby McRae,' across state borders and preventing her from seeking termination of the pregnancy."

He waited until the murmur in the courtroom had subsided. Rich could tell by the way the judge puffed up his chest behind the bench that he was enjoying it. Scrap the champagne. He'd given the old guy enough of a gift today.

"I have not taken this decision lightly. Guiding this ruling is the importance of the marital relationship in our society as shown in *Griswold v. Connecticut* and *Maynard v. Hill*. It is this court's belief that the institution of marriage can only continue to prosper if the rights of both partners are considered to be equal, and it is this court's opinion that the father's right to protect his child's life should be placed above the mother's right to destroy it. We recognize that when a woman decides to terminate a pregnancy without the consent of the father of that child, she is violating not only the rights of the father but also the rights of the unborn child, for whom the father advocates. I believe it is the state's role to protect the lives of its citizens at all costs, and I believe that

Texas should be following in the footsteps of the great states of Alabama, Kansas, and Missouri by protecting the rights of our most vulnerable citizens, those who have not yet been born. As Baby McRae cannot argue for his or her own protection, I understand that Mr. McRae is acting on the child's behalf. Should Mrs. McRae violate this decision by taking Baby McRae across state lines without the express permission of both Mr. McRae and this court, and should she seek to terminate the life of Baby McRae without the express permission of Mr. McRae and this court, she will be in violation of the court's mandate and will be subject to prosecution."

Another murmur from the court. Rich saw Patrick's shoulders begin to shake and moved to stop him before checking himself. *Fine, let the guy cry. The public loves a politician who shows emotion, as long as he's a man. Housewives around the state will be swooning when they see his handsome, tear-streaked face. What a father, they'll say to themselves. What a man!*

Yep, he was playing this one right out of the ballpark. Rebecca thought she was smarter than he was, thought she didn't need to listen, that she could do whatever she wanted and somehow get away with it.

He smiled to himself.

She was about to learn that nobody outsmarts Rich Cadogan. Nobody.

They know about Adam.

That was Cait's first thought when she saw the cop leaning through the Jeep's window and shining a flashlight in Rebecca's stricken face. She tossed a twenty at the gas station clerk and burst through the door just in time to see the police officer pulling Rebecca from the passenger seat by her elbow.

Cait ran up to him. "What the hell do you think you're doing?"

The officer—a tall, stony-faced man with his cap pulled low over his eyes—held up a hand to stop her. "Ma'am, please take a step back."

Cait took another step forward. "Not until you explain to me what you're doing. This is my car, you know. I have a right."

He raised an eyebrow, unimpressed. "Ma'am, you are currently interfering with an arrest, which itself is an arrestable offense, so unless you two want to be sharing a jail cell, I suggest you take a step back." He smirked at her, and she had to hold her hands behind her back to keep from slapping him.

"At least tell me where you're taking her."

"Down the road, to the Yoakum County Jail. You're welcome to follow."

Cait's eyes sought out Rebecca's. "Are you okay?"

She expected Rebecca to be terrified, but instead she looked preternaturally calm. Almost like she'd been expecting this. "I'm fine," she said quietly. "It's okay."

Cait nodded. "We'll figure this out, I promise. I'll be right behind."

She watched as the officer lowered Rebecca into the back of the cruiser, one hand resting on the top of her head. Cait wanted to scream at him not to touch her, but she held herself in check. She had to play by his rules for the moment, whatever they were. If she made a scene, she'd only be making things harder for Rebecca.

Cait jumped behind the wheel of the Jeep, shoved the plastic bag full of snacks under Rebecca's empty seat, and sparked up the engine. The cruiser put on his lights, and Cait followed them out of the parking lot.

Her mind raced as she followed the cruiser through town. The officer wouldn't tell her why he was arresting Rebecca, but it had to be about what had happened out on that mountain. Had they found Adam's body? The charred remains of his truck? How would they have linked Rebecca to his death so quickly? They'd been careful to wipe the prints off the gun before they left it next to his body. Cait had harbored the hope that whoever stumbled across the scene might think it was a suicide, though that felt naive now, absurd. They should have been more careful when cleaning up the site. They might have wiped the prints, but their blood would be all over.

Blood. Shit, their bloody clothes were still stuffed in the back. She glanced in the rearview mirror. She could explain the rest of it—the smashed-out windows, the bruises on their faces—by saying they'd been in an accident, but she couldn't explain how someone else's blood ended up on their clothes. She should have gotten rid of them back in New Mexico. It had been stupid of her to think it would be better to bring them back with her. How could she have been so careless? If they tested them, they would find traces of Adam's blood. How would they talk their way out of that one?

It was self-defense. He had tried to kill them.

But how could they prove it?

Stop. Calm down. She was getting ahead of herself. Adam's death had happened only a few hours earlier. Even if someone had found his body as soon as they'd left, how would the police have been able to pull together the evidence that fast? She couldn't imagine why Rebecca's prints would be in the system. How had they traced her?

Her own prints, though . . . Back in high school, during her shoplifting days, she'd been picked up outside of Walgreens for stealing a curling iron. The officer had taken her down to the station, printed her, even put her in a cell for a couple of hours until her mom could get off work and collect her. They'd said at the time that she wasn't being charged—the officer had done it more to scare her than anything else—but how could she know for sure that they hadn't kept her prints on file?

Even if they didn't have her prints, if they had enough evidence to arrest Rebecca, surely they would have enough to arrest her, too. They'd been driving in the same car, and any witnesses would have seen the two of them together.

It just didn't add up.

Again and again, the same question circled in her head: why had Rebecca been arrested while Cait was still free?

YOAKUM COUNTY JAIL, PLAINS, TEXAS—
72 MILES FROM LUBBOCK

Rebecca stared at the man's head through the screen. It was her first time riding in a police car, and she was struck by the smell: Armor All mixed with sweat.

She knew she should be more frightened, but it all seemed so inevitable. This was what Rich had warned her about when he'd come to the house that morning. It was what Patrick had hinted at, too, though he hadn't had the guts to say it outright. As soon as the man had dropped the summons into her hands, she'd known the clock was ticking. Now it looked like she'd run out of time. If she'd been the type to find irony funny, the fact that she was being arrested for making a decision that was supposed to be legal when she'd helped commit a murder not even twelve hours earlier would be enough to make her laugh. As it was, all she felt was a dull sort of anger.

It all felt like such a waste. Rebecca and Cait nearly dying, all the miles they had driven together, all the plans she had made for her baby. It had all come down to this: a man in a uniform driving her through a one-horse town on the way to the county jail. And her baby still alive inside her, inching toward inevitable suffering.

The jail was a two-story brick box lined with rows of tiny, darkened windows, brutal and austere. A lick of fear went up her spine as the officer came around the side of the cruiser and opened the door. He held out a hand and she took it, making sure to look him in the eye and smile. She wanted him to like her. She needed all the friends she could get.

He caught her elbow when she stumbled slightly on the lip of the curb, her hair blowing across her face. "Careful, now," he said, and steered her gently through the glass double doors of the jail. He nodded to a man behind a large wooden desk. "Hey, Bill," the officer said. "Can you process her for me?"

Bill looked up and gave her a long, cold once-over. She knew at once that she wouldn't be able to get him on her side, no matter how many smiles she offered. "Bring her out back," he grumbled.

The officer led her down a long corridor to a windowless room at the end. There was nothing there but an ancient Formica table and a few folding chairs. "Do you want water or anything?" he asked before closing the door behind him, but she declined. She didn't want to waste a favor on a glass of water.

She sat down on one of the chairs and stared up at the flickering fluorescent light. She wondered if Cait had arrived yet. If she had, she was probably giving the gruff man behind the desk an earful. That thought was enough to make her smile, if only for a moment.

The officer came back into the room, joined by a second officer, who introduced himself as Lieutenant Walker. "You've already met my colleague Sergeant Bakerson," he said, nodding toward the officer who'd brought her in.

She smiled at them both. The lieutenant was older than Sergeant Bakerson—she guessed mid-fifties—with a head of close-cropped gray hair. He didn't smile back.

"Mrs. McRae—"

"Please, call me Rebecca."

"Mrs. McRae, do you understand why you've been arrested?"

She widened her eyes. "No, I don't."

"You were served a summons to appear in Lubbock County Court. Is that correct?"

She was silent.

"And you understand that the hearing went ahead this morning at eleven a.m. in your absence?"

Silence.

"Ma'am, do you understand that failure to appear in court following an official summons is a criminal offense?" She said nothing. The officer shifted his weight onto his other foot. "Mrs. McRae, can you tell us what you were doing in New Mexico?"

"I was on a trip with a friend."

"Yes, we've had the pleasure of meeting your friend." The two men exchanged glances. So Cait had arrived. "Was your husband aware of your trip?"

She shook her head. "It was a last-minute thing. He was away on business, so I didn't want to bother him."

"Mrs. McRae, I understand that you're with child. Is that correct?"

"I'm pregnant, yes."

"Mrs. McRae"—she wished to God he would stop saying her name like that—"your husband has filed an injunction preventing you from crossing state lines with his unborn child. That was the subject of the hearing this morning. The judge granted the injunction, and you are now in violation of it, which is why we brought you in." He fixed his eyes on her. "Did you travel to New Mexico with the intention of terminating your pregnancy?"

A fizz of anger traveled through her. "I don't see why that's any of your business. Abortion is legal in this country, you know."

"Ma'am, the judge also granted an injunction preventing you

from seeking an abortion, which means that any attempt to do so would be in violation of the court order, and therefore a criminal offense."

She gripped the table with both hands. She knew that Patrick was desperate, but she hadn't anticipated that he would have sunk so low. "I haven't done anything wrong."

"Am I to understand that you've terminated the pregnancy?"

She was silent. She wasn't about to give him the satisfaction of knowing that she had failed.

He shook his head. "I'm not here to debate the morality of your actions," he said, though it was crystal-clear from the look on his face that he had already made his judgment. "I'm here as an officer of the law, and in that capacity, I am informing you that you have violated at least one of the terms of the injunction, and therefore you have been arrested accordingly. You will spend the night here in Yoakum before being transferred to Lubbock, where you are scheduled to appear in court tomorrow morning. Do you have any questions?"

"Can I see my friend?"

He shook his head. "Visitors aren't allowed until tomorrow morning."

"What about a phone call? I'm entitled to a phone call, aren't I?"

The lieutenant ran a hand across his stubble. "Phone's down the hall. Make it quick, though. It's lights-out in an hour."

Sergeant Bakerson led her to a cubicle with a single pay phone at the end of the hallway. Through the double doors beyond, she could hear the faint din of the other prisoners. "Dinnertime," he said, nodding toward the noise. "Don't worry, I'll make sure they save you a plate."

"I'm not hungry."

He tilted his head toward her. "You're going to need your strength," he said, more gently than she would have expected.

"Anyway, here you go." He gestured toward the phone. "I'll give you some privacy."

She held out a hand to stop him. "I—I want to call my friend, the one who followed us here."

He hid a smile. "The one with the mouth."

She nodded. "I don't know her number off the top of my head. I know it's a big thing to ask, but do you think there's any chance you could give me the number for the pay phone in the lobby?"

He stared at her for a moment, then sighed. "Wait here."

"Thank you!"

"Just don't say anything to my boss," he muttered as he disappeared down the hall. He came back a few minutes later holding a scrap of paper in his clenched fist. He pushed it toward her. "Make it quick," he said. "You heard what Walker said about lights-out."

"I will," she said, unfolding the scrap of paper and punching the number on the keypad. "Thank you again. I really appreciate it." The small kindness was enough to make her want to cry.

The officer shrugged. "For what it's worth, I think what they're doing to you is criminal. I hope that husband of yours gets what's coming to him."

"Me, too," she said, gripping the phone tight in her fist. "Me, too."

YOAKUM COUNTY JAIL, PLAINS, TEXAS—
72 MILES FROM LUBBOCK

Cait ignored the pay phone that was ringing next to her head until the police officer who'd led Rebecca away poked his head around the door and motioned toward it. "It's for you."

She jumped off the plastic bench and lifted the receiver from the cradle. "Are you okay?"

"I'm fine." Rebecca was trying her best to sound strong, but Cait could tell that she was scared. "They're taking me to Lubbock tomorrow."

"Is it"—she lowered her voice to a whisper—"is it about Adam?"

"No, it's nothing to do with that. It's my husband and his snake of a campaign manager."

Cait was hit with a mixture of relief and confusion. "What are you talking about? How did Patrick manage to get you arrested? You haven't done anything wrong."

"Tell that to the judge in Lubbock." An official-sounding voice was shouting something in the background. "Listen," Rebecca said hurriedly, "I don't have much time. I need you to do me a favor."

Cait straightened up. "Anything."

"I need a lawyer—a good one—by tomorrow morning."

"Leave it to me. Are you going to be okay in there for the night?"

"After last night?" Cait could hear the laughter in Rebecca's voice and felt a bit better. Maybe she really was okay. "Yeah, I think I'll be okay. Where are you going to stay?"

"There's a motel down the street." A dusty-looking place she'd spotted on the drive to the station. "I'll get a room there. Do you know what time they're taking you to Lubbock tomorrow?"

"They haven't said."

"Okay, well, I'll be back here as soon as the sun comes up. Take care of yourself until then, okay?"

"You, too. And, Cait?"

"Yeah?"

"Thanks for sticking by me on this."

Cait allowed herself a smile. "That's what I'm here for, right?"

She hung up the pay phone and fished around in her bag for her cell. The screen flashed in her hand: thirteen missed calls, all from the same number. There was only one person she knew would be able to help, but first she had to face the music. She hit the call button and waited.

Lisa picked up on the second ring. "What the fuck, Cait? Where are you?" The anger in her voice made Cait flinch.

"I'm at the Texas border. Somewhere called Plains."

"Is Rebecca with you? Is she okay?"

"She's here and she's okay. Look, Lisa, I know what I did was—"

"Stupid? Dangerous? Irresponsible? Illegal?"

"Yeah, all of those things, and I'm sorry. I know it was a shitty thing to do."

"I don't want to hear it. Do you have any idea what you've done? You've jeopardized the entire organization. I told you specifically to stay away from Rebecca, but you couldn't do it. Instead, you tricked poor Pat, who feels terrible, by the way, because she's not some *psychopath* like you."

"Look, you can yell at me all you want when I get back to

Austin, and trust me, I know I deserve it. But right now I need your help. Actually, it's Rebecca who needs your help."

"I thought you said she was okay."

"She is, physically, at least. But"—Cait took a deep breath; now came the hard part—"she's been arrested."

"Shit. I thought we'd have more time."

"You knew about this?" Cait asked, incredulous.

"It's all over the news here. Rebecca's husband has filed an injunction preventing her from getting an abortion. He went down the personhood route, and the judge was stupid—or attention-seeking—enough to buy it. I just didn't think they'd get to her this quickly."

Suddenly, it all clicked into place. Rebecca must have known this was waiting for her—that was why she'd said what she had, when they were waiting for the Jeep to be repaired, about running out of time. "Did Rebecca say anything about this when she made the appointment?"

"Nothing. She must have known, though—the press is saying she ignored a summons to appear in court." Lisa took a sharp breath. "She could be in deep shit, Cait."

"That's why she needs us to find her a good lawyer. They're taking her to Lubbock tomorrow. She's scheduled to appear in court."

"They move quick when it's a big politician pulling the strings, don't they?" Lisa didn't bother to hide her disgust. "I'm on it. I'll call Cathy Rebuck and see if she's available. They're keeping her overnight?"

"Yeah, at Yoakum County Jail in Plains. I'll follow them to Lubbock tomorrow."

"Good. I'll meet you at the Lubbock courthouse and let you know the plan. You did the right thing by calling me. We're going to figure this out, okay?"

Cait drove to the motel, a low-slung stucco affair with a cardboard sign tacked out front announcing vacancies. She parked in the lot and rang the bell outside the reception door. A tall, rangy man in a button-down and jeans appeared. "Can I help you?"

"I'd like a room for the night, please," Cait said, trying her best to sound respectable. She knew how she must look—like she'd been dragged backward through a hedge—and she knew that if the man turned her away, she'd be screwed. She fumbled for her wallet. "I can pay up front, in cash."

He waved her away. "There's no need for that. You can pay tomorrow morning; I don't think you'll be skipping out in the middle of the night. Rooms are basic, no frills or anything, but you'll get a hot shower and a warm bed."

She smiled at him. "That's all I need."

The place wasn't so much a motel as a couple of rooms at the back of the man's house. He led her through his living room past the kitchen, where his wife was making supper, to a small, tidy bedroom. "The bathroom's down the hall," he said, pointing toward it. "You hungry?"

She shook her head. "I don't want to impose . . ."

"I wouldn't have asked if you weren't welcome. Terry always makes too much anyways. Dinner'll be ready in about twenty minutes or so. Make yourself comfortable and holler if you need anything."

Cait took a shower in the green-and-pink-tiled bathroom, watching as the dirt and blood sluiced off her skin and down the drain. She was careful to wipe down the tub and the floor afterward—she could tell they kept things clean, and she didn't want them to think she was dirty—and then pulled on the same leggings and sweatshirt and headed into the kitchen.

The smell of frying onions and garlic and spices hit her as soon as she walked in, and all at once she realized her hunger. She thought of Rebecca in a jail cell and felt a pang of guilt as she was ushered to the dinner table. Would they give Rebecca something to eat that night? Would they lock her up with a bunch of criminals, or would she be all alone? Would she get any sleep? Was she terrified?

The man's voice interrupted her thoughts. "You're not one of those vegetarians, are you?" he asked as he picked up her plate and moved toward the stove.

She laughed. "Nope. I'll eat just about anything."

"Good. I'm Jim, by the way, and this is my wife, Terry."

The woman at the stove gave her a wave. "Nice to have you here. Tonight's chili night—I hope you came hungry."

"Cait. And chili sounds great, thank you."

The three of them sat down to dinner and ate in companionable silence. They asked her a few questions—where she was from, what she was doing out here—and she answered them as politely and vaguely as she could muster. The chili was good—spicy and warming—and by the end of the meal, she felt a little stronger. She insisted on doing the dishes. They invited her to watch TV with them, but she begged off as tired and went straight to her room.

She lay in bed, listening to the faint murmur from the TV in the next room, and stared up at the ceiling fan. She was bone-tired, but now that she finally had the opportunity to sleep, she was wide awake and jittery. All she could think about was Rebecca in her jail cell across town and what she might be facing the next day.

Cait pulled her phone out of her bag. Lisa had mentioned that the story had been in the news. She wondered now if she could find something about it. She pulled up the Internet—a strong signal, finally—and typed Rebecca's name into the search engine.

There were three dozen news hits from the last twelve hours alone.

"Senate Hopeful Hailed as Pro-Life Hero After Suing Wife"

"Rebecca McRae Arrested Following Injunction Order Preventing Abortion"

"Antiabortion Activists Make Gains in Texas"

"Is This the End of *Roe v. Wade?*"

"McRae Rises in Polls Following Legal Action"

"Ten Things to Know About Rebecca McRae"

As Cait scrolled through the sound bites and hot takes, the sick feeling that had come over her began to deepen. Rebecca wasn't just facing a judge tomorrow morning; she was facing the public. And Cait knew better than most that the public had the power to act as judge, jury, and executioner far more than a court of law.

She needed to do everything in her power to make sure Rebecca was prepared.

She jumped out of bed and ran down the hall to the living room, where Jim and Terry were watching a repeat of *Law & Order*. They looked up as she came through the door. "You need something, hon?" Terry asked, hitting the mute button.

"This is going to sound like a weird question," she said, "but is there anywhere around here where I can buy clothes tomorrow morning?"

"There's a Family Dollar on Cowboy Way. They usually have a few things. You suddenly struck with the shopping bug?"

Cait smiled at her. "Something like that. Do you know what time they open tomorrow?"

LUBBOCK COUNTY COURTHOUSE, LUBBOCK, TEXAS

The cameras were rolling when the police cruiser pulled up to the Lubbock County Courthouse. Rebecca knew she looked awful—the scrape on her forehead had scabbed over, and her hair was slicked back and dark with grease—but she was wearing the outfit that Cait had dropped off at the Yoakum jail that morning, and wearing it made her feel slightly more in control.

They'd placed her in a cell by herself, but she could still hear her fellow prisoners muttering and shuffling and moaning and snoring, punctuated by the clank and scrape of metal doors opening and slamming shut. She had spent the night staring up at the stained ceiling above her bed, wondering how it was possible that twenty-four hours before, she'd been climbing into Cait's car, scared as hell but convinced that the worst of it was likely over, that the plan she had so carefully put in place was finally coming off. How stupid she'd been, how naive. She should have known as soon as Rich had turned up on her doorstep that he would find a way to stop her. Even when she'd received the summons, part of her hadn't believed Patrick would go through with it. Surely it was political suicide to sue your own wife? But she no longer recognized the waters they were swimming in. The tides turned so quickly these days, sweeping everything familiar out to sea. Now she was out there, alone and drowning.

That wasn't true. She had Cait. She hadn't been able to speak with Cait this morning—the clothes had been left at the front desk—but she'd seen the Jeep parked in the lot as they bundled her into the cruiser, and she'd watched it following all the way to Lubbock. So, no, she wasn't alone. She had a woman she'd met only the day before, but who she knew now would stay by her side.

Rebecca straightened her back as she watched the police officer circle the cruiser and open her door. Time to go.

Flashbulbs popped as the officer pulled her from the backseat and escorted her through the crowd. The courthouse looked like most courthouses in America, built to intimidate and impose. A woman in a dark suit was waiting at the entrance and smiled when she shook Rebecca's hand.

"I'm Cathy, and I'll be representing you in court today," she said in a calm and reassuring tone. "Cait alerted us to your situation. I've had a look at the case file and I'm confident we can get the ruling overturned. Judge Duley is going to be presiding today, and he's good: tough but fair, and a real stickler for the letter of the law. There's no legal basis in Texas for your husband's case, and frankly, I'm shocked that the injunction was allowed in the first place." She leaned in conspiratorially. "That said, I've known Judge Proctor a long time, and I have no doubt he thinks this is his ticket to the circuit court." She straightened up and put a reassuring hand on Rebecca's arm. "Do you have any questions?"

Rebecca swallowed a wave of nausea and shook her head. "Thank you," she said weakly. "For doing this."

The lawyer smiled at her. "It's my pleasure. I live to give people like this hell." She squeezed her arm. "I think it's very brave, what you're doing."

Rebecca shook her head. "I don't feel particularly brave."

"Well, you are. You have to be. We all do." Cathy gestured toward the entrance. "Are you ready?"

Rebecca looked through the doorway into the marble foyer, where a bronze relief of Lady Justice was mounted on the wall. She took a deep breath. "As I'll ever be."

LUBBOCK COUNTY COURTHOUSE, LUBBOCK, TEXAS

The bailiff cleared his throat and a hush fell over the courtroom. "All rise for the Honorable Jonathan Duley."

Cait watched Rebecca's back straighten as the judge walked into the courtroom. Cait was in the back row—the front was reserved for family and the press—already sweating into the polyester button-down she'd bought at Family Dollar. She'd remembered Rebecca had been wearing Cait's old leggings when she was arrested, so she'd bought her an outfit, a black cardigan and pants that she noticed, with some satisfaction, fit her perfectly. The clothes made Rebecca look polished and confident, though Cait could see even from twenty feet away that her shoulders were shaking.

Her husband was standing across the aisle from her, looking like a jilted groom with his dark suit and stricken expression. Good. Cait hoped he felt like the shit that he'd proved himself to be.

Next to him was a smarmy man in a too-tight suit, trying not to look pleased with himself and failing. *That must be the campaign manager Rebecca mentioned*, Cait thought. *Asshole*.

Judge Duley asked them to sit down, and the proceedings got

under way. Cait tried to follow the back-and-forth between the lawyers, but most of it went over her head. It was clear to her, though, that the lawyer provided by the Sisters of Service was a very good one. There were moments when it felt to Cait like she was using a scythe to slice down the opposing counsel's arguments, one at a time. After a particularly savage disemboweling of Patrick's lawyer, Cait had to sit on her hands to stop herself from clapping.

"Your Honor," Cathy said, knifing the air with her hands for emphasis, "there is no constitutional basis for granting this injunction, and doing so is in direct violation of *Roe v. Wade*. Judge Proctor's ruling is, frankly, the work of a rogue judiciary member who wishes to promote his own political agenda and career ambitions over his duty to adhere to the letter of the law. My client"—she gestured toward Rebecca, who was sitting very straight and still in her seat—"has been the victim of a campaign of harassment at the hands of her husband. The fetus she is carrying has been diagnosed with a rare genetic condition that makes it incompatible with life. My client has been forced to come to terms with the reality that her much-wanted baby will not survive longer than a few hours outside the womb, should it survive a childbirth that has the potential to put her own life in grave danger. She has made the extremely difficult decision to terminate this pregnancy—a decision that it is her constitutional right to make—and yet she's being treated like a criminal. I ask you now to right this wrong and throw out Judge Proctor's unprecedented and reckless injunction."

Judge Duley gazed out across the courtroom. "Before I give my ruling on this case, I'd like to urge both parties to come together outside the courtroom and engage in an open and honest dialogue. It always saddens me when a matter as personal and emotionally fraught as this ends up in front of someone like me to decide. The two of you are married, which means you must love each other. I hope you will remember that love going forward." He paused to take a sip of water.

"As much as I am sympathetic to Mr. McRae's concerns as a father, the injunction granted by Judge Proctor has no constitutional precedent in the state of Texas and therefore cannot be upheld in this court. I wish the best for both Mr. and Mrs. McRae, and I will hold them in my thoughts during this difficult time." Judge Duley reached for his gavel. "Case dismissed."

Cait leaped to her feet. She wanted to burst into applause, to shout for joy, but she saw Rebecca walk across the aisle, her face streaked with tears, and pull Patrick close and whisper something into his ear. His face crumpled, and the man began to sob, and Rebecca turned around, her beautiful face savaged by grief but her head held high, and walked out of the courtroom.

LUBBOCK COUNTY COURTHOUSE, LUBBOCK, TEXAS

As soon as she was out of the courtroom, Rebecca broke into a run. She felt the familiar panic starting to build in her chest, and she knew she had to get away from everyone—the lawyers, the gawkers, the reporters, even Cait—before it broke.

She pushed through a metal door marked "Emergency Exit" and hurtled up a flight of stairs. Another door opened onto an empty corridor, and at the end of it, she saw a sign for a bathroom. She hurried in and locked the door behind her.

The air smelled like recirculated air freshener and bleach. She turned on the tap and let the cool water run across her wrists, then splashed her face and neck with it. The panic started slowly to subside, replaced with something that felt heavier and more permanent. Dread. Relief. Regret. She couldn't tell what it was yet. She just knew that it would live inside her from now on.

She stared at her reflection in the mirror. Under the fluorescent lights, her skin looked yellowish and waxy, and her eyes seemed to have sunk deep into her skull. She stared at this woman in the mirror and tried to make sense of her. What did she know about her?

She had almost died at the hands of a lunatic.

She had spent a night in jail.

She had ruined her husband's life.

She had destroyed her marriage.

Her baby was still alive.

Her baby was still doomed.

The question she would be forced to ask, over and over, when the dust had settled and she could see clearly again, if that was even possible, would be: had everything been worth it?

She touched a hand to her abdomen and felt the flutter of butterfly wings. The adrenaline that had pulled her through the past twenty-four hours had abandoned her, and she was left with nothing but a sick, hollow feeling. The grief was still there, and the hurt, and the rage at the unfairness of it all. Her daughter had already been through so much, and she would still never feel the comfort of her mother's touch or be cradled in her father's arms. Some facts remain unchanged even if the world has been tipped on its axis.

Would she do it again? For her baby, yes. She would go through anything to save her from a life that not even the cruelest person would wish on another. So of course she would do it again. In a single fluttering heartbeat.

Rebecca braced her hands against the edge of the sink and leaned in toward the mirror. She locked eyes on herself, and for a while all she saw was pain and exhaustion, but then it came to her. It was just a glimmer, but she knew it was there, and she felt it flood back into her veins and knew that she had the strength to do what still needed to be done. Her daughter had given that to her, and she couldn't betray her now.

There was still a fight to be won. She wasn't done yet.

STEPS OF LUBBOCK COUNTY COURTHOUSE, LUBBOCK, TEXAS

A swarm of reporters engulfed Rebecca as soon as she stepped outside into the fresh early-winter air. For a second, she stumbled back, but then she felt strong hands grip both of her arms and she regained her sure footing. She turned and saw her lawyer standing to her left, steely and confident in the face of the press, and Cait to her right, fearsome and protective.

"Are you okay?" Cait shouted over the din, and Rebecca nodded. It was true, she realized. She was okay. She had proved to herself that she was strong and that she could survive.

"Ladies and gentlemen," her lawyer was saying now, "my client is not going to make a statement at this time, but we are happy that—"

Rebecca put a hand on Cathy's arm and stepped forward. "Actually," she said, her voice surprising her with its steadiness, "I'd like to say something."

Her lawyer leaned in. "Are you sure? You don't have to."

She shook her head. "I know. I want to."

Cathy moved aside, and Rebecca stepped forward into the throng. Reporters surged around her, thrusting cell phones and cameras in her face. She tilted her face up to the sun and looked out across the clear morning sky.

"The past few weeks have been the most difficult of my life. My husband and I both desperately wanted a child, and finding out that our baby was sick and would not survive was the cruelest blow I could have imagined. I don't blame my husband for the actions he's taken—his grief is as real and as pure as mine, and I know that he was acting out of love—but I am grateful that the laws of this country protect my rights as a woman and as a mother to decide what is best for my body and for my child. No woman should have to go through what I've gone through. No woman should have her judgment called into question over this most intimate and emotional decision. I stand before you today as one of millions of women who have been faced with this decision. The reasons that have brought us to this decision are as myriad as we are, and we don't make the decision lightly, or without conscience, or without pain. But the one thing that unites us in our decision is that we make it because we believe it is what is best for our bodies and our lives and our futures, and that is something that only we can know."

The reporters began shouting questions. "Mrs. McRae, can you tell us what you told your husband following the ruling?"

"I told him the truth, which is that I love him and that I love our child."

Another microphone was thrust in her face. "Do you plan on filing for divorce?"

She was careful to keep her face neutral. They didn't deserve to know everything that was in her heart. Especially when she herself was unsure what it held. "I'd like to ask for privacy for me and my husband at this time."

A reporter at the back of the crowd pressed a phone to his ear and held up his hand. "Something's happening in Dallas," he shouted. A murmur went through the crowd as reporters began frantically making phone calls and refreshing Twitter. Just like that, her moment was over.

Her lawyer reappeared at her elbow. "I think this means the press conference is over. That was a beautiful speech you made. You should think about going into politics—you've got a knack for public speaking."

Rebecca shook off the suggestion. "I don't think so."

Cathy shrugged. "Hey, never say never. I've got to take off. I've got a hearing in Amarillo this afternoon." She thrust out her hand. "It was a pleasure working with you."

Rebecca shook it. "I can't thank you enough. Honestly, you saved my life in that courtroom."

"That's what we women are here for, right? To save each other's lives." She reached over and squeezed Rebecca's shoulder. "Don't forget what I said about going into politics. If you're interested, Sisters of Service can help get you connected." She waved as she set off down the court steps.

Rebecca felt Cait's arm around her waist. She turned to see Cait beaming up at her. "You were amazing!"

"Thanks. And thank you for setting me up with the lawyer, and . . . well, for everything. I couldn't have done it without you."

Cait rolled her eyes. "That's a total lie. You're stronger than you think, you know. You're a fucking badass. Now, are you ready to get out of here? The Jeep's waiting around back, ready to take you wherever you want to go."

Rebecca let go of the breath she hadn't realized she'd been holding. "Let's go."

They started making their way down the steps when one of the reporters blocked their path. "Excuse me, Mrs. McRae? We've just learned that an abortion clinic in Dallas has been bombed. Could I have your reaction?"

Mike loaded the last of the boxes in the back of his truck and clipped the tarp shut tight over the load. He checked his watch. Ten past noon. He was ahead of schedule by a country mile, but he'd been eager to get started.

When Ken first floated the idea, he'd been skeptical. He understood that something drastic needed to be done—he'd read the literature, after all, and watched that documentary Ken had loaned him—but what was being proposed felt extreme even to him. Ken had talked him around to it over time. All the pamphlets and protests in the world weren't enough to stop the evil happening right under their noses. The courts were changing things, sure enough, but progress was slow and uncertain, and in the meantime, thousands of lives were being lost. Didn't Mike want to do something to stop it? Didn't a moment like this require a man to act?

That had really gotten him thinking. How many times had he wished he'd killed the man who had killed his Bonnie? He could still remember the man sitting in that courtroom, sniveling in his cheap suit, pretending to be filled with remorse so the judge would go easy on him. The judge had been fooled, but Mike hadn't been. The only thing that man had been sorry about was the fact that he'd been caught and was going to prison. He should have gotten a death sentence, in Mike's opinion, and Mike should have been allowed to do it with his bare hands. Instead, he'd gotten three years in a federal prison out of state, where he was given a bed and fed three square meals a day. How was that justice in anyone's eyes?

In the end, he agreed to Ken's plan. It didn't take much to convince him. He didn't have much to live for, and if he could use what little time he had left to make a difference . . . well, how could he not agree?

He didn't ask about the logistics. Ken told him to leave all that to him—said he had a network, whatever that meant. True to his word, he'd turned up at Mike's place in Columbus a couple of weeks ago with a crate of explosives and a detonator and a full plan of execution. Mike had asked him once over one too many beers if Ken didn't want to come along, see the action for himself, but Ken shook his head and said, "I'm a family man." Mike understood that, no questions. There was no better reason for not taking risks with your own life than a family at home relying on you.

In the end, Mike was glad he was going solo. It gave him the chance to get creative with the plan Ken had put in place for him. He was supposed to just park the truck by the entrance and run, but Mike had no intention of doing that. He'd be sitting in the front seat when that bomb went off, and the last moment of his life before he was reunited with Bonnie would be knowing that he had helped to extinguish just a little piece of evil on this earth before he left it.

By tomorrow, it would all be finished. The thought gave him a sense of comfort. By this time tomorrow, he'd be free.

The papers were still filled with news of the bombing. Two nurses had been killed, along with a janitor. No patients, thankfully—the bomb had gone off before the doors had opened—but the man driving the truck filled with explosives had been killed. Cait had stared at his photo for a long time, sure that she had seen him before, but the name, Michael Chambers, failed to ring any bells. Politicians—including Patrick McRae—had been quick to denounce his actions, but he was already being hailed as a hero and a martyr on the darker corners of the Internet. Cait switched off the talk radio station and snapped her phone into the speaker jack. She scrolled through her music until she found something she wanted to hear—an old Ani DiFranco song she used to listen to on repeat in college—and she listened to it as the engine idled. She glanced at the clock: plenty of time to get to the clinic. Rebecca was inside getting herself together. Cait didn't want to rush her.

The Jeep was in the shop—the repairs the mechanic had made back in New Mexico turned out to be a temporary fix—so she was in a loaner. A little hatchback, low to the ground and with a transmission that took its sweet time changing gears. It made her miss the Jeep.

She glanced over at Adam's apartment. The windows were dark, and his Corolla was parked out front. She hadn't seen anyone go inside since she'd been back, and the yellow police tape she'd expected to see cordoning off the area never materialized. No one knocked on her door asking questions. It was almost as if he'd never existed. She figured at some point the landlord would get wind that the place was empty and rent it out to someone else, though considering she'd never met the landlord herself and the monthly rent flew directly from her account to some anonymous property management company based in Cedar Park, it might be a long time before anyone learned that Adam wasn't living there anymore. Wasn't living, period. She wondered if his body was visible out on that mesa or if the birds had picked his bones clean.

She checked the time again. Getting close now. Another five minutes and she'd go inside and get Rebecca.

After they'd left the courthouse, Cait had driven her back to the house in the Lubbock suburbs and sat outside while Rebecca ran in and packed a bag. They'd been staying together in Cait's apartment since, Rebecca taking the bed while Cait slept on the couch in the living room. Cait had insisted on that. She wanted her to be as comfortable as possible, and anyway, Cait wasn't sleeping that much at the minute.

She blamed herself, if she was being honest. She knew deep down it wasn't her fault that Adam had come after them, but there was a little persistent niggle at the back of her mind that said it had been punishment for what she'd intended to do on the trip. Rebecca kept saying that she'd forgiven her, and part of Cait believed her, but she chalked that up more to Rebecca's good character than having atoned for her own sins. She had a ways to go on that front.

This was a start, at least. Giving Rebecca a home and a bed and a clean set of sheets. Giving her a ride to the clinic. Cait would look after her once it was over, too: she already had a stack of magazines and a stocked refrigerator. She was starting to find she liked taking care of her. Was maybe even good at it.

Her front door opened, and Rebecca emerged. To the average pair of eyes, she looked the same as she had the night Cait picked her up a week ago, all blond hair and patrician beauty. With the exception of the cut healing above her eyebrow, you would never know she'd just been through something like she had. Was still going through, really. But Cait could see the difference. The past week had toughened her up, hardened her to the world. A fact that made Cait both proud and deeply sad.

Rebecca slid into the passenger seat without a word.

"Ready?" Cait asked, but she was already pulling away from the curb. She knew Rebecca was ready for this.

The two women drove in silence for a while, lost in their own thoughts but comforted by the other's presence.

Eventually, Rebecca turned to her. "I've been thinking," she said quietly. "Do you still have your notes for the story you were going to write about me?"

Cait felt the familiar heat of shame flood over her. "No! I mean, yes, I do, but I'm going to get rid of them, burn them. I just haven't had the chance. I promise you I will, though. I'm still so sorry about—"

Rebecca held up a hand to stop her. "I don't want you to destroy them. I want you to use them. I want you to write my story. All of it."

Cait raised an eyebrow. "All of it?"

They were both thinking about Adam's body lying in the desert.

One corner of Rebecca's mouth twisted up. "Maybe not *all* of it." She looked at Cait and held her gaze. "I want people to know what happened to me. I think maybe it could help other women. Let them know that they're not alone. Would you do that for me?"

"Of course. I'd be honored."

There were armed policemen stationed at the clinic gates, a temporary measure due to the heightened risk. Lisa said that they'd be gone by next week and it would be back to business as usual, with volunteers in high-vis vests to guide patients past the protestors and shield them from harm.

Rebecca tugged on a baseball cap, and together they made their way through the throng of protesters. Cait held her breath and waited for one of them to recognize Rebecca from the news, to say something particularly personal and cruel, but they just shouted their usual slogans and waved their usual signs.

They reached the clinic door, and Rebecca paused on the threshold.

Cait looked at her. "You okay? We can take a minute if you want . . ."

Rebecca shook her head and touched a hand to her stomach. There it was, the tiny flutter of butterfly wings. She closed her eyes.

I hope you know I love you. I hope you know that I'm doing what I think is right, and that it's breaking my heart to do it.

She opened them and nodded. "I'm ready."

Cait reached out and took her hand. "I'll be here when you get out," she said as she led Rebecca through the sliding doors. "I'll be waiting. We'll get through this together."

Rebecca squeezed Cait's hand and smiled. "I know we will."

ACKNOWLEDGMENTS

Thank you, as ever, to my brilliant agent and friend, Felicity Blunt, for her constant support and guidance, and for not firing me when I refused to set up my voicemail. Thanks, too, to the wonderful Alexandra Machinist at ICM, and to Katie McGowan, Cal Mollison, Rosie Pierce, Luke Speed, and everyone at Curtis Brown.

Thank you to my US editor, Sara Nelson at HarperCollins, who didn't so much as bat an eyelid when I told her the idea for this book, and whose confidence and enthusiasm has been so helpful along the way. Thanks also to Heather Drucker, Katie O'Callaghan, Mary Gaule, and Lisa Erickson. Thanks to my UK editor, Jade Chandler at Harvill Secker, for her invaluable notes and feedback, and to Sara Adams, Sophie Painter, and Jasmine Marsh. Thanks to KM, for finding the heart of the story and for giving me the push I needed to dig it out.

This book wouldn't have made it out of the gate without the steady wisdom and encouragement of two people: Simon Robertson and Katie Cunningham. I love you both so very much.

I researched a lot of dark corners of the internet for this book, and while much of what I was found was maddening, sobering, infuriating, and terrifying, I also found countless instances of sacrifice and support, bravery and defiance, of women holding each other up and protecting each other, both online and out there in the real world. I'll carry these moments with me.

penguin.co.uk/vintage